scapegoat of strath glen

also by jerri chisholm

praise for the sordid selection

(Pretty Little Robots Book One)

"A must read for fans of Allie Condie's Matched trilogy and Kiera Cass's Selection series!"

— Caroline P., *NetGalley Reviewer*

"I am not one that has dabbled in Sci Fi very much and especially not YA Sci Fi, this was my first. Let me just put it out there, this book gave me all the feels! I would love book 2 now, please and thanks! If you are intimidated by Sci Fi, give this one a go because I do feel like it is digestible and easy to manoeuvre through. The concepts covered in this book feel relevant to today and I think that's why it's so easy to follow. The world building is good, the characters are interesting, and the plot is mysterious....There is tension, emotion, mystery, an overall really good plot, and a CLIFFHANGER (you've been warned – but it's worth it). I am super excited for book 2!"

— Carly W., *NetGalley Reviewer*

scapegoat of strath glen

Pretty Little Robots
Book Three

jerri chisholm

WISE WOLF
BOOKS

WISE WOLF BOOKS
An Imprint of Wolfpack Publishing
wisewolfbooks.com
9850 S. Maryland Parkway, Suite A-5 #323, Las Vegas, Nevada 89183

Cover design by Wise Wolf Books

Paperback ISBN 978-1-957548-33-3
eBook ISBN 978-1-957548-32-6
LCCN 2023943997

one

. . .

I OPEN my eyes to dazzling sunlight ushered in with the dawn of spring—that and a thunderous headache. It's the sangria to blame. Sangria, along with that *thing* that I did. That thing that right now—cocooned between sheets, in the quarters I now share with Wolfe Rocksavage, my fiancé and the viscount of Airo-Aurora—seems so otherworldly, so foreign, I can hardly believe it's true. In fact, maybe it was nothing but a dream...

I close my eyes and consider the previous evening, openly and honestly. No, it wasn't a dream. It happened following Agnes' wedding. Wolfe and I had enjoyed the evening, and even each other—surprisingly so. And then Patrick had arrived, there had been tension, and Wolfe and I left. And then, standing on the sidewalk in the midst of an argument, I had thrown myself at him. I had *kissed* him. Kissed the very man that I typically go to great lengths to avoid.

So. What the hell had I been thinking?

And what does Wolfe possibly make of it?

At the time, he seemed neither bothered nor pleased. He had assured me, there, on the sidewalk, that we never had to discuss it again. And then, true to his word, had paid me no attention in the behemoth as Monsieur Sawyer chauffeured us home, instead burying his nose in the paper and forgetting my existence entirely.

I can't help but feel a rush of gratitude toward him. Because not only had I already rejected the man in my heart, I'd laid it bare to him, as well. I had made it clear that ours would be a marriage by contract alone, and that he was the reason for this—no other. And yet *I* had leaned forward, *I* had placed my lips right there, right on his. What on earth could I have been thinking? Why *that*, of all things?

Sangria. Yes, there's no doubt the sangria is to blame. Entirely.

Then I sigh. Because I can only imagine what he must be thinking. Crazed and unpredictable are two of the kinder adjectives that come to mind. I had never wanted to be the type of girl to play games, and yet how else could he possibly interpret all that had happened? A rejection, followed by a kiss...

If that wasn't toying around, what was?

Maybe I really am becoming far too much like the Rocksavage clan. In the past couple of weeks, I'd been kissed without consent by one royal, and I'd taken it upon myself to do the same to another. At this pace, I'm fitting right in with palace life.

To make matters even more perplexing, before that disastrous exchange with Patrick, I'd actually been enjoying Wolfe's company. Things had returned to normal between us, as normal as could be. Things had been peaceable, too—we had joked with my friends, and he had made a real effort with my aunt, a gesture that, at its core, meant more to me than any amount of jewels ever could.

He was right about one thing, though. The accusation I leveled at him before the kiss—that he cares not for me but only the role that I occupy—isn't one he can easily sidestep.

Either I'm completely on the nose with the accusation, or I'd laid a problem for him that is completely unsurmountable. Either way, the outcome is the same: a loveless marriage on paper alone.

So then, *why* had I kissed him?

————

THE EMBARRASSMENT EASES EVER SO SLIGHTLY as I begin the day, life returning to its normal ebb and flow. Though Wolfe had already left for work by the time I woke, I passed him in the corridor as I headed to the library. As promised, he hadn't mentioned the kiss. In fact, he behaved just as cool and aloof as always, nodding curtly to me as though none of it had ever happened. Now I sit surrounded by dusty books and cords of sunlight funneling through the towering library windows, carrying on with my work, slowly and thoroughly cataloging each title.

Eventually, though, I throw down the book I struggle to document and sigh. It's an illusion, my productivity. My heart isn't in it, and my mind isn't, either. It's not simply the kiss that distracts me, or that troubling and megalithic discovery I had made in the wee hours of the morning—that my best friend Agnes is the leader of the controversial White Ribbon Movement—no, it's my evening plans, too. Because tonight isn't a regular evening, not in the slightest. Tonight is a busy one, and hopefully, one that proves to be even more monumental than what transpired last night.

A meeting with Neo in the stables before dinner—that's first on my agenda. And then, even more significantly, a meeting with Agnes, Timothee, and Neo in Battery Park at 11:30, once the palace is slumbering. A high-stakes meeting, at that. A chance for Timothee and Neo to plan precisely how they will do the unthinkable: hack into the override chips during King's national address and expose to all that people are being interfered with. My skin prickles with excitement, and anticipation. Nerves, too.

It's also a chance for me to corner Agnes on that theory of mine—that she's the one behind the White Ribbon Campaign—a risky endeavor to induce change against the ruler. One already branded as a terrorist organization by King, too.

Yet all that excitement and anticipation I feel grinds to a halt when I think about my friend Jill. Not just a friend, according to Neo, but an outlier, just as I am. Someone who should want to induce change. Someone who has suffered great hardship, who is distrustful of the system, of the status quo. And yet she had declined my invitation to attend tonight's meeting, she had refused to get involved in the business of revolution. I'd be lying to myself if I said I wasn't disappointed. And yet I can't exactly blame her, either. Not when there's so much on the line. Not when things are finally going well for her too.

And then, from the other side of the shelves come the rustling of fabric and the echoing of high heels, drawing me from my thoughts. The strong scent of jasmine wafts through the air, and then a cloud of pink emerges with a towering pile of yellow hair made to look like a swirl of icing. "I thought the ditch piggy might be here, curled up with these dull, old books," Aubrey declares, fanning herself. A dozen strands of pearls of varying lengths wrap around her neck, and she plays with them as she strokes her burgeoning belly. "Evie-darling tells me you've another dress fitting fast approaching," she pouts. "My oh my, it's a nonstop parade of extravagance for you, hmm? Never did I think when you first put that Quire toe into my realm it'd be Alex, Alex, Alex."

"That was never my intention," I begin, but she isn't listening.

"And now I hear that my beloved Strath Glen keeps

chickens—*chickens*. And all thanks to your hillbilly hands looking for some old-timey fun."

"Actually, the kitchen staff will use the eggs for—"

She waves her hand, dismissing my words. "As for me, now that Butch has been officially banned from the palace by Papa, I must meet him off-site, and how it pains me," she adds with a sigh.

I go still. It was just yesterday she had been wailing about Butch, about how he had changed, even accusing me of predicting such a change. And, of course, I had suspected something, with Doctor Lebwitski on site, but I thought it was Aubrey who was the target of the override chip. Turns out it was her illicit lover instead. "Er, is he feeling more like himself?" I ask tactfully.

Her face falls. "Not yet, mon petite ditch-pig. Not yet. But I'm sure in a few days he'll be back to normal, don't you think?" She blinks at me with false extensions.

"Of course," I lie.

She nods, then considers me carefully. "I still say you knew something was about to happen, and that's why you were urging us to go. And my great brain tells me something, ditch-piggy. That if you knew something was about to happen, you knew what, in fact, did happen, whereas I have been kept painfully in the dark."

I rub my head. This isn't a problem I have time for, and yet it's not one that can be dismissed, either. Not when the risk of King finding out that I know about Lebwitski and the override chip program is so great. "I don't know what happened to Butch," I assure her. "I was simply urging the two of you to go before you were discovered with your lover here when everyone knows you're married to Dear Matthew."

It's a good lie; even I'm impressed. Aubrey just sighs in a trinkling way. "If you say so, little piggy." Then she pulls out smelling salts, takes a whiff, and spins. "Do you envy me in my new dress? I've had to revamp my entire wardrobe with a muffin on the way! Butch will find me so radiant he will be back to his usual vibrant, virile self in no time, I promise."

"I'm glad to hear it."

"Aubrey, darling," comes a new voice, and suddenly Morocco emerges from between the bookshelves holding a martini in one hand and a Cabriole cigarette holder in the other. "My new gown finally arrived, isn't it exquisite?" She spins elegantly.

"Darling," gushes Aubrey. "Whatever is it crafted from? And the emeralds hanging around your neck?"

"New as well. My James has spoiled me. As for the dress, it's crafted entirely from the tusks of endangered elephants, isn't that splendid?"

"Grand, absolutely."

My heart sinks. I know what this dress and the new emeralds mean. James has bought Morocco's complacency concerning King's vast weapons order from her father's weaponry business. An illegal, suspicious order. An order that Wolfe and I know is to arm the Mavericks, the group of woods people that King has enslaved through the use of override chips to act as his personal army. Soon to be a weaponized army too, unless Wolfe's ingenuity has bought us more time. He did, after all, choose weapons whose parts were in short supply—our only hope, seemingly, of stopping the innocent Mavericks from becoming killing machines and seeing our beautiful Airo-Aurora reduced to ashes.

"James must adore you to the moon and back, and yet he's always whispering in this one's ear," says Aubrey in a conspiratorial way, and she juts her chin my way.

Morocco's gaze narrows. "Think you're going to nab yourself a prince, do you? A prince soon to be King?" she continues, growing in height alongside her anger. "I'll destroy you—"

"What on earth is all this chatter?" comes yet another new voice, and this time, none other than Claudia bursts into view. Her eyes narrow as she spots me, and I'm reminded that only a couple days ago, she was making similar threats to me for standing between her and her ex-boyfriend—Wolfe. "An unusual place for a party," she continues, glancing at the dusty books with disdain. "And with a Quire mouse, too? I thought you ladies had finer taste."

"I was simply showing off my new dress," Morocco explains.

"A dress that simply slays," gushes Aubrey. "But alas, I can't stay for the party—my loins are bursting! Tah!"

"Tah," I say, hoping that Morocco and Claudia follow her out.

Instead, Morocco leans over the desk and lowers her face close to mine. "I can't even begin to explain what I'll do to you, dearest, if I catch you sniffing around my James once more."

"Oh, I never—"

"James?" Claudia interrupts, stifling a laugh. "She desires James? But—that's perfect! The viscount shall be all mine for the taking—"

Morocco rounds on her. "How dare you speak such vile words," she shouts. "Why, James is my husband, and what—"

"Miss, the butler needs you straight, like," comes Rebecca's voice from around the corner. She winks.

I stand, immensely grateful to the young girl who used to be my adversary. "Thank you," I whisper as I stream behind her through the columns of shelves.

"Thought you'd need a break, aye, from those two."

"Indeed I do. Tell me, Rebecca, how was King yesterday while Wolfe and I were gone to the wedding?"

"What do you mean, Miss?"

"Well, do you think he's still bothered by the White Ribbon Campaign protest a few days past?"

"Oh, aye, I'd say, like. He's been eatin' double the biscuits, and in a bad mood, to boot. Even canceled his singing lesson."

As we push out of Counterdown and between the Ming vases, a tall, lithe figure stalks out of Devonshire. Wolfe, and for a minute, we stare at each other with widened eyes. It's as if he's as shocked to see me as I am to see him. Too shocked for curt nods and a façade of niceties. No, this is exposed and raw, two people staring nakedly at one another. I think of that kiss. I swallow.

And then Rebecca is curtsying and retreating into the shadows so it's just the two of us, and I consider the delicate carvings on the towering vase I stand next to rather than feel so bare as when I meet his gaze.

"Erm, yes, well." He clears his throat. "How goes the cataloguing?"

I tuck my hands politely behind my back and turn to him. "Well. Thank you," I reply, still averting my eyes. Already I can feel that dreadful feeling of blood blush filling my face. If I wasn't kicking myself earlier for leveling him with a kiss, well, I certainly am now.

And then Morocco and Claudia are tumbling out of the library behind me, hurling insults at one another and spurring both Wolfe and me away. But with both of us ascending the imperial staircase, once again alone together and this time in close proximity, the awkwardness becomes even more unbearable.

Eventually, I clear my throat. "The library houses many rarified editions."

"Is that so?"

"Indeed. Most impressive."

More awkward silence, punctuated only by the clicking of his expensive loafers. "The hens have begun to lay eggs."

"Excellent."

He coughs lightly into his fist. And then, at the top of the stairs, he adds, "I'm off to Bishop's Aisle," and I breathe with relief.

"Goodbye," I say as I head toward the House of Mirrors.

And then we're angling away from each other, and I'm speeding past a hundred mirrors through the black and white hallway, wiping sweat from my brow as I go.

two

. . .

WITH THE ARRIVAL of early spring, the days are longer and dusk is prolonged, meaning there will hardly be any time for my meeting with Neo under the cover of darkness before I'm expected in Carnegie for dinner. All I really need to tell him, though, is that we're to meet as a group this very evening at 11:30, and with that in mind, I push out of the quarters I share with Wolfe, grateful that he still remains tucked inside his office upstairs. Then I slap my forehead. Monsieur Sawyer—I'd completely forgotten. I'll need him to act as watchman if I intend to sneak out of the palace tonight. Sighing, I rush down the servants' stairs and turn for Devonshire, the easiest way to reach the underground garage where Monsieur can typically be found. But I pause just outside it—I listen to a party underway, one that has yet to move to Carnegie.

Another sigh, and then I step inside, hoping to pass through the room undetected. My attempt to blend into the tapestries, however, doesn't work, and almost immediately, the eyes of the entire room are upon me. James makes cawing sounds at me as a decanter is readied above his mouth, Morocco passes around Jell-o shots, and the rest of the vultures—guests from neighboring estates—cackle as I sprint to the awaiting doorway.

Through the door and down the stairs, into the damp expanse that houses the palace's limousine and other automobiles. Workers huddle in the corner, apparently in the midst of changing out lightbulbs, which form straight lines along the ceiling and number in the thousands. A deafening Shop-Vac echoes from the behemoth, and I head there, finding Monsieur with his sleeves rolled up to his elbows, vacuuming out the backseat.

"Blimey," he shouts upon seeing me. He hits his head on the ceiling, then retracts it, grumbling. He switches off the vacuum. "Shouldn't you be at dinner, Miss Alex?"

"Actually, it's early yet. There's still a party in Devonshire, as a matter of fact."

"Fascinating."

"May I ask what you're doing?"

"What I'm doing? Why—I'm cleaning up the mess from your blasted chickens, that's what. It was your hair-brained idea, I gather?"

"A hair-brained idea? On the contrary, having a source of fresh eggs to feed the palace with is both economical and a sustainable—"

"Spare me the lecture, Miss Alex. I've spent all of yesterday lugging you and yours around, not to mention far too many trips with those hideous, filthy creatures than I ever could've dreamed. Now, duty calls."

He switches the Shop-Vac back on, but I immediately switch it off again. "May I trouble you with one more favor, Monsieur?"

"Yet another one?"

I give him a look. "I believe the chickens had more to do with Evie and Wolfe, if memory serves me."

"Ah, and yet the common denominator is you, you, you. Quite a hold you've got on people, hmm, Miss Alex?"

"So I've been told. Nonetheless, I really could use some help. This evening," I add tactfully.

"Go on."

"I was hoping to slip out of the palace for a little while—"

"And you want old Sawyer to play watchman, is that it?"

"Precisely. A favor for a friend, and all that."

"Oh, yes. And all that."

"One I'm happy to repay, I might add."

He licks his teeth and considers me. Then he rolls his eyes. "Oh, fine. What time is this little outing of yours?"

"11:30."

"Be back by midnight."

"Can we say 12:30, Monsieur?"

"You really do know how to push your luck."

"Nevertheless—"

"Yes, yes, fine. Take care not to let word get back to your fiancé that I had any hand in your rule-breaking, hmm? I don't need his wrath, thanks for asking, and good day to you." He tips his hat.

I wave goodbye as the Shop-Vac once again whirs noisily, and when I return to Devonshire, I find it blissfully empty. Only the parrot remains. "Once a killer, always a killer," it says wisely as I pass.

Out the window, only the dim outline of shapes remain, and streetlights already flicker to life in the city below, so I pick up my pace, not wanting to be late for my meeting with Neo. Faster and faster, I push through corridors I now know like the back of my hand, grabbing a cloak from the back closet and positioning a brick along the doorjamb before bursting into the night. Adrenalin has me now, and after scanning the woods for beasts, I rush over the grass made sopping by the melted snow and into the darkened stables.

Empty, but almost immediately, the soft braying of the

horses is interrupted by the sharp squeal of weathered hinges.

"Right on time," I whisper excitedly to Neo, who pokes through the near-darkness toward me.

"I come bearing news," and I note how somber his voice is.

"You do?"

He nods. "Edith, the technician holding your files, she's been tampered with. She's only just back from a two-week vacation, or I would've noticed sooner."

I'm silent as I digest this, and my excitement withers. Another victim, right on the heels of Butch. Lebwitski, evidently, has been busy, and my stomach dives at the thought. "Why?" I finally ask.

"I imagine it's because she saw what you and your fiancé saw in Ashville Range. A development known to King, naturally, since she was the one who alerted him to the disturbance."

The sinking sensation in my stomach worsens. Because this one is on me—it was my reckless decision to do the flyover, after all.

"She must've been asking too many questions," Neo continues. "Or she didn't believe that it was simply an army, I'm not sure."

"You mean the technicians don't know what's happening?"

"Of course not. King and Lebwitski are the only ones who know, and they both had their transmitter chips deactivated a couple years ago."

"So how did you come to know such information?"

"I held King's files before, during my first year on the job. Sometimes I'd get bored and enter his feed out of curiosity—he is the King, after all. Not something technicians are allowed to do, by the way, but I guess I'm not the best at following the rules. Anyway, pretty soon, it became obvious that something fishy was happening, and then, before I knew it, I was monitoring his feed by design. I was able to listen in on his early conversations with Lebwitski while they were laying the groundwork for their plan. The rest I've pieced together by illegally tapping into various feeds."

"Why wouldn't King mask his conversations the way you and I do?"

"He wouldn't know how, I doubt. Rumor is, he's never once visited the memory bank. Still, it was a stupid mistake, wasn't it? I'd chalk that one up to arrogance—thinking he's untouchable and all. Still does, I'd say, although I'd wager the recent protest knocked him down a peg."

"I think he's more neurotic than you realize if he bothered with the override chip program in the first place. And an army."

"Good point. So—did you talk to Timothee and Jill?"

I hesitate. "Yeah. I mean, yes, I did. But first, well, since we're on the subject of Ashville Range—did, um, Wolfe know what was happening there before that helicopter ride?"

Through the murky darkness, I see that he looks surprised by the question. "I very much doubt it. It would seem from the surveillance I continue to conduct that he's been brought fully on board by the King ever since, however."

I nod. I had suspected that. And King himself had said that Wolfe had been helping him with a couple important dossiers. "Do you trust him?" I ask next, dimly aware that the longer we take talking along tangents, the later and, therefore, more conspicuous I'll be arriving for dinner.

"Don't you? Geez, Alex, if it weren't for his quick thinking, you'd have been tampered with at the Sky Center then and there."

"So he said."

"You don't believe it?"

"I do. It's just—no, I do. For the most part."

"Look, it's not like I'm saying you have to love the guy—in fact, that was something I worried about, actually, when I first put you here."

"What do you mean?"

"If you fell for him, you wouldn't exactly be incentivized to take down a system that gave you your love, right? I was particularly worried when he made you his pilot."

I frown. "It sounds like you do a lot of 'surveillance'."

"I do what has to be done. And speaking of that, you spoke to Jill and Timothee, you said? Did you schedule a meeting?"

"Tonight. At 11:30 in Battery Park. Can you make it?"

"That's quick turnaround. But yeah, I'll be there."

"Jill opted not to come," I add carefully. "She doesn't want to risk her job and her engagement—things have been going well for her lately." Neo is silent, but I can sense his disappointment. I press on, "You should know I invited my friend Agnes too. I believe she's the person behind the White Ribbon Campaign."

"Are you serious?" he asks immediately, no longer seeming disappointed in the least. "What's her last name?"

Once again, I hesitate. Telling Neo her full name would mean he'd conduct 'surveillance' on her too. "We'll know for sure if it's her or not tonight," I say instead. "Either way, she's trustworthy and unhappy with the system. In other words, a good ally."

He nods. "I have to say, I'm surprised about Jill."

"I don't really blame her," I say eventually.

"We could really use a greencoat though. Keep trying to convince her—whenever you see her, keep on her case. Anyway, I have to go. Since I hold your file now, if you need me again, write a message and look at it at noon each day. I'll check in on you then."

"And only then," I clarify.

"And only then," he agrees. "See you tonight."

I wave goodbye, then make my way carefully back to the palace, my brain whirring with thought. I hang up my cloak and smooth my wrinkled gown. I wipe my boots on the mat and draw in a shaky breath. I try to focus on the evening ahead of me, one which will culminate in a risky and high-stakes meeting, but I can't stop replaying everything that Neo had said. Another technician turned. Wolfe, having saved my life at the Sky Center. Jill, and the need to recruit her. And, finally, a new way to communicate with Neo.

I'm surprised indeed when I finally push into Carnegie to find it completely transformed since when I was here two days ago. Floral wallpaper now adorns the walls where the elaborate wood moldings don't reach, bird cages full of chirping songbirds hang from the rafters, and bouquets by the dozen fill every nook and cranny—an ode, I suppose, to spring. A life-size rendition of King has even been added, crafted from rosebuds. And instead of profanity-laced gospel music, a palace favorite, the chorus sings nursery rhymes.

"A strange way to fashion a dress," speaks a voice in my ear. I turn to see the duchess staring coolly down at me.

"Forgive me, madam," I say at once, remembering, of course, that it was this very woman who ordered away my riding ensemble. "My feet still haven't recovered from yesterday's high heels. These boots are far more comfortable."

"And the cardigan?"

"It's chilly, madam, seeing how it's the early days of spring."

"You make no attempt to dress accordingly, do you." She poses the question as a statement.

"According to what?" I query.

"According to palace norms, child. Do you not see the way other ladies fashion themselves?"

"It doesn't appeal to me," I say frankly, but immediately I regret it.

Her eyes narrow. "Does it ever cross your mind that you are now a representative of the Rocksavage family?"

"Well—"

"Are you unconcerned with looking the part of Viscountess?"

"Again—"

"Do you not wish to present yourself properly for the sake of your soon-to-be husband?"

"Mother," comes Wolfe's icy voice from behind us. "Let her be."

The duchess' left eyebrow lifts as if hooked; she contemplates him, then bows her head. She gestures to us both. "Tell me, how was the wedding you attended yesterday? Your first official outing, I believe?"

I glance at Wolfe, then away again. It's the last thing I wish to discuss, but with the duchess waiting expectantly, say, "It was, er, an interesting time. Your son was most gracious." I add, attempting to ingratiate myself with the woman, who's dislike for me has only intensified with the passage of time.

"Oh?" She lifts her gaze to her son, but already he is speaking with his father about business matters. "How so?" she asks me, stepping closer.

I swallow. "He, well, he was very friendly with my aunt, for one. He even asked her for a tour of Quire, along with my aunt's house."

The surprise I spot across her face dissolves almost immediately, hardening into something else. "Is that so?" she levels at me.

"Have I offended you, madam?"

"Not in the least. I wonder, though—would my son be able to say such things about you?"

"I—I should hope so, madam," I stutter, even as it hits

me at the base of my stomach that he can't. I've attempted to avoid all contact with my soon-to-be in-laws since day one. However, admitting as much seems misguided, so I return to proclaiming my innocence. "Certainly, I've always tried—"

"Sister, there you are! How I missed you yesterday at dinner, my! Tell me all about darling Agnes' wedding. Was it splendid? Were there any design aspects you'd like to weave into your own upcoming nuptials? Did you and Brother enjoy yourselves?"

"It was a wonderful event," I assure her, relieved to have her here instead of being alone and in the crosshairs of her mother. "And yes, the two of us did enjoy ourselves," I say tactfully, keenly aware that the duchess is reading into my every word while I also try not to think of the embarrassing kiss I had proffered to her son at the end of the night.

"Splendid," gushes Evie.

"And what about the other question, child? Did you see any décor you'd care to have at your own wedding to my son? Do you care about that wedding in the slightest?"

The tone of her voice isn't lost on me, and I nod. "As a matter of fact, yes," I lie. "The fairy lights woven through the park were lovely once the sun went down. I'm not sure if we have it in the wedding budget, but—"

"Consider it done, sister!" Evie cries. "Oh, it's so wonderful you're taking an interest in the big day, my! I can hardly believe it's only a few weeks away!"

"Six weeks," I clarify, a little too quickly, judging by the look on the duchess' face. I must try harder, I remind myself, to feign interest in the upcoming nuptials—his mother might hate me less if she thinks it's something I want, rather than the truth: that it's something I'm begrudgingly going forward with because I have no choice.

And then King's moon-shaped face drops into position directly in front of mine, and all thoughts of the duchess, Evie, and the wedding go flying from my mind. I blink, King laughs. "My cute little petal," he sighs in a whimpering voice. Over his shoulder, I see the duchess and Evie walk toward the punchbowl together, leaving me alone with the ruler. "Tell me, since you seem to know everything, where is my darling Aubrey this evening?"

The assertion makes my jaw drop open, but I do my best to disguise it with a cough. "I don't know, sir."

"And yet, according to my daughter, you sound like quite an accomplished fortune teller!"

My stomach tightens into a knot. Surely—no.

"Why, isn't it true you knew her illicit lover, that common scoundrel, would be removed from the palace imminently?"

"What? Not at—"

"According to Aubrey, you warned her and that boy to flee at their earliest convenience." He flutters his eyelashes at me as he awaits my response.

My response. How can I think up an adequate one when the room spins around me and the nausea is overwhelming?

Finally, without averting my eyes for even a second, I say as calmly as can be, "I will admit, sir, that I've taken a liking to your daughter. And as much as I respect Dear Matthew, I didn't want Aubrey and her lover to be found together, so, yes, I did advise them to take their, er, amorous activities elsewhere."

He considers me, then squints his eyes and pushes his round face close to mine, looking, it would seem, for any sign that I'm being untruthful. I give him nothing, and after an eternity, he claps his hands together. "Then you admit to rule-breaking, you mischievous imp! You ought to know, dearest, that the Mainframe selected Dear Matthew to be the perfect companion to my darling Aubrey, so why in heavens would you go against the Mainframe and try to protect the most unholiest of unions?"

"Really, King," I say breezily. "I was simply looking out

for my sister-in-law."

With that proclamation, I think I've stumped him. Indeed, a moment later, he sighs, then follows after a passing chip bowl.

I can hardly believe my luck. Not only have I avoided being outed for knowing about the override chip program, but I've just avoided punishment for going against the Mainframe too. My ability to play the game of Strath Glen improves by the day.

As the party swirls around me, a riotous one—the enthusiasm for the end of winter and the start of spring evident, I stand alone, finally taking the opportunity to study the profile of my soon-to-be husband, who stands across the room speaking to Dear Matthew. And once again, my mind wanders back to that revelation from Neo, a week or two past, that Wolfe and I, aside from our differing stations, are ideally suited to one another.

Funny. It's a piece of data that shouldn't matter in the slightest. The Mainframe is nothing but a machine, and romantic matches should be left to the human heart. And yet I can't shake the thought. Me and Wolfe are good matches, for some strange reason. Me and him. Him and me. That vastly tall, ice-cold aristocrat that Neo believes to be trustworthy, that I believe to be trustworthy, for the most part, who managed to stop my fate from being sealed at the Sky Center—*he* is my ideal mate, according to the Mainframe and its unending mine of data.

Just then, Wolfe catches sight of me staring at him in his peripheral vision. His gaze snaps to mine, but suddenly it falters. We look at each other as if for the first time.

I fumble my wine glass at that very moment, and it smashes into pieces along the floor. I step back, horrified, as a team of servants swoop down in front of me, and another glass is pushed into my hand.

A seamless transition, and I shiver.

three

. . .

AFTER DINNER IS FINISHED WITH, I waste no time rushing back to my quarters. I root around the closet for the animal pelt that Wolfe typically sleeps under and set about making up a bed for myself on the couch. Next, I throw open the window, just the way he likes it, turn out the lights, and cover myself under the pelt, still fully clothed.

Waiting under here for two hours until it's time to go meet the others doesn't exactly appeal. But seeing and speaking to Wolfe appeals even less. I think about kissing him and groan into the hide. Thinking about this evening's meeting is little better, as every time I think of that, nerves erupt in my stomach so bad they make me nauseous.

Finally, a full hour and a quarter later, I hear the echoing of crisp footsteps, the opening and closing of a door. Wolfe enters our chambers a moment later, and I think he hesitates. He has probably noticed me on the couch, a shapeless lump, visible under the still-healthy fire. Then the wind whistles loudly through the open window, and the door to the closet clicks shut. It would seem he believes me to be asleep, just as I wish him to. Still, with just forty-five minutes until I have to go, things are getting down to the wire. What if he isn't asleep when the clock edges close to 11:30?

But there's no need to worry because it's shortly after Wolfe retires to the towering bed tucked around the corner that his breathing grows longer, more even. Eventually, I throw the pelt off, bracing myself against the jolt of icy air that takes my breath away.

With ten minutes to spare, I silently arrange the pelt on the couch so that it looks like a small body lay buried beneath, then tiptoe across the room.

Wolfe's rhythmic breathing is uninterrupted, and I slip from the room feeling more confident than before.

"A time, Miss Alex, that you'd like to return home?"

"You startled me, Monsieur," I exclaim quietly. "You're punctual, as always."

"As always, indeed. As is required at this fine institution, I'll remind you," he adds. "So, a time when you'd like me to start playing the watchman?"

"Uh, well, it's difficult to know precisely—"

"I'm not asking for precision, Miss Alex."

"Half an hour?" I finally suggest.

He tips his head. "Then here I'll be," and with that, he turns on his heel and heads toward the servants' stairs. "Do remember, Miss Alex," he says before disappearing downstairs, "that I was up all hours of the night last night, chauffeuring you and the viscount here and there, hmm?"

"I won't be late, I promise," I assure him, stifling a yawn as he does the same. Then Monsieur disappears down the servants' stairs, with me not far behind him.

At the back door, I grab a cloak, then push out into the damp night. I pull the cloak's hood over my head, an attempt to disguise myself even further from prying eyes, and delve into the tree line so I'm less conspicuous to anyone who happens to be gazing out a window right about now. There's danger here, in the woods—wild and ferocious beasts, but right now, I readily take the risk. I like my chances better with a wolverine than with King, anyhow. And then I'm scaling down the sharp slope to the east of the property and, several minutes later, find myself off palace grounds and only a few blocks from Battery Park.

As the dark grounds lift into view, I fasten the cloak to my chin and pull the hood down low over my eyes. Not only will it help to stop me from looking at my friends, it will stop their feeds from having footage of me. Then I walk between shadowy outlines of trees, the ground underfoot spongey with recently melted snow, my eyes peeled for any sign of life. My pulse is quick with anticipation, with some blend of excitement and fear.

There. Up ahead, barely visible through the blanket of darkness. A figure, I'm sure of it. Then there's a flurry of activity behind me, and before I can scream, my shoulder is grabbed.

I pivot, my eyes wider than the mottled orb known as the moon hanging overhead.

Jill's face breaks into a grin, and I immediately roll my eyes. "You just about scared me to death."

"Sorry, princess."

"I thought you weren't coming," I continue.

"Guess I changed my mind," she replies, shrugging. "Where's everyone else?"

"I'm looking for them now," and I motion her forward through the darkness. "What made you change your mind?"

"Meh. Looking at photos from when I was a kid, that sort of shit." She spits. "Don't want any other kids growing up like I did. Free choice matters. My mom and I would've ditched that drunk bastard years ago, if we could."

"Well, I'm glad you're here. Neo will be relieved, too."

She chuckles, then nudges her chin in the direction of a nearby clearing, where I'd first noticed the outline of a figure. Voices, I realize, and a minute later, we step over thicket and find Timothee and Neo sitting on the bench, speaking in hushed voices.

"Hi," I say, edging closer. "No looking at each other," I remind them. "No using names, either."

"Thanks, Mom," Timothee jokes. "This guy was just letting me know all about the Mainframe's computer system. Fascinating stuff."

"Yeah?" I say, sounding hopeful. "And? Is our plan doable?"

"Oh, it's definitely doable, but it means I'll have to be physically present inside the Mainframe, that's all. I might go with a mad scientist disguise—thoughts?"

"You might want to go in a different direction," says Jill. "You know, if you don't want anyone recognizing you."

"Very funny—"

"So, you decided to come?" Neo interrupts, turning in Jill's direction.

"Yeah, I mean, I had second thoughts about saying no, that's all," she responds, sounding defensive.

"Thank goodness, too," I say, "because you guys will want a greencoat by your side if you're breaking into the Mainframe."

Neo nods. "Definitely." Then he says in a hushed voice, "And what of your friend?"

"Oh, is she coming, too?" Timothee asks. "That's super— the more, the merrier, although it would be handy to have someone else with coding experience. This program I'm writing for the national broadcast is taking up every spare second I have. My gaming console has a layer of dust on it for the first time in years."

Jill snorts, but I just scan the empty park, my gaze lingering on every shadow, wondering where indeed Agnes is.

Neo, meanwhile, is whispering to Timothee. "...problem is that it's not the type of program that can be thoroughly tested in advance, but I'm happy to review the code to look for gaps or other errors that could—"

There, through the trees, walking along the sidewalk. A small figure, big hair. I dart around the others to get Agnes' attention, waving my arms until she spots me.

"Sorry I'm late," she whispers. "Miller and I had a huge fight about me going out so late. Like, he's not my dad, hello."

I nod. "Sorry. I didn't mean to cause a fight between the two of you, but I can't really sneak out—"

"It's not your fault. So, who's that?" she whispers, nodding in Neo's direction.

"That's Neo," I say quietly. "He's the technician at the Mainframe who's been sending me the scrolls. The four of us have been working on a plan to expose King during the next national address, a week from now."

"Expose him?"

"Oh, right," I say, suddenly remembering that Agnes isn't yet up to speed on all that's been happening in our beloved Airo-Aurora. "The past couple years, King has developed an override chip program," I begin. "Basically, he has these override chips inserted into people's brains when they're too much of a nuisance. I'm talking about folks who are unhappy, angry, or don't agree with King's reign or the Mainframe's supremacy in the first place. The override chips effectively shut off a person's brain, making them powered by Artificial Intelligence. It can be difficult to recognize, though, since the Mainframe has so much data already collected from that person's life."

"So he's turning people who don't like the system into robots that do like the system?" Agnes sums up, sounding incredulous.

"Exactly. Which brings me to the White Ribbon Campaign."

She's silent. So are the others, but I can tell they're listening intently.

"It struck me," I continue pointedly, "that perhaps you aren't simply a member of the campaign."

"What do you mean?" she asks.

"I mean…it's *your* Campaign, isn't it?"

More silence. Then she sighs. "How the hell did you figure it out?"

"It doesn't matter," I say quickly. "The important thing is that you realize how risky it is. I'm not kidding—even wearing the ribbon, and having others wear it—it creates traceable data that King and his cronies can access, making it really easy to identify all those in the city that are dissenters."

"But it's peaceful, what we're doing. Even the protest—"

"It doesn't matter. It's going against King, meaning it's incredibly dangerous."

"So are you saying we should just give up? At some point in time, people have to stand up to this guy, or things will stay the same forever."

"That's true," Timothee pipes up. "And, knowing what we do, we absolutely need to take action."

"I think your Campaign should definitely continue," I assure her, "but it should be a secret, underground movement. Not something that's so visible—at least not yet."

"How's that supposed to work?"

"Well, you could use the network you already have to spread what you've learned tonight, for instance. And then, after the national address—scheduled eight days from now, we're hoping the entire population will be so outraged, there won't be a need to keep the Campaign a secret anymore."

She takes a moment to digest things, then asks, "What exactly is happening at the address?"

I turn to the others, pointing at Timothee and Neo, I say, "Right now, the plan is for them to access all the override chips from inside the Mainframe and insert a program that will run during King's speech. The Queen is one of King's victims," I add, "so she'll be on camera."

"Wait—what kind of program are you thinking?"

"Let's just say," says Timothee, "it's going to be very obvious that folks with override chips are, as you said, robots."

"And just in case it doesn't work," I add, "I think you should try to spread as much information to your group as you can. Everything you've heard tonight. And that it's the bluecoats—the Mainframe police—that people have to watch out for. More than that, even, it's a doctor dressed in white who goes by Lebwitski. He's the one who actually performs the operation."

"This is heavy stuff," Agnes says. "Like, really crazy shit. What if it starts, I don't know, a mutiny?"

"Good," says Jill. She shrugs.

"I'm not so sure," I say. "Don't forget the army King's working on."

"Army?" Agnes echoes.

"Made up of Mavericks with override chips. As far as I know, King's working on getting them weapons."

"Weapons? How the hell are we going to fight that?"

"We can't," remarks Timothee. "Not without weapons of our own."

I nod. "Hopefully, we can cause such an upset during the national address that change happens before the army can be weaponized. Or even called in. Right now, they're a hundred miles north of the city."

"I'm really hoping that when the entire nation demands change, King will capitulate," explains Neo.

"But is that realistic?" Timothee asks.

Neo and I shrug. "Nobody can survive at the top without any support from the masses," I point out. "If things are bad enough, I don't think he'll have much choice."

"What if people decide to storm the palace?" Timothee asks me. "Technically, you're part of the royal family, meaning you could be in danger."

"I'm in danger anyways," I say, thinking of King. "We all are."

The group is silent as we digest all this. As we digest the magnitude of what we're trying to do, and the gravity of the risks too.

"So, what now?" Agnes finally asks. "I'm supposed to move my Campaign underground and start dispersing everything I've learned tonight, correct?"

"Right. And both of you will keep working on the override program." I say to Timothee and Neo. Then I turn to Jill, "Can you make sure you're assigned to the Mainframe or Strath Glen the day of the broadcast? We'll need you in the vicinity. And I'll try to get an update on any progress King's made in arming the Mavericks. Maybe I can find a way to further delay it, I'm not sure."

"Wouldn't it just be easier to kill the King ourselves?" Jill asks. "I mean, he's evil, so I think we'd be able to stomach it."

I snort. "I don't think it'd be easy to stomach in the least. Not to mention all the repercussions we'd face since the rest of the system would remain in place. Plus, the throne would pass to his son, who isn't much of an improvement."

She sighs. "Let's keep it as our backup plan, then."

"A backup plan, it is."

"We should meet again soon," Neo says. "To update each other on what's going on."

"Good idea. Same time, in a few days?"

"Wednesday night works for me," agrees Timothee.

We part ways a few minutes later, and I feel lighter than before. There's relief, definitely, that things are going according to plan. There's relief that there is a plan. But mostly, there's relief to have a team working alongside me—

I'm no longer alone in my quest to take down King and the Mainframe.

As I cross the street, I think of Agnes' concern about a mutiny, about the possibility of Strath Glen being stormed by an irate population. And as scary as the thought is, as much danger as I'd be in, part of me still hopes it comes to fruition.

I look at my watch and pick up my pace. Monsieur won't be happy—I've already doubled the length of my excursion without even meaning to.

Once I'm close to the palace, I lift my gaze to the east wing, second floor. There, faintly noticeable through the vastness of the windows and their ornate cornices, I spot the minute figure of Monsieur Sawyer, and I find myself smiling. I think of the meeting I just attended—with not just allies, but friends—and the network I have inside the palace too, and it strikes me that despite King's presence, despite the draconian rules he enforces that limit my mobility, I have managed to craft a reasonable life here at Strath Glen. A life I don't hate.

Have I changed? Or is there simply good in every situation, and I've managed to find it? I'd like to think it's the latter, but something tells me it's a combination of the two. And then there's the revelation I had last night in Quire Park to contend with. That I never had much of a true community back in Quire. That I'm close to remarkably few people, considering how much time I spent there. Then, of course, there's the no-small-matter that by being betrothed to royalty, I've effectively ostracized myself from all the inhabitants of Quire, who incorrectly and unfairly assume either that I look down my nose at them now, or that I weaseled my way into palace life to begin with.

So, what will things look like if the population of Airo-Aurora does rise up? If King is forced to backtrack on not simply the override chip program, but the entire Selection system, too? I'd no longer be betrothed to the viscount or be obliged to serve as his handmaid—a goal I've been working toward since day one of my post-Selection life. And even though I don't rightfully belong here at Strath Glen, I think to myself as I scale the steep slope to the east of the palace, it would be strange to leave it. Returning to Quire, too, would be strange, and, judging by the behavior of some of those at Agnes' wedding, I wouldn't exactly be welcomed back either.

I sigh. It would seem that despite solving the mystery of the scrolls, life hasn't become any less complicated.

The kiss—*the* kiss—whispers through my mind, the most complex element of it all, but quickly I snuff the thought away, instead focusing on my footing and scanning the woods for beasts.

"Took your sweet time, hmm, Miss Alex?" calls Monsieur quietly into the night.

I smile. "It wasn't intentional, I can promise you."

"Do hurry. My beauty sleep awaits."

I grab the door he holds open, hang up my cloak, and follow him into the heart of the palace. "Thank you," I say before he can disappear down the servants' stairs to his sleeping quarters. "I'd like to return the favor, and quickly."

"Quickly?"

I scratch behind my ear. "Well, you see, I've made plans with the same friends to meet again in a few days' time—"

"Didn't you just, Miss Alex. I'll be thinking on that favor until the sleep fairies find me. Until next time," and he tips his head and vanishes from sight.

Not wanting to risk seeing anyone on the imperial staircase, and with Carnegie Reserve eerily quiet, I take the servants' stairs up to the House of Mirrors, trying to ignore the rush of nerves that makes my hair stand on end. And no sooner do I step foot onto the black and white checkerboard floor do I hear the sound of soft thuds echoing in the distance.

My head swivels, my heart pounds, and there he is—King of Airo-Aurora, walking along the House of Mirrors in the west wing, wearing a blood-red silk night coat that stands out even with the torches dimmed to their lowest setting.

The shiver starts at my shoulders, it traces its way down my entire spine.

A Cheshire grin, and he bypasses the imperial staircase and heads straight for me. I swallow, my feet cemented to the floor as I watch him stride ever closer, the fact that I broke the rules and snuck out of the palace tattooed plainly across my face. But really, that's nothing. Because what I and the others are planning is far, far worse than that. Far more scandalous, far more consequential, far more criminal.

The shiver intensifies.

"Dearest, dearest," he coos, adopting his often-used impression of a very old man. "Whatever are you doing out of bed in the middle of the cold, old night, hmm?"

Two things strike me at once. The first is a reminder that the palace is theater, and right now, I need to put on a show. The second is that even though I no longer wear a cloak, my face must still be flushed from the outdoors. Thinking quickly, I laugh in a sheepish way. "Why, I slipped downstairs for a glass of milk when the strangest thing happened!"

"But tell me, dear one!" King cries, looking, for the moment, genuinely amused.

"The torches on the wall flickered in the most unusual way, and—well, I don't know what came over me, but I sprinted up these stairs just now as though my life depended on it!"

"A spook, and a good one!" King exclaims happily. "Such

a funny thing when our mind plays tricks on us," and he taps me on the head.

"Indeed, it is. I better try to get some rest," I add, turning away.

A beat of silence, and then, "Is that typically what you wear to bed, my dearest?"

My heart jumps into my throat, and I freeze. But when I turn back to King, the breezy smile is once again plastered across my face, matching his with precision. "Have you never shared a room with your nephew, sir?"

"Indeed, I haven't."

"He has the most peculiar habit."

"Oh?"

I nod. "He insists on throwing the window open as wide as it will go—no matter the temperature. As you can imagine, a nightgown simply won't suffice."

"Ah, that is rather peculiar. Perhaps one I'll care to query him on in the morrow, hmm?"

"Indeed, sir," I say, waving goodnight and walking to my quarters with a steady gait. Locked inside though, I grip the wall and curse under my breath. Just my luck to run into King. And yet, I had played my cards well, and the interaction hadn't exactly been ominous, aside from that parting statement—that he'd query Wolfe about the open window in the morning.

It begs the question—why?

The most obvious answer is because he doesn't trust me...

I sigh, suddenly exhausted. The dying embers of the fire offer enough light for me to tiptoe across the room and to the awaiting sofa. And even though the wind howls through the open window, dropping the mercury to glacial temperatures, I'm careful to position the hide over me in such a way that my outfit remains ever so slightly visible. Just in case King thinks to ask Wolfe what it is I wear to bed.

four

. . .

THE NEXT MORNING, I find myself cocooned completely under the hide. Overhead, I can hear the continued whistling of the wind, along with footsteps and tinkering—Wolfe, it must be. Then again, perhaps I've over-slept—it wouldn't be surprising considering my late-night rendezvous. So perhaps it's Gerard, the butler, tidying the room and making up the bed.

"Alexandra."

The sound of my fiancé's voice somewhere above me, on the other side of the animal pelt, causes my eyes to widen. Muscles relaxed from a night of rest seize up. Once again, I think of that damn kiss, and I pretend to be asleep rather than face up to him.

"Alexandra," he says again, louder this time.

With no other choice, I pull down the pelt enough that I can peer—through coarse fur—up at a face that hovers several feet above mine, the brow scrunched sharply in the middle. "Good morning," I mutter.

He sighs. "I believe our current routine of systematically avoiding each other despite sharing a room is unsustainable.

This business of retiring to bed at separate times and pretending to be asleep to avoid each other—it's childish."

"I don't do that."

"You were doing so just now."

I sink down lower beneath the pelt. "So, what do you propose?"

Before he can respond, there comes a knocking at the door. Wolfe, looking put out, hesitates for a moment as he continues to hover over me, then withdraws to the far side of the room. I hear him muttering to one of the servants.

"I have a phone call to take," he says curtly from across the room. With that, he walks out the door, and slowly I exhale. Really, our routine of systematically avoiding each other isn't so bad, is it?

Simultaneously grimacing and blushing at the conversation, I lift myself from my hastily-made bed on the sofa and begin readying for the day, a task made all the more arduous by the removal of my preferred riding wear. I choose both a gown and cardigan at random, pull on the riding boots that Wolfe had returned to me, then head to the washroom, where I brush my hair and contemplate my reflection.

Even worn so haphazardly, the cardigan and gown give me an air of legitimacy. I look far more at home amongst luxuries than when I first arrived at Strath Glen, though the thought gives me no comfort. Well, Wolfe had said repeatedly that the others would ease up on me after the wedding, didn't he? Perhaps that will include the freedom to dress as I wish. I twist my heavy locks into a long braid that hangs over my shoulder and wonder if there will even be a wedding, following the address.

Slipping downstairs to the kitchen is the first task of the day, and with two bacon rolls in hand, I set out for the front doors. I hand one to Jill. "Any regrets about joining us last night?" I ask in an undertone.

She gazes at the highest bank of windows. "It was the right thing to do."

I nod, then consider the sparkling city laid out like a tapestry beneath us. Even from our spot on high, I can see the flashing of the screens lining Central Boulevard, cycling through news clips and ads. Cars and buses hum along the avenues, and factories around the perimeter of the city send up chutes of smoke to the warming sky. A typical day in Airo-Aurora, during not-so-typical times.

"How are you going to find info on the army?" Jill asks between bites.

"What—whether they're armed?" I shrug. "I guess I'll start with the prince's wife. Her father owns the only munitions factory in the nation-state."

"Better be careful, princess," she warns. "Asking questions makes people suspicious."

I can't help but agree. It's a risky endeavor, and maybe a pointless one.

"How was your friend's wedding, by the way? It was this past weekend, right?"

"Fine," I say quickly. Heat rises to my face. "It was a nice event," I add.

Jill gives me a curious look but says nothing more about it. I pop the last bite of the bacon roll into my mouth and wave goodbye, intending to track down Morocco. What to do when I locate her, though, leaves me unsure, especially with Jill's warning fresh in mind.

I don't make it very far when I notice voices emanating from Devonshire Commons, so I slow my gait and peer around the elaborate doorframe accented with gold leaf. A group of ladies play poker as the parrot looks on, but nowhere amongst them is Morocco. I tiptoe away before any of them can notice me, particularly Aubrey, who puffs on a cigar with her feet up.

It's not that I disdain her, not really. But I know how

emotional she's been since her lover, Butch, was taken by Lebwitski. I had seen her sorrow on Saturday, right before the wedding, when the two of them finally reunited and she found that he had changed. And right now, with too little sleep and too much stress, I'm not sure I can handle it all over again.

Past the Ming vases I go, barely acknowledging Counterdown with my gaze, despite how much I'd like to be inside right now, working on my cataloging project. Up the imperial staircase to the second floor, just like usual, except right now, I turn for the west wing, where Morocco and James reside.

The corridor is quiet, apart from the drilling in the ceiling, but—just my luck, it's James who pulls open the door when I finally muster the courage to knock.

"A splendid angel gracing my doorstep!" he exclaims happily. "I was just about to fasten my stirrups and prance in the most princely way off to work."

"Don't let me keep you."

"Indeed, Papa has decided to entrust me with the most important of dossiers—I've just received word. It seems your cantankerous fiancé is no longer the favorite!"

Now he has my attention, and I freeze. "Why do you say that?"

He winks. "Thought that'd tickle your fancy. Seems that dear old cousin did something he shouldn't have—how about that!"

Something he shouldn't have. My brain rings with alarm bells. "What did he do?"

"Heavens! These aren't matters you need to concern yourself with, my dearest angel."

"It's no matter," I assure him. "I'm simply curious—"

"A curious cat will get broken like that," he chimes—a phrase I've heard his mother use before.

"Does that mean you're no longer pushing for the throne?" I finally ask, changing tactics.

He waves his hand, one that sports a dazzling array of rings. "Now that I'm numero two? I think I shall wait to inherit the throne like a good little boy," and he winks again.

I nod as my thoughts race. Wolfe, in trouble? What on earth could he have done? After all, the man doesn't typically make mistakes, of that, I'm sure. And what about the jumble of emotions I feel?

Sure, the biggest impetus to fully trusting Wolfe all this time has been his loyalty to King. So, is that happiness in my chest? Relief? And yet, there's something else there, too. Something I can't put my finger on.

Concern, that's what.

Because if Wolfe really has been acting as a double agent all this time, losing his position as King's number two is a blow indeed...

James taps me on the head. "I'll see you later, dolly. A celebration is in order, I'd say," and then he's off, and I'm left standing alone in the east wing of the House of Mirrors.

I turn to the door and rap upon it once again.

"What?" Morocco snaps a moment later as she wrenches the door wide. "Oh—it's you," and her lip curls as she considers my ensemble. "What in holy hell do you want, Quire rat?"

"It's Alex," I remind her. "I was—" It strikes me how out of place I am. How suspect it is to show up here demanding to know details about her father's arms deal, just like Jill warned. So I switch tactics, swallowing my pride and saying, "I was hoping to—to spend some time together."

Her eyes narrow. I think she's going to laugh, but she yawns instead. "You're not trying to sell anything, are you?"

I shake my head.

"Fine. I'm having my breakfast. You can watch me eat."

I follow her inside, finding that her quarters are even

more lavish than Aubrey's. Most surfaces are coated with gold, but the touches of red lend a regal feel that I suppose is fitting for the second in line to the throne. My mouth twists at the thought, alongside my stomach, and once again, I mourn what was once my beautiful Airo-Aurora.

Morocco positions herself at a gold table laid out with a fantastic array of breakfast items—from Danishes, to scones, to omelets, all served on well-polished silverware. She lays a napkin across her lap, and I notice for the first time that she sports a velour tracksuit, as opposed to her typical scanty gowns. She picks up a croissant and calls to a maid named Honey, who appears from the shadows and begins at once straightening Morocco's blunt bob, aided by an abundant amount of hairspray.

I tentatively take a seat across from Morocco, who barely seems to notice my presence, or Honey's. Instead, she spoons jam inside her crumpet and dresses her tea.

"So," I begin, feeling more foolish by the second. "How have you been?"

She shoots me a sharp look. "Is this how those in that derelict Quire district you're from make small talk?"

I shrug. "Is it very different than other small talk?"

"I wouldn't know," she replies indifferently. "I don't do small talk."

"Very well. Tell me, are you reading any good books?"

She slumps back in her chair and groans.

"Uh—the wedding. The upcoming wedding between Wolfe and me. Have you, er, decided what you're going to wear?"

This, I can see, is the right conversation vein to land in, and immediately Morocco sits straighter. "Funny you should ask, you Quire dumpling, because I was just thinking about that very conundrum. Something spring-themed, that's a must—a terribly obvious one, indeed. But, what, then, of your chosen theme? Bohemian, says the birdie?"

I nod.

"Not my style in the slightest," she says with apathy. "Me? I like the bolder things in life, and bohemian is just the opposite—hum-drum and hempy."

"You're welcome to ignore the theme," I begin, but she just waves my words aside.

"I've been thinking a dress fashioned entirely from roses might be splendid. Oh, not the stems, of course—could you imagine?"

I force myself to laugh alongside her.

"And I'm also eyeing the ultimate in bohemian—a dress fashioned after that ridiculous creation story."

"Sorry?"

"The creation story," she reiterates, rolling her eyes as if I really am slow-witted. "You know, the one starring Adam and Eve, hmm?"

"Right."

"In the story, Eve always wears a leaf right over her crotch, her bottom, and her breasts. It's a fetching outfit, frankly, and certainly on theme." She chomps on a biscuit and fixes me with a piercing stare. "Don't you agree?"

I nod enthusiastically. "And how is Aubrey doing?" I ask, deciding that if there's ever a moment to bond with someone over gossip, it's now, no matter how lowly I consider it.

"An absolute puddle." She shakes her head.

"That's too bad," I offer. "Although she seemed in better spiri—"

"And it's her own doing," Morocco continues, as though she didn't even hear me. "What a stupid thing, to take a lover. It never ends well, did she really not realize?"

"I don't know what she was thinking," I say in an agreeable tone. "I suppose she wasn't."

"You're absolutely right. Thoughtless, completely."

I nod. Then, with a tightening in my stomach, I say,

"That meeting in Carnegie that King called recently was rather unpleasant. Have you quite recovered?"

She pulls a face. "*Such* dirty business."

"Your family business must be powerful indeed for King to have such a reaction."

"Oh, it is," she says with utter earnestness. "The Moody House of Weaponry is simply renowned the world over."

"I understand, then, why you wouldn't want it to be tarnished by a bad business deal."

Morocco swats Honey away and swings her hair from side to side, testing its bounce. After a quick nod at Honey, who promptly vanishes straight after, she pierces a strawberry and points it at me. "If only my husband could wrap his pee-wee-sized brain around that," and she sighs. "But, father-in-law has personally assured me that everything is aboveboard, so I suppose that solves the matter."

Another nod, given placidly, but inside, I reel. It sounds as though Morocco hasn't officially opposed the arms deal as I had hoped. "Have the weapons already been delivered, then?"

She eyes me, and I do my best to act nonchalant. "Why do you want to know?"

"I'm simply wondering what all that nonsense was about in Carnegie, I suppose. You see, if the weapons have already been delivered to the recipient, whoever that is—well, that just proves that things were aboveboard all along, doesn't it? I mean, it's not like there are helicopters bearing down on Strath Glen as we speak."

The two of us share a chuckle at something so outlandish.

Then she clears her throat. "I suppose I never thought of that angle. What did Father say? Oh, that's right—they're to be delivered this week. They changed the order to a more popular model allowing for far speedier delivery. Did you know it was your fiancé of all people who chose the original weapon? My, it would have taken past summer for those to arrive. Talk about egg on his face. I heard our angel the King was none too happy."

I blanch. Then, unsticking my lips from my teeth, ask, "Is that why Wolfe was demoted?"

"Was he? Heavens, no wonder my James was in such high spirits this morning. And speaking of him, that brings us round to you. Why is it every time I open my eyes, my husband has you wrapped up in his clutches like a pastry around a sausage?"

I'm too busy thinking to reply. The weapons deal did go through. The weapons are to be delivered in the coming days. Wolfe's actions—choosing the weapons with the longest delivery time in order to buy us time—were discovered. Caught by *King*. This is worse than I even imagined.

"Hmmm, little Quire rat?"

"Oh, yes—uh, James. I don't know why he bothers speaking to me in the first place, frankly."

"Nor do I. You're really rather plain."

"I should be going. I, er, enjoyed our chat."

"Let yourself out, doll. My feet need a rest," she adds as she pierces a waffle smothered in syrup.

I pull the door closed behind me and stand stalk-still in the west wing of the House of Mirrors. Right now, I feel shaky and unwell. Wolfe—I need to talk to Wolfe. Except he won't be in any mood to talk, not right now. In fact, I can only imagine how cantankerous he must be, knowing how much his position of power meant to him. Yes, best to avoid him. Between the kiss and the demotion, that's two good reasons to keep my distance.

And yet I need to speak to someone about what I've just learned. I turn once again for the front doors.

"I need to speak to you and the others about something," I declare a few minutes later.

Jill spits, then lifts a brow. "You supplying lunch?"

"I'd think the provision of breakfast earlier would suffice," I say, elbowing her. "Anyhow, it's too risky for me to sneak off palace grounds in broad daylight."

"Not another late-night meeting," she says, yawning.

"This evening. Can you make it?"

"I guess so. Same spot?"

"There's another park just up the street from here, off of Central Boulevard to the east."

"Skelton Park. Yeah, I know it."

After a few more minutes of chitchat, I take off for Devonshire Commons, now empty. With no Monsieur in sight, I head down to the underground garage. There, on his hands and knees, Monsieur Sawyer polishes the rims of the gleaming behemoth.

"So, this is why it always sparkles," I observe as I near him.

"Miss Alex. You look well-rested, considering."

"And so do you. Surely it wouldn't be too much trouble to do the same thing, tonight?"

"Surely you jest."

"I wish I was."

He glares at me. "Do this for me, do that for me. Shouldn't you be rearranging that library of ours?"

"After a quick outing in this," and I tap the limousine, "if you would be so kind."

"Oh, isn't that the cherry on top. It's two favors you ask for? And this outing—is it sanctioned by your loving fiancé?"

"You do know we now share a suite, Monsieur."

"Ah, so that's a no, then. Quick, off you go."

"I am no longer subject to those ridiculous sanctions he imposed, making his express permission necessary for you to take me from the palace. Please, Monsieur."

"And where are we going?"

"Hallah. A short drive and an even shorter mission."

"That being?"

"Does Monsieur always ask so many questions of his patrons?"

"Does Miss wish to walk?"

"If you must know, I'd like to inquire with a friend who works there about the creation of software for use in the library," I lie, simultaneously proud of my quick thinking and ashamed of my deceptiveness.

"That seems in order, I suppose."

I nod.

"I'll take you, but on one condition."

"Sir?"

"Let me in on just what transpired at the wedding between hers and the great Lord."

"Excuse me, Monsieur?"

"Don't think for even a second I didn't pick up on the tension clogging up this beautiful machine on the drive home." He strokes the behemoth with great fondness. "Heavier than a wet blanket sewn with weights and alight with electricity. Something large transpired between the two of you, I'm sure of it."

"Hallah, please, monsieur."

"The lady won't indulge me?"

"The lady, so to speak, doesn't wish her messy personal life splashed about the entire palace. It was you who warned me, did you not, how fast word at Strath Glen spreads?"

He flashes me a mischievous grin as he throws open my door. "You really are growing accustomed to life around here."

"More than you know," I agree, once buckled into the backseat. "I hate to repeat myself," I continue as we charge into sunlight, "but this short journey isn't my only request."

He throws a look at me through the rear-view mirror. "Indulge me."

"I really would like to escape the confines of the palace

tonight, using the help of you or the other servants. I wasn't joking."

"I didn't think you were. In fact—another favor? Why, nothing would surprise me less, my lady. Lucky for you, it's my evening playing watchman for the others, Miss Alex, or you'd be high and dry. You've been ingratiating yourself to some of the help, so I've heard, but still, many consider you to be a generously betrothed soon-to-be royal."

"Is that a yes?"

"Consider it your lucky day."

"Thank you, Monsieur. I really do owe you one."

"Several, by this point, Miss Alex. Here we are—Hallah awaits."

"I won't be long," I assure him, sliding out of the seat and ignoring his grumblings. Since the workplace has already been mentioned between the chauffeur and me several times, I don't bother averting my eyes as I enter the square, glass-covered building, and when I step inside the large office space dotted with computers and bursting with the symphony of a thousand clicking keys, I throw caution to the wind and call Timothee's name.

"Long time, no see," he jokes as he sets down his coffee mug and starts toward me. He stumbles over a loose shoelace.

"I just wanted to say hello," I say casually, then I lean closer to him and lower my voice. "Can we meet again tonight? Same place?"

He arches an eyebrow. "Already? Must be important."

I nod.

"Okay. I mean, yeah—I guess I can squeeze it in."

"I know you're busy," I say pointedly. "Is it, er, coming along?"

He grins. "It's a work of beauty, if I may say so," and he bows deeply.

Relief and excitement follow me back to the limo, but

once I'm buckled in the backseat, I wonder how much further I can push my luck with Monsieur Sawyer. I clear my throat.

"Oh, what now?" he cries.

"My aunt. It's almost lunch, so she's likely to be home—"

"Off to Quire we go," he shouts gaily before I can finish the sentence.

"Thank you, sir. That's very—generous of you."

"You've hit the nail on the head with that comment," he replies as he arcs the behemoth up Central Boulevard. Immediately, I press my nose to the window, though this time, it isn't the fancy shops I'm trying to glimpse. No, I'm looking for any sign of the White Ribbon Campaign. Ribbons pinned to jackets, flyers tacked to lampposts—but the limousine hums along far too quickly for me to do a thorough examination. Eventually, I lean back in my seat and close my eyes instead. It's Quire I want to block out. Not only has the sight of it become that much more painful recently, given the memories it drags up from before the accident that took my parents, but there are too many fresh memories of Agnes' wedding, too. Like, the revelation that maybe Quire isn't my rightful place. That maybe I was never as close to the community as I'd assumed. I think of the kiss with Wolfe and sink even lower in my seat.

"Ah, here we are," says Monsieur, switching off the engine. He bounds from the driver's seat before I can move and throws open my door.

"Thank—"

"I'll see you inside, no worries about that," he continues, ushering me up the drive and to the front door of the small circular house that I've called home for the past few years.

Aunt Jo throws open the door on the first knock. "Another visit, so soon? It's my lucky day!"

"Mine, too, Aunt. Monsieur Sawyer has been most obliging this morning."

Monsieur, beaming, dives into a bow. "My lady," he adds to my aunt. "One Madam Josephine, if memory serves me?"

"That's right. Are you two coming inside? Beautiful turn in the weather, but all the same—it is lunch. Can I fix you something?"

"No—" I begin, but Monsieur cuts me off.

"Lunch would be most appreciated, Madam," and he offers another bow.

I stare at him, then reluctantly follow him inside. Having Monsieur here hadn't exactly been part of the plan—how am I supposed to ask Aunt Jo what she thought of Wolfe now? And then I smack my forehead and scramble around the corner to the kitchen. Two minutes to noon. I grab a pen and paper and rush to the guest room.

"Alex?" Aunt Jo shouts. Concern touches her voice.

"I just have to do something," I call. Hurriedly, I write out tonight's meeting time and location on the paper and spend the next ten minutes staring at it, just like Neo instructed.

Finally, I scrunch the paper into a ball, throw it in the trash bin, and return to the kitchen just as my aunt serves up steaming slices of lamb pie. I pick up a fork and smile. "Did you enjoy yourself at the wedding, Aunt?"

"More than I should have. I'm still catching up on sleep. And you? You must've slipped off early, or so Agnes said."

Agnes. Damn. Someone else to track down, and I shoot a look at Monsieur. He doesn't seem to notice. "Uh, yes— Wolfe had work he needed to do," I explain, another lie. "I'm sorry, I should've found you first—"

"No need to apologize to me," she says merrily. "And God knows, we got to spend some time together before the ceremony, wasn't that nice?"

I nod. "You enjoyed—" and my eyes dart to Monsieur and back again—"that? The tour, ahem, and everything?"

"With your fiancé, you mean?" she asks, completely

missing my cues to be cryptic, and, indeed, I spot Monsieur's eyebrows dash up. "I sure did. Mighty nice chap, that one. Do you know him well, Monsieur Sawyer?" she asks, turning to him.

"Oh, indeed I do, madam. A good man and well-suited, I think, to your beloved niece."

Aunt Jo beams, and for the rest of the meal, the two of them chat amiably. Once we return to the behemoth, I ask Monsieur to stop at the Quire nursery, where I learn that Agnes neglected to show up to work that morning.

———

ONCE WE PULL up the drive to Strath Glen, my insides twist. Smoke curls into the sky from a third-floor balcony, and I can see the large outline of King standing there, puffing his cigar like a chimney, watching the hulking behemoth glide past the entrance statues—lions with serpents' tongues—and toward the underground garage. How much trouble will I be in when he discovers it was me enlisting Monsieur to leave Strath Glen? Worse yet, how much trouble will Monsieur be in?

Still, it's not like I left palace grounds without a chaperone, and wasn't that the issue from the very start?

Then the twisting in my stomach grows worse as I remember what I gleaned this morning: that King is cross with Wolfe, that Wolfe has been demoted, and that James has taken over the role as King's right-hand man. Not only does it make me worry over Wolfe, but it makes me worry about myself, too. For without the protection of the country's number two, I'm more exposed than before.

Then there's the reason why Wolfe has fallen out of favor, and its myriad of implications. The weapons deal— that damn weapons deal. King had discovered Wolfe had selected the weapon with the longest shipping time, so how much trust has been lost? Or had Wolfe managed to convince his uncle that it was nothing more than an oversight? An error, yes, but one made without intention?

I can only hope so, I think to myself as I step inside the palace.

I'm accosted immediately by Evie. "Oh, sister, did you hear the news?"

"What news?"

"It's Dear Matthew—he's missing!"

"Missing? But I thought—"

"His family has been in touch and everything—he's absolutely nowhere to be found! Isn't that terrifying and tragic all at once?"

"Perhaps he doesn't want to be found," I suggest. After all, living here wasn't something he wanted. And, frankly, now that everyone knows about Aubrey's lover, he has some justification to vanish. But it's difficult to vanish in Airo-Aurora. Impossible. "Have his chips—"

"Uncle's on the phone with the Mainframe as we speak. The palace is absolutely buzzing, my!"

"And Aubrey? Is she alright?"

"She's not here," Evie whispers conspiratorially. "Rumor has it she's gone to visit with Butch. He isn't allowed on the premises anymore, did you know?" Before I can reply, her face turns glum. "It makes you think, doesn't it? If only we could choose our mates, none of this would ever have happened. Sister, please—you have more connections outside palace walls than I. Whatever is the state of the White Ribbon Campaign?"

I hesitate, my natural proclivity to protect Evie the cause. Finally, though, I say in an undertone, "I believe it's continuing, despite being designated a terrorist organization, but will be conducting most of its business underground."

"But whatever will being discrete accomplish?"

"I'm not sure," I admit, "but it's better than the alternative."

"What is the alternative?"

"Uh—nothing."

"No, tell me, sister. What would happen to people should they be known members of the campaign?"

I stare at her and feel a push-pull sensation deep inside my chest. She deserves the truth—everyone does. But I couldn't live with myself if something were to happen to her.

"Where were you?" comes a cold, chiding voice, and I'm distracted from Evie's round eyes by the clicking of approaching footsteps. Wolfe strides along the corridor toward us, a frown bending his face. "My uncle, though currently distracted by other matters, will soon get wind of your outing."

"Monsieur Sawyer took me to have lunch with my aunt," I reply. "You can tell your uncle that Monsieur dined with us, so I was chaperoned the entire time."

Some of Wolfe's cantankerous mood seems to ebb. "I assume Evie's filled you in on the latest palace drama?"

I nod. "A husband on the run."

"Not for long. His location was easily surmised just now, as any halfwit would expect."

"So where is he, Brother?" Evie asks.

"The Sky Center. He'll be returned to Strath Glen shortly."

And then, as if on cue, there comes a commotion from around the corner. The three of us glance at one another, then start forward.

The front door is flung open, and Dear Matthew is being marched inside by a pair of bluecoats, looking put out. "What kind of insipid treatment is this?" he shouts. Then, upon seeing Wolfe, he asks, "Can a man not charter a flight from time to time?"

"You can take him to the third floor," Wolfe advises the bluecoats. "His father-in-law will be most anxious to see him," and a thin smile curls Wolfe's lip.

"Please, no!" Dear Matthew shouts, his eyes wide. "Alex, Evie—I implore you!"

I turn to Wolfe, even as the shouting continues. "That was rather cruel," I inform him.

"You think he should be applauded for trying to skirt his responsibilities and flee the country?" he counters. "Besides," he adds into my ear as Evie scolds the bluecoats, "this should deflect attention from you, and I'll take any opportunity I can to do that."

"Evie!" cries the duchess, who appears suddenly from Devonshire. "Why in heavens aren't you completing your studies?"

"There is so much excitement, you see, with—"

"Right now," her mother continues, just as a stern-looking woman with a tight bun appears from the study tapping her watch.

"How boorish and unfair," Evie pouts, dragging her feet along the polished floor. "I'll see you at dinner," she adds over her shoulder before disappearing through the doorway, looking defeated.

And then we're alone, just Wolfe and me, and memories of that kiss come roaring back. Quickly I glance at him, I find him staring straight at me, and then his gaze is on the floor. He plays with something in his pocket, and I clear my throat and consider the wall. Finally, I draw up the courage to address what needs to be addressed. "I spoke to James this morning."

"Ah. Then he'll have brought you up to speed on my uncle's displeasure with me."

"A worrisome turn," I say pointedly. "Especially considering the reason for his displeasure."

"How did you come to know such things?"

"Morocco."

In my peripheral vision, I watch his gaze narrow. "I didn't realize the two of you were so friendly."

I don't bother to respond. Instead, I zero in on the most pressing matter—the one that crisscrosses my chest like a knot. "Does it mean he is now suspicious of your allegiance?" I ask in an undertone.

"I don't know," Wolfe murmurs, shoving his hands into his pockets. "In any event, now that I've been replaced by James on his special dossiers, I'll have time to complete my own work for once. On that note, I'll be working late the next few nights as I play catch-up." He promptly turns on his heel and disappears up the stairs.

Working late, I think to myself with a groan. So, how am I to sneak out of the palace now?

five

. . .

WOLFE HADN'T BEEN at dinner, and, despite the clock drawing ever closer to eleven o'clock, he hasn't returned to our quarters yet, either.

Finally, with nothing else to do, I roll up a house coat and some cardigans, arrange them under the animal pelt, throw open the window near the sofa so Wolfe doesn't have to, and slip out the door.

Monsieur and Rosa once again stand near the window, chatting in an amiable way as Rosa dusts the spotless window frames. A ruse, I suppose, if a royal does indeed stream past, late to bed. With a wink at them both, I dive down the servants' stairs, skittish at the possibility of bumping into my fiancé or, worse yet, King. Careful around corners, particularly since music still emanates from Carnegie, I dart to the backdoor unseen and pull on a cloak.

Out the back door that latches itself securely behind me, around the palace to the east, through the tree line where the guards stationed at the front door can't see. Walking along the city sidewalks is easy, flooded with light as they are, but once I reach Skelton Park, the light stops, and the park looks like a pit of blackness—more so than the previous night.

A good thing, I remind myself, since less stimuli to the visual feed prompts less automated surveillance. Still, I'm timorous as I stick a toe in. A large sculpture I hadn't noticed before plunges upward from the ground, torquing itself in a way that looks downright sinister swallowed by darkness. The fir trees that dot the park seem to suck up any whisper of light gifted from the stars, and the dampness brought by spring reaches my bones.

Despite beginning to lament my decision to call a meeting, I push forward into the heart of the park, even as the darkness quivers.

"Did you bring a flashlight?" comes Jill's voice.

Timothee starts to respond, but he bumps into something and groans instead.

"Wouldn't a flashlight rather defeat the point of meeting under the cover of darkness?" I ask, smiling.

"Would save us some bruises, though," moans Timothee.

"Is the other guy coming?" Jill asks.

"I think so, but we'll have to wait and see. I have a way of communicating with him, but he has no ability to communicate back."

"And you're sure about this guy?" she continues.

"What do you mean?"

"I mean, he's sort of been playing god, hasn't he?"

"I suppose he has," I say slowly. "Certainly, I wouldn't have wound up at Strath Glen if he'd let the Mainframe decide my fate like everyone else."

"No shit. And it doesn't make you mad?"

I consider the question but finally shake my head. "He's trying to do something bigger than that. Bigger than me. Bigger than my life."

"Maybe. But why did this Neo fellow think to target a bunch of teenagers with something so important?"

"Because only they could marry into the royal family," Timothee responds. "Right, Alex?"

"And because so long as we're shy of eighteen, we're subject to less automated surveillance, giving us more leeway to poke around—maybe even interfere with the status quo. Exactly like we're doing."

"Don't forget," adds Timothee, "that the national address plan wouldn't work without Neo's help."

And then we're silent at the sound of approaching footsteps. "I saw your message," Neo says to me as he joins us. "Sorry I'm late. What did I miss?"

"Nothing," I say quickly. "I mean—we haven't started yet. We were waiting for you."

"Great. So, how's the program coming?" he asks Timothee.

"It's coming together nicely, but it's slow work. If I use the wrong angle, someone could strain a joint. Make the movements too fast, and they could tear a ligament. On the flip side, if the movements aren't extreme, it looks too natural."

"Sounds like a real balancing act."

"It is," Timothee agrees, then he turns to me. "Why'd you want to meet again so soon?"

"I did some digging around," I explain, "and I discovered that the army of Mavericks—the ones with override chips that are at King's beck and call—will receive weapons this week."

"Crap. I thought the ones with the slowest delivery were ordered—"

"It was caught. And he's been demoted," I add in a somber voice.

"Wow, that's not good. Is he in trouble?"

"I don't know," I admit. "He won't say. I'm hoping King chalks it up to an innocent mistake."

"Is there anything we can do to stop the weapons from

reaching the army?" Jill asks. "Because once that happens, we're pretty much screwed. Nobody's going to cause a stink if they're faced with robots with guns."

"That's why I wanted to meet. There must be something we can do. The weapons were ordered from the Moody House of Weaponry—probably everything to do with that sale is digitized."

"So you'd like to hack into the system and cancel the order," Timothee correctly surmises.

"Is it possible—"

"Doubtful. It would take weeks to do that properly. Don't forget I'd need to develop a way in and create a way to cover my tracks. Plus, I'm already working full-time on the program for the address."

Slowly I nod. "There has to be another way, then. Even delaying delivery by a week may be all we need."

"You said the army is about a hundred miles north of here?" Neo asks.

"Yes—in Ashville Range. Why?"

"I'm wondering how the King plans to deliver the weapons to such a remote location. Will they be shipped to Strath Glen first?"

"That's a good point. I have no idea where they're being delivered, but I could try to find out."

"Even if they are delivered to the palace, what's princess going to do about it?" Jill asks.

"That's another good point," I say. "I don't know how to destroy guns. I could hide them, maybe..."

"Even if you did manage to hide them, don't you think the King would suspect you?" Timothee asks. "Plus, it would be all over your feed."

I'm forced to agree. "But I can't exactly sit back and do nothing about it," I continue. "Don't forget the people the Mavericks shoot aren't the only victims—the Mavericks are becoming killers against their will, too."

Our four are silent as we digest the magnitude of this last statement.

"Could there be a way to sabotage the guns without making it obvious?" Timothee wonders.

"That's what I'm wondering," I say, my brain churning.

"Was it the bluecoats or the blackcoats that rounded up the Mavericks in the first place?" Jill asks.

"The bluecoats—Mainframe officers."

"So it's likely they'll be the ones distributing the weaponry," she continues. "I work at the Mainframe from time to time, plus I know most of the greencoats that are posted there. Assuming they do take delivery, I can let you know when they arrive."

"That would be per—"

"That would be perfect if you knew how to sabotage a bunch of guns," Timothee reminds me.

Jill shrugs. "Switching out the ammo would buy us some time."

"Switching out the ammo?"

"Yeah, you know—with the wrong-sized bullet."

"Where could we get different-sized ammo?"

"The bluecoats would have a supply of whatever ammo their guns take." She yawns. "I'm damn tired, princess. Is that enough of a plan for you?"

I yawn myself. "I think it's going to have to be."

"Are we still meeting Wednesday night?"

"Let's, but see what we can find out about the status of the White Ribbon Campaign in the meantime," says Neo. "The leader/Your friend may prove to be very useful. On that note, why isn't she here tonight?"

"I went to her work to invite her," I explain, "but she wasn't there."

We say our goodbyes a minute later, and I break free of the blackness and emerge back onto Airo-Aurora's well-lit streets. It hadn't been the most productive meeting, and yet I feel a surge of fondness for the others—their willingness to listen and to help. Besides, we have the makings of a plan, or the start of one, to delay the delivery of weapons to the innocent Mavericks. Perhaps I can even do some research of my own in the palace's library, to see if I can learn anything about guns and their ammunition. My mind whirls over the possibilities as my eyes scan the second-floor windows for a familiar figure.

There. I lift an arm to him, then follow the tree line back up around the palace, the same way I came down. A few minutes later, the back door inches open, and Monsieur ushers me inside.

"Did you enjoy your little slice of freedom, Miss Alex?"

"Immeasurably. Did the viscount retire?"

"About a half hour ago."

"Excellent."

"Is it time for your beauty rest?"

"Does this mean it is time for you to get some sleep?"

"I wish. Instead, another still roams the streets, likely getting pissed at one of the pubs. I envy you your slumbers, Miss Alex," he adds as we climb the servants' stairs.

"I'll stay up and wait with you, then. It's no trouble—"

He waves away my words. "The viscount will have my head if he gets wind of it. Skuttle off to bed—don't make me repeat myself."

I say goodnight, then move with exceptional quiet as I slip into the walnut-lined entrance hall of my chambers and then through the next door. The fire still burns brightly, so I have no trouble at all seeing the towering figure of my fiancé sitting on top of the animal skin on the sofa, the very one I'm supposed to currently be under. The cardigans and housecoat I had stuffed in my place now sit folded up neatly next to it.

I go still, frozen in place near the door.

Slowly he turns that morose face to mine, his gaze so

piercing under the flickering light that it stops my heart. I almost wish it wouldn't start up again. Instead, I'm left to drag my feet forward, nothing to do now but accept my fate.

Still, he says nothing. He just watches me with those inhuman eyes.

The heat of the fire slowly becomes suffocating. I pull off my cloak and then my boots, relieved to have something occupy me. Something to distract me from that look he levels my way.

Still, nothing.

Then he stands to his full height and, in two long strides, reaches me. He seems taller than usual, I think, as I angle my head way back. He clasps his hands together and says in the calmest voice I've yet to hear from him, "Where were you?"

I wince. "Me?"

"Yes, Alexandra. You."

My heart hammers. "I was meeting with friends, not far from here. Best to go under the cloak of nightfall where King is concerned."

His gaze narrows. "So why deceive me? Why leave sweaters where your body should lie?"

"How is it you came to realize—?"

"Alex," he growls.

"Right—not time for questions of my own. As for yours, well—I didn't think you'd be all that keen—"

"Were you sneaking out to meet with that boy?"

"What boy?"

He slowly folds his spine in two so that his face pushes uncomfortably close to mine. "That boy that keeps showing himself at *my* palace. That boy who couldn't stop *gushing* over you at the wedding. What other *boy* would I be talking of?"

"You're frightening me."

His mouth presses together, as though I'm the most frustrating thing he ever had the misfortune of encountering. But he draws himself upright, turns to the fire, and puts some space between us.

"Patrick, you mean," I say eventually. "Yes, I suppose I should have figured that was who you were talking about. Forgive me for having other things on my mind."

"Answer my question, then."

"It's an easy answer. No, I wasn't with Patrick. What I'm curious about is why you're so distrustful in that sense."

"Your curiosity doesn't interest me at the moment," he replies. "Who were you meeting with and why?"

I drop my voice to a whisper. "I was meeting with Jill, Timothee, and the Mainframe technician to discuss the weapons destined for the Mavericks. Happy?"

He sighs loudly. "I suppose there's nothing I could do or say to stop you from playing detective?"

"No, there isn't—and I don't appreciate your condescension."

"Fine. Regarding your meeting, is there anything else that was discussed? Anything...plotted?"

"You know of my desire to right this wrong."

"Meaning?"

"You know what it means, sir."

"Always Wolfe, didn't I tell you? You intend to interfere somehow, I take it?"

I say nothing.

He gives me a hard look. "Alex?"

"You cannot control me, just as I cannot control you. You don't hear me commanding you to share what precisely happened with King following the weapons debacle, do you?"

"That doesn't concern you."

"On the contrary, I feel it's relevant to our united desire to stop King and, at a minimum, his override chip program."

He grips me around the arm and stares down at me with a pensive look on his face. "You finally believe me?"

I speak plainly, "We're allies, you and me. That, I accept —wholeheartedly." Then, because the viscount looks consumed by this turn of affairs, I use the time to go to the closets and get changed. "If memory serves me, I have a dress fitting first thing in the morning," I announce. "Goodnight."

He half-nods, as though he only half-hears me.

six

. . .

THE DRESS FITTING TAKES place in a room designed just for the purpose. Shaped like an octagon, a triple-pane mirror that reaches the ceiling stands in the middle, and in front of it is a small platform painted black. Various tape measurers hang along the wall, along with a variety of ribbon and a basket holding pin cushions. The room, tucked behind a plain-looking door, is situated near my old residence, the guest room, and right now, it's inexplicably full of people.

"Evie?" I shout, just barely avoiding the elbow of a small man dressed dazzlingly well and holding a ball of white fabric. Upon closer inspection, I discover it's, in fact, a dress on a hanger, folded into eights. Soon, I count seven others holding similar garments, while a trio of tailors ready their tools. A team of servants dust the floor and walls while the royals and their guests drape across the furniture, sipping mimosas.

"Isn't this splendid, sister? I told you this fitting would make the last one pale in comparison, didn't I?"

I force myself to nod. "It's...wonderful."

Evie laughs gaily. "I can see right through you, though I

must say, I do appreciate the attempt at enthusiasm! Come now—it's just a few dresses to try on, sister," she continues, steering me toward the mirrors. "Once you pick your favorite, we'll have it sized here and now, splendid? We really are getting down to the wire—my!"

Before I can respond, the duchess grips me around the shoulders. "I ran into my son this morning," she says in my ear. "You heeded my words!"

"I'm sorry, madam?"

"I haven't seen him look so well-rested in ages. Can you even comprehend how that makes me feel?"

"Happy?" I try.

She gives me a woeful look in the mirror. "Not *happy*, child. *Relieved.*"

"Well, madam, he is deserving of a restful night," I say, masking my confusion. After all, he was kept up late by none other than myself.

"Excuse me, everyone!" trills a voice from the far side of the room. A woman with a bun resembling a pin cushion walks from her spot alongside the window to the platform, where she places two fingers inside her mouth and whistles. The room quiets to a tomb.

"My name is Monique, and I am the chief executive officer of today's operation. Would a Miss Alex of Quire please join me?"

The duchess gives me one last knowing squeeze, and, with Evie by my side, I step onto the platform. For a moment, Monique is quiet—examining me, turning my face side to side, lifting and shifting my braided hair, peering down my cardigan.

"Dress Uno, please proceed forward. Graced *A Bed of Flowers* from House Barnaby!" she proclaims, stepping down from the platform as one of the giant balls of fabric pushes toward me. Monique wastes no time stripping me of my cardigan and then pushes me around the mirrors with

Evie holding the fabric ball, which now resembles a real dress. A dress covered in fabric-sewn flowers in various shapes and sizes. As I begin to remove the gown I'd thrown on at random that morning, a string quartet begins to play in the far corner of the room, and the realization that this will take a while begins to sink in.

"What was mother going on about?" Evie asks as she helps pull the flower-covered dress over my head. She smooths out the bodice, blows hair from my neck, then zips it tight.

"She discovered your brother had been sleeping on the couch, leaving me the bed, and she was none too happy about it."

"And now?"

"And now we've switched, and this morning he appeared exceptionally well-rested."

"You switched just last night?"

"No," I admit. "It was several nights ago."

"So what transpired last night to make brother rest so easily?" Excitement glints in the girl's eyes.

"Nothing like that," I scold. And, in truth, I don't know what would have caused him to sleep so well.

Then, as Monique starts tutting her tongue impatiently over the violin solo, I round the corner, and the room inhales as one. I'm helped onto the platform and stare at myself from all angles as the others in the room do the same, some pinching the gown, others prodding my body.

"What do you think?" Monique queries. "Give your most honest opinion, don't be shy."

"I think it's beautiful," I acknowledge. "But I'm afraid this train is more formal than I was picturing for a bohemian affair." I glance at Evie, who nods knowingly. Even the duchess looks impressed.

"And yet the flowers are perfectly fitting, don't you find?" counters the dressmaker.

The fitting room door flies open at that moment, and there stands James. "Thought I heard voices. Ah—a beautiful bird is born!" he cries, and the crowd parts for the prince of Airo-Aurora. "You know what I'm starting to think? You're far too sweet to be marrying that skulking old man to whom you're betrothed. I propose a switcheroo—I simply can't shake the candy-coating that has covered my lips since our kiss."

"A kiss?" the duchess demands, looking instantly scandalized.

"Please, madam—" I begin.

"James forced himself," Evie explains efficiently, shooting her cousin an indecent look.

He merely shrugs. "Your brother didn't take it so well himself. I must say, I think resorting to violence was quite beastly and hereunto unnecessary, but, to each his own." He steps on the platform next to me and positions his hands on my waist. "I like her, come Jupiter!"

"Cousin," interrupts Evie, "she has twenty-seven more gowns to try on, do you realize? Would you please let us be?"

With a peck on my nose and on Evie's, he walks out the door as Monique announces the maker of *Dress Deux.*

"Tell me what's going on between you and brother, won't you?" Evie whispers once we're hidden behind the mirror again.

I turn my eyes to her as I step into the next gown. "What do you mean?"

"You know what I mean! I always tell you what's happening in my love life, don't I? Tell me all about what happened at the wedding between you and brother, won't you?"

My eyes widen, and the dress falls around my ankles.

Evie gasps.

"Whatever is wrong?" shouts Monique. "Has a dress torn? Quick, answer!"

"No," I assure her. "No, everything is fine. I'll be out in just a moment." Evie grabs the dress and fastens it, which turns out to be a daring number with a plunging neckline. "The whole thing is a mess—one lost in a blur of regret," I mutter.

"Regret?"

I give her a look. "I honestly don't know what my feelings are toward him, Evie. And yet we shared a kiss. I can't even begin to think what he must think of me."

"Mademoiselle, are you quite ready?"

"Coming!" I call.

"It will all work out," Evie assures me as she draws back the curtain. "I simply know it will."

I round the corner as the room once again inhales in unison.

So the morning goes until, finally, after hours of the same monotonous routine, I reach the final dress, one that turns out to be the most casual of the lot and is immediately my favorite. Monique scribbles notes on her clipboard as I observe the floor-length gown fashioned of white satin, a ribbon of lace encircling my waist and capping my shoulders. My arms are bare, but otherwise, no skin shows. I nod enthusiastically to Evie, who studies it for several more minutes before giving it her seal of approval. The duchess looks satisfied, too, and the tailor approaches with a series of pincushions tucked between her fingers.

And then, from the House of Mirrors, there comes a ruckus, and I think James has returned, but no, because the door is being banged upon, and suddenly, as the room quiets, a servant screams, "Security breach!" at the top of her lungs.

Immediately the room swells with panic.

Mimosas are dropped, glass shatters. Morocco and Aubrey scream, the duchess grabs Evie around the wrist and pulls her through the door, Monique hot on her heels along with the rest of the royals. The dressmakers and tailors follow suit, leaving me alone standing in my wedding dress.

I sigh. Just five more minutes and the fitting would be over, and I would be free to spend the rest of the day tucked inside the library, researching ammo and working on the catalog system, daydreaming about King's downfall following the sabotaged national address.

"RUN!" a servant screams at me, who happens to be sprinting past the fitting room.

Reluctantly I poke my head into the corridor. Servants rush toward the stairs, some looking genuinely concerned, others giggling with excitement. An unknown person has breached security and entered the palace, that much I glean from their conversations. Made it past the two guards flanking the entranceway and disappeared amongst the tapestries.

The panic from one intruder, I reason, is really overblown. Of course, as one of the least fascinating folks in the palace, that's easy for me to say. The rest of the royal family are high-profile public figures, and vaguely I wonder if Wolfe's been notified of the breach, if he's locked inside his office along Bishop's Aisle.

Lifting the dress carefully around my ankles, I take the servants' stairs down to the kitchens, hours of trying on dress after dress leaving me famished. I take a sandwich from a large spread being prepared for King and some businessmen he hosts, and I consider my reflection in the shiny steel appliances. I have to admit, it really is a beautiful dress, and I decide to head back to the fitting room and wait for the tailors there.

I don't get very far down the corridor, however, when I spot a figure dart along the adjoining corridor, cast in shadows. Still, her taffeta dress and towering yellow hair leave little doubt—Aubrey.

"In here!" she shouts a moment later, and for a second, I wonder if she's shouting at me.

Then there comes another flash. This time it's a large and hulking figure. The very same one I had spotted on the float at the Winter's End parade—Butch.

I lunge forward and shove my nose around the corner in time to see the princess pull him inside a dark room, kicking the door closed with her diamond-crusted high-heeled shoe.

I stand stalk-still until sounds of amorous activity propel me up the stairs. Well then. There's the source of the security breech, mystery solved. Still, it's strange, though.

Because Butch already had the override chip implanted in his brain. So, why would someone being controlled by the Mainframe break the rules and behave so scandalously? Isn't that what the override chip works to prevent? Perhaps the question isn't why—it's *how.*

This is what occupies me as I traipse up the stairs, and I barely notice the shadow cast across the main floor landing. Then Dear Matthew grabs me by the wrist. "It's him, isn't it?" he asks. "You saw their sickening display at the parade, I spotted you shivering along the sidelines—always the bridesmaid and never the bride, huh?" He seems to notice my dress at that moment and does a double-take, but already his legs propel him down the stairs, a series of greencoats tumbling after him.

I stare after them, more bewildered by the second. Matthew refused to even live at the palace with Aubrey until the pregnancy was announced, so why should he care so deeply about Aubrey's lover now?

"Alex," comes a cold and scolding voice. I turn to see the tall frame of the viscount bearing down on me, his brow drawn into a stern line. Suddenly he goes still. He pulls back and folds his hands away, blood blush tinging his cheeks.

The dress, I realize, and immediately I turn away. "You... You weren't supposed to see."

He turns away, too. "There's been a security breach, haven't you heard?" he says, eventually.

"Indeed."

"And you're strolling casually about the palace, why?"

"I was hungry." He rounds on me, but I lift my hands to placate him. "Alas, the intruder is Aubrey's lover, Butch. Nothing more terrifying than love roams these halls."

He glances at me, looking exasperated. "I'll let you get back to things, then," he says, vanishing a moment later.

I continue upstairs, sitting on the edge of the black-painted platform in the fitting room as I wait for the entourage to slowly file back inside. Once the room is full—minus Aubrey, of course—tea is served, and then pins are pushed and pulled as the dress is readied to fit like a glove.

After a short speech by Monique, thanking everyone, and after readying a short list of invitees for Evie so that invitations can be sent out, I'm released back to the day. I pull my oversized cardigan around me, then busy myself at the back of the library, working once again on my catalog.

seven

· · ·

"SISTER!" Evie hollers from the other side of the dining hall, her voice barely noticeable amongst the swell of frenzied ones.

Ever since the intruder earlier, a man quickly confirmed to be Aubrey's lover and the father of her baby, the palace has been in an uproar. It has been made no better by the most recent news that Matthew has once again fled the grounds, such was his devastation. Aubrey isn't in attendance for tonight's meal—from what I've heard, she's been sent to her room and grounded, much like a young child. But really, despite the gossip circulating at full force, my mind lingers on one person: King.

King, of all people, must be thoroughly perplexed. He must be confused, bewildered, stressed. For Aubrey's lover, Butch, shouldn't have broken into the palace after being banished from it. Not with the chip implanted in his brain that allows the Mainframe to control his every move. But every time I try to lay eyes on King, to assess his mood and mental state, an elbow catches me in the side, or the crowd grows too thick and frenzied to see much of anything. It doesn't help that the decor tonight is macabre, that the lights are deliberately set low.

Voices continue to shriek around me: Aubrey, Butch, Dear Matthew—again and again, and again.

Then my arm is grabbed, the room ceases to spin, and a Cheshire smile alights just inches from my face.

My throat goes dry as I blink at King. In my peripheral vision, I see a towering figure—Wolfe, his spine straightening as he watches us.

"Fitting trimmings tonight, hmm?" he queries, nodding at the decorations. "A dark time in Strath Glen, indeed. Is little Alex scared?"

My eyes widen ever so slightly, but otherwise, I keep my composure. "No, sir. Not now that the intruder has been caught."

"And yet it goes to show, little one, how easily this beautiful home of mine can be breached. Count me concerned!"

"Perhaps more greencoats are needed," I say with a bow of my head, playing along even though I know perfectly well that isn't what bothers him. That isn't what causes the deep lines drawn between his brow, or the sweat that glistens across his forehead. Even his eyes have lost their luster— that way they shine with sinister humor. And that Cheshire grin looks as false as I've seen it. Butch's override chip must not be working correctly, I'm almost certain.

"Bad business, baaaad business," King continues, shaking his head. "That poor Dear Matthew is heartbroken, did you hear?"

"I'm sure the whole thing will blow over soon."

He smacks his lips on the side of my head and I almost choke at the undeniable stench of sweat. "Your optimism is contagious, my Alex!" He turns away and starts toward the duke, who double-fists scotch.

I stare after him, my mind whirling. Neo. Neo might know what's going on. He might know how it's plausible for an override chip to fail, and whether it's happened before. And then another possibility strikes me—that perhaps there was never a chip there in the first place. That Doctor Lebwitski might be rebelling in his own right—pretending to do a procedure when, in fact, all he does is twiddle his thumbs. And yet, working against that theory—Aubrey had been devastated at first. Yes, she had noticed a change in Butch—

"Good evening," says a cool voice from above me, one that draws me immediately from my thoughts.

I stare up at my fiancé, and for the first time in days, I don't feel my face warm with embarrassment. The kiss, in fact, as foolish as it was, pales in comparison to the recent turn of events. "Good evening."

"I take it the dress fitting wrapped up without further incident?"

"Indeed it did."

"My apologies for—"

"None needed," I say hurriedly, knowing he's talking about spotting me in my wedding dress, and not wanting to discuss our upcoming nuptials in the least. I step closer. "Rather interesting, isn't it, that Aubrey's lover should break the rules?" I look pointedly at him.

Wolfe's dark eyes scan the room, until finally they land on his uncle. Confirmation that he knows precisely what it is I speak of. Confirmation, too, perhaps, that he's had the same thoughts.

"An unexpected turn," he mutters as a roving spotlight illuminates his face, casting it in shadows. "And not one you should attempt to probe."

"Will you attempt to do so? Do you have theories of your own?"

His eyes narrow. "I fear you aren't using the utmost discretion."

I gaze around at the crowd, one growing more inebriated

by the second. The juicy gossip making its rounds has made everyone lightheaded and giddy. "Indeed, I'd think now would be the perfect time to discuss things," I counter. "May I hear your theories?"

He peers at me as revelers push against his well-crafted suit jacket. He says nothing.

"I'll share my own, then," I continue, undeterred. "Is it possible that the chip was never implanted in the first place? That Doctor Leb—"

Wolfe grabs my wrist and takes up the small sliver of space directly in front of me. He drops his head all the way down to mine and places his mouth next to my ear. "You are taking unnecessary risks during a time of great uncertainty. Anyone could eavesdrop at any moment. I urge you to show far more discretion."

"We can continue this conversation later," I agree.

"Arousing suspicion at this time would be markedly stupid," he continues.

I raise my hand. "I get it."

"Do you, Alexandra? Because things have changed between me and my uncle, not for the better. More discretion than ever is required. And, for the record, I believe your theory is wrong." With one last cantankerous look, Wolfe turns and heads toward his father.

Evie appears from within the dense crowd and swats me across the arm. "Let's start with the basics. When and where."

"What are you talking about?"

"The kiss between you and Brother, of course. Surely you don't consider our conversation closed on the matter?"

"But it was just a drunken bit of silliness—nothing of worth transpired. Besides, you already know when and where it happened. At Agnes' wedding, of course. Don't you wish to discuss Aubrey and Matthew?"

"Don't try to change the subject, sister, you rascal! We'll

get to Aubrey and Matthew as soon as dinner is served. Right now, I need to hear precisely what transpired between you and Brother. So, back to the wedding. Were you admiring each other all evening? Were you dancing when it happened? Swept away by the music? Was it at the very end of the night? A kiss goodnight? Was it a long kiss? Close-lipped or open? Was tongue involved? What was said directly prior? And immediately after? Oh, come now, sister —*please*."

Taking Evie's fingers between my own, I stifle a bite of laughter. "It happened at the close of the evening, when we were waiting for Monsieur."

She squeals. "And paint the picture for me. What were you discussing? How did it happen?"

"That's just the thing. We weren't discussing anything, and, in fact, we were fighting. Things weren't *romantic* in the slightest, if that's what you're thinking. I can assure you yet again that we don't have those sorts of feelings for each other."

"Yet my brother took it upon himself to smack you right on the lips?"

I blink at her, astonished. "N—no."

"No?"

"It was—it was rather me," and that familiar feeling of warmth crawling up my neck and flooding my face takes hold. "It was me who decided to, er, smack him, you know —right *there*. I did it completely without thought, and...and I can't figure out how it came to transpire." I scratch my head. "Has such a thing ever happened to you?"

Evie looks too shocked to respond.

"I suppose it was simply the alcohol to blame," I continue. "Or perhaps I was swept away by the evening, after all."

Evie, meanwhile, continues to stare at me, flabbergasted. Then she bursts into a fit of riotous laughter that draws looks from nearby revelers. "My," she finally sighs, allowing her head to drop onto my shoulder as she angles us in the direction of our usual table. Servants sweep through the shadows with steaming plates balanced on their shoulders. "I didn't think in any iteration that you'd be the one doing such a thing, sister. Really, I can't tell you how delighted I am. Was brother shocked? I imagine he must've been. What was said following? And what has come of it since?"

"Of course, he was shocked," I agree. "*I* was shocked. Right afterward, I blamed it on drink, and we haven't discussed it since."

"Truly, you were shocked by your very own action?" She fixes me with an astute stare.

"Truly," I say, returning her gaze.

She shrugs her shoulders dramatically. "Then it's clear."

"What is?" I ask as we take our seats. Wolfe approaches the table slowly from across the room, speaking with a man in a top hat. Both of us have our eyes set on him.

"Why, sister—isn't it obvious? Your body knows something your brain doesn't."

I consider her silently as she greets her brother with a knowing smile, one that makes his brow furrow and his gaze teeter back and forth between us.

With great exactitude, I study the tines of my fork, I shrink smaller in my seat.

But all the while, I wonder...could Evie be right?

———

I THROW the window open wide and feel the rush of wind push back my hair. No longer biting; the air. Just damp, with the faintest whisper of warmer days to come. Yes, change is coming.

And then, just a minute after my own arrival, the door flies open, and Wolfe steps inside, locking the door behind him and removing his jacket in one motion. He strides across the room toward the couch and takes a seat.

I shift the animal pelt and join him as the wind whistles across our shoulders.

"You found Butch's behavior as bizarre as I did, I take it," he murmurs, getting directly to the point with his typical efficiency.

Carefully I maneuver myself so that I can speak directly into his ear, pausing when I catch the scent of his aftershave. Blocking it from my mind, I say, "Have you ever heard of, or suspected, the chips to malfunction?"

"Not once," he replies swiftly, and we exchange a meaningful look.

"Your theory about Lebwitski, I must admit, is an interesting one," he continues.

"So, you think it's possible Butch never had the chip implanted?"

"Possible, yes. Likely? No. Not only would Lebwitski be risking his own life in favor of someone completely unknown to him, but there's the inescapable evidence that Butch was, in fact, behaving according to plan after he was taken. We saw Aubrey's reaction ourselves," he reminds me.

"Yes, I wondered about that myself. Perhaps, then, the chip came loose shortly after it was placed."

His gaze rakes the ceiling. "I suppose that is a possibility. A happy twist of luck for him and my cousin, though if he deigns to break in again, I can only assume the procedure will be repeated, or worse."

Yes, the risk is real. And yet, as I learned last time, warning him and Aubrey is futile.

"I'd urge you to leave the matter alone," Wolfe continues. "My uncle is already on edge because of all this, not that he'd admit as much. It's best not to arouse suspicion, particularly when he's so agitated, and that's saying nothing about the reduced sway I now hold over him."

I feel myself nodding in agreement. Inwardly, though, I know I won't be able to turn my mind from it. The question of why the chip implant failed in Butch is simply too curious. And the implications are too vast to let it slip by without another thought.

"I can sleep on the couch tonight," he says a minute later.

"No," I say, smoothing my dress. "No, I insist that I'll take the couch. Besides, your mother has been markedly more friendly with me ever since she noticed you looking more rested." I head to the closet before he can protest.

eight

· · ·

BY THE TIME Wednesday night rolls around, and the time for my secret meeting with the others is upon me, the palace uproar and its tidal wave of associated gossip have cooled to a simmer. Dear Matthew had been located and once again returned to Strath Glen, though looking more put out than last time. Quickly Butch's forced entry becomes yesterday's news, and Aubrey makes her way from room to room in a bustle of gauze, no different than usual, apart from the baby bump that has now taken shape.

It's a good thing the panic has passed, too. Had more greencoats been added, I realize, along with other heightened states of security, it would be much more difficult to sneak out of the palace as I currently do.

Making my way to Skelton Park is easier this time with experience behind me, but not less ominous. The dark is even more impenetrable than last time, and as I pick my way along the forest line, it's hard not to conjure up ferocious beasts in my imagination, waiting in the deepest dark.

Once I finally make it to street level, where lampposts offer pockets of light, my mind wanders to the meeting ahead of me. I wonder whether Timothee has had success with his programming, whether we're on track to expose King in five days' time. I wonder if anyone has received word on the weapons shipment, too, and if Neo has the answers about faulty chip implantation that I'm looking for.

The whole thing makes my pulse tick along quicker than normal, and I feel butterflies in the base of my stomach. What we're attempting to do is exciting, but dangerous too. After all, I have endured enough warnings from Wolfe on the matter since arriving at Strath Glen, and I've seen up close and personal King's cruelty on plenty of occasions. Should anything go wrong, should we be exposed, it wouldn't simply be a smack or two on the shoulder, oh no. Our fate would be death, even if our bodies continue to function.

And then there's Jill, Timothee, and Agnes, three people I've dragged into this, three people I feel responsible for. If the override chips are installed in their brains, that's on my conscience—nobody else's.

"Hi."

I barely manage to stifle my scream. Then I spot a pair of eyes that catch the light from the nearest streetlamp. Neo.

"Are any of the others here yet?" I whisper as we head deeper inside the park.

"Not that I know of—"

"Boo," comes a voice behind me, and once again, I have to fight the urge to scream.

Timothee laughs. "I knew you didn't see me, clomping through the leaves like that."

"I wasn't clomping, I was—"

"Shhh," Neo says, pointing through the shadows. Timothee and I are silent, and I hear it too. The faint murmur of voices. Neo motions us forward, and a minute later, we find Jill and Agnes chatting near a water fountain.

"So we meet again," Jill says through a yawn.

"Yeah, third time this week—my fiancé's getting suspicious," adds Timothee.

"Third?" Agnes echoes.

"Yeah, we met Monday night—an emergency meeting about the weapons deal. I stopped in at the nursery to tell you, but you weren't there."

"I wasn't feeling great. So, what'd I miss?"

"The Mavericks are set to be armed this week. I was hoping to find a way to delay that, but so far, we haven't had much luck. Have you guys heard anything?" I ask the others.

"Nothing," says Neo, "and I've been looking."

"As of this morning," says Jill, "the weapons haven't arrived at the Mainframe, but that doesn't mean they never will."

"Why would they go to the Mainframe?" Agnes asks.

"Because that's where the bluecoats are housed," explains Neo. "And it's the bluecoats who will most likely be delivering them up north to where the Mavericks are."

"It's a working theory," I add. "The Moody House of Weaponry may deliver them straight to the Mavericks, for all we know—in which case, we're screwed."

"What if the White Ribbon members protest the army and—"

"I think it's too risky," I interrupt. "Don't forget you guys are now considered a terrorist organization. That means everyone at the demonstration can and will be thrown in jail."

"It's for a good cause, though, right?"

"True, but the more people who are locked up, the fewer we'll have to take to the streets after King's address."

"And hopefully," adds Timothee, "those protests are so widescale and well-attended that they couldn't possibly lock everyone up."

"How's the program you're writing?" asks Jill. "You gonna have it done on time?"

"You bet. So long as I can install it, every affected person will be bleeping, booping, and dancing the robot alongside nobility."

"It's no problem to open up the channel from inside the Mainframe," says Neo. "The only issue is getting you in past the greencoats. But that's what she is for." He said, pointing at Jill.

"Let me know what time you need in, and I'll make sure it isn't an issue," Jill grunts. She spits into the trees and continues, "If we have access to these override chips, can't we install some sort of self-destructing bug and kill the override program?"

Neo shrugs through the darkness. "I'm not a programmer, so don't ask me. Is this self-destruction-thing a viable option?"

"I've already considered that," says Timothee, scratching his chin, "and I'd have to say no—too risky. If I introduce a virus targeting the override chip, it would definitely destroy the link between the chip and the Mainframe, but it wouldn't necessarily destroy the override chip itself. That would leave an empty chip running, with no data, executive controls, or anything."

"There's also the possibility that even if the virus kills the current program running the override chip, it can be reprogrammed," Neo adds.

"Speaking of override chips," I say, "is it possible for them to malfunction? Or to stop working?"

"You mean, on their own?" asks Neo.

I nod.

"I suppose it's possible. Personally, I've never seen anything like that happen. Why?"

"The princess' boyfriend had an override chip implanted recently. Initially, she was heartbroken by how different he was. But he seems back to himself now—and he's willing to break the rules to be with her."

"That's odd. You're certain he was taken by Lebwitski and the bluecoats?"

"Positive."

"I guess the power of love overcomes all," Timothee adds dryly.

"If you hear anything about it, let me know," I tell Neo. "His name is Butch."

He nods. "The national address is scheduled for Monday evening. We should probably meet one more time before that, to make sure everything's organized for game time."

"Let's meet the night before, on Sunday," Timothee suggests. "We can decide what time to meet at the Mainframe," he adds to Neo and Jill.

"And if you hear anything about those weapons in the meantime, let me know," I say.

"I'll start spreading the word to the White Ribbon members to tune in Monday night," Agnes adds.

We all nod, then splinter off into the dark.

nine

. . .

TRAPPED by a crown taller than I.

King, circling me, his claws primed.

My friends falling over a ledge, never to hit bottom.

These are the images that plague my sleep. Snippets of an unending dreamscape, a fever dream where I'm neither awake nor asleep.

Wolfe's boot stomps me between the floorboards.

My wedding dress crawling with maggots.

Claudia naked in my chambers.

I try to drag myself away from the unending sequence, I try to wake up, but the merciless pull of sleep drags me back under.

Now King has returned. He sits in a darkened room, staring straight at me, wielding a scalpel and a mischievous grin. "Plotting, plotting, I hear the pitter-patter of your feet," he sings. "What I really fear is the influence you exert over my nephew."

Now I see that Wolfe is there, too, tied up on a nearby chair, tie stuffed between his teeth. Blood trickles down his forehead, and I scream.

"Plotting, plotting—"

A cold hand has me by the face. "Alexandra."

I groan, then start, and finally, I'm free of sleep. I pull myself upright in the darkened room, the embers of the fire alighting Wolfe's outline.

"You were having a nightmare, yes?" He speaks curtly.

"How did you know?"

"You woke me with your...breathing."

"I'm sorry."

He clears his throat suddenly and stands to his full height. "Well, then," he says gruffly. "Goodnight."

"Wait."

He half-turns, staring down at me.

For a moment, I'm not sure why I called to him. Quickly I realize that I was contemplating confiding in him the plan to disrupt King's upcoming national address. We are allies, after all. And I trust him, I think—I trust that he too wants to stop the override chip program, and King's reign. But his natural proclivity towards protecting me, whether it's the true me or the mere fact of me being his fiancé, stops me. He will deem it too risky. He will insist that I pull the plug, allow him to clean up the matter in due time himself. So I hesitate, then, finally, shake my head. "Never mind."

He must misinterpret my call, or be referencing my nightmare, because he says to me, "There will come a time when you will dismiss your fears. I'll see to it."

I stare at him through the murky darkness of our shared quarters, realizing that perhaps he misinterpreted nothing, and nod.

ten

. . .

I PUSH a stack of books away and sigh. Three hours of searching the library for information on guns and interchanging ammo, and I have nothing to show for it. I suppose none of it matters, really. Already it's Thursday, meaning the guns have probably already been delivered to the Mavericks. My plan didn't work, and the King's robotized army is now equipped with lethal weapons. Perfect.

I stretch my legs and walk to the nearest window seat. How many times did I sit in this very spot in my early days here at Strath Glen? When I wasn't allowed to leave the palace, much like now, and I didn't have anything to occupy me, either? Too many times to count, but now, at least, I have plenty to occupy me. Plenty to think about, plenty to do.

Except, right now, I don't feel like working on the catalog system, or readying for my fast-approaching nuptials, or contemplating the plan concocted by me and the others to expose King at his own national address. I push my nose to the window, surveying my beloved Airo-Aurora, and sigh.

It's the waiting that bothers me. Waiting for the days and hours and minutes to pass, so that the national address is upon us. So that the moment is now. Twiddling my thumbs doesn't exactly help. With the plan already in place, there's little for me to do, except hope that Timothee crafts a program that will work, and that Jill will find a way to grant them access to the Mainframe on Monday evening. And me? I won't be doing anything, aside from observing it all with my fingers crossed.

The sense of uselessness tastes unpleasant against my tongue.

Eventually, my gaze lands on the Mainframe, the building that holds the data of all citizens, those still with us, and those long past. Secrets, too. Dark ones.

My eyes comb the back of the building, where the mainframe officers—the bluecoats—work. Officers that are complicit in the override chip program. Active participants in wrongdoing. Because surely they know what they're doing when they apprehend someone with Doctor Lebwitski breathing over their shoulders. And even if they don't have all the details, surely they'd suspect something sinister...

But what if they don't? What if they've been fed some lie instead? Perhaps to change the course of history, perhaps to change the future of Airo-Aurora, all I must do is speak to them. Explain the injustice they're perpetuating against innocent citizens. Perhaps that will be enough to cause a revolt amongst the force, stripping King and Lebwitski of the ability to apprehend an individual in the first place.

And then my gaze tightens, my thoughts are interrupted, and I watch a vehicle pull into the Mainframe parking lot, then continue down the lane running alongside the Mainframe and out of sight. I pull my lip, for that hadn't been just any vehicle, nor any delivery truck. No, that had been an armored car, an unmarked one, and my skin prickles.

I stand up, sit down again, my gaze sweeping back and forth, looking for any signs of the mysterious vehicle, but there's nothing. I focus my attention more firmly on the spot where the bluecoats are stationed, all the way down there, silently counting off each passing minute.

Finally, after sixteen of them, I spot the armored car emerging from the Mainframe, rejoining society along Airo-Aurora's bustling streets.

Once again, I stand, then promptly sit down again. Calm down, I urge myself. You don't know. You don't know if that was the weapons delivery or not, of course you don't.

Except my stomach lurches in a knowing way.

Jill. I need to find Jill. She'll know what to do, she'll know what it means, or doesn't, and immediately I dart between towering columns of books, out of Counterdown, and through the front doors. I barely notice the warmth in the air, or the cacophony of birds in the distance. Spring may well be in the air, but right now, I set my sights on my friend.

"You okay, princess?" she asks, surveying me. "Looks like you just saw a ghost."

"More of a truck, actually," and I explain what I witnessed, along with my suspicions.

She turns and faces the Mainframe, peering over the railing at its low-slung white roof. She spits, then turns to me. "It's almost lunch. Most of the bluecoats will be buggered off eating if you want to do some poking around. I can walk over with you, if you want. Show you where every-thing is, maybe even distract one or two staff if it works out that way. I'm not looking to lose my job over this, though."

Immediately I nod. "Totally understand," I assure her.

"How are you going to sneak out?" she continues, eyeing the palace.

I check the other guard, to make sure he isn't listening. "I'll go out the back door and take the woods down to street level. Meet you there at noon?"

"At the back of the building, sure. Don't get too close, though, until the bluecoats clear out," she advises. "And you better think up a pretty damn good excuse why we're there."

"Right. On it," I assure her, though nothing springs immediately to mind. I head inside the palace, feeling more alive than earlier, revived with the promise of action, of contributing. How, though, to explain our presence in the bluecoats' quarters? I stream past the Ming vases, thinking. I could pretend I'm a representative from the Moody House of Weaponry, there to perform a Quality Assurance check.

But if I do manage to switch out the ammo and it's caught, it wouldn't take long to be outed as the culprit. A disguise would be much safer, but how to craft—

"Look who it is—my fellow captive," drawls a voice from behind me.

I turn; Dear Matthew strides from Devonshire with his hands in his pockets and a frown across his face. "Sorry?"

"Surely you don't think you're fooling me?"

"I'm not sure what you're talking—"

"You don't want to be here any more than I do. At the palace. At Strath Glen. In this very spot. Can I be any clearer?" A vein protrudes from his forehead. "At least your betrothed isn't stepping out on you for all the world to see. You know, if I'm being frank, I never cared much for Aubrey. But now that she insists on humiliating me time and again with that ridiculous oaf? Why, I downright disdain the woman," he says between clenched teeth.

"What about your insistence that the palace is theater?" I ask him. "Can't you continue to play the part?"

He scowls. "After my manhood has been dragged so thoroughly through the mud? I think not."

It strikes me that Dear Matthew, now angry and unwilling to play along, will be the next victim of the override chip. "I think the advice you gave me to play the game of the palace is good advice indeed," I say pointedly. "A heartbroken husband who manages to forgive his beloved wife for her adulterous ways would endear you to King and all the rest who frequent this institution, I'm sure."

"I tried to go, you know," he says, dismissing my well-veiled words of warning. "Tried to go abroad to start fresh. They located me in mere minutes and swiftly put a stop to it. There's now a stop-travel warning with my name on it at the Sky Center. Can you fathom it? There's no out. There's simply no out!"

It's difficult not to roll my eyes—he's just realizing it now?—even considering his current state of desperation. "Since Princess Aubrey is seeing that oaf, as you put it, perhaps you can relocate back to your own residence, much as you did earlier in your marriage?"

He shakes his head. "King has his tethers in me now. I never should've come back in the first place. You know, for a fraction of a second, I actually thought that babe might be my own." He shakes his head wearily. "Anyway, now that I'm here, there's no escaping it. Not for you, either."

It strikes me that Dear Matthew might be an ally. That he might wish to work toward a free Airo-Aurora. But confiding in someone so dubious is unwise, I can see that a mile away, so I simply nod and start toward the stairs.

"If only I could be so simple, so impassive, so content to accept an unwanted future," he calls after me.

Inwardly I laugh—if only he knew. But what Dear Matthew thinks isn't my concern, so I carry on, up the stairs and along the House of Mirrors toward my quarters. What I need is to think. Think of a reason to be at the bluecoats' quarters, and during lunchtime, to boot.

Lunchtime—lunch.

I could pretend to be part of lunch service, delivering food. I spin on the spot, about to rush down the servants' stairs to the kitchens, but the familiar echo of small thuds makes my blood run cold. I go still.

Yes, there he is. King and his walking stick, and he pauses when he notices me. "Come, come, little Alex," he calls.

Unable to think of a reason to politely disobey or dismiss the ruler, I stumble toward him, finally dropping into a clumsy curtsy as my brain spins with panic.

"Whatever are you up to, cotton-eyes?" he asks, twirling my hair around his finger.

"Uh—just returning from the library, actually," I tell him. "It really is a spectacular space."

"Indeed it is," he shouts gaily. Complements, I've noticed, tend to be well-received by him. "And now?"

"And now I'm about to go find something to eat," I explain, pivoting away from him. A perfect out, and I can hardly believe my luck.

"Come, come! Feast with me, muffin. After all, in just a month, you'll officially be family!"

My stomach twists. "Uh—I appreciate the offer, truly, but unfortunately—"

"Do you have somewhere more important to be than with your King?" he asks, and his voice turns candy-coated and simpering.

"No, sir."

"Daises. Come, Miss Alex," and he does a pirouette, then sets off for the imperial staircase with his walking stick thudding rhythmically against the black and white tile. I follow behind him, my head hanging, my stomach churning with fright.

Up the stairs we go, past the shriveled heads floating in glass jars that line Bishop's Aisle. My eyes scan behind every open door, searching desperately for Wolfe, someone who'd help me find an out to this most unwanted date, but the rooms prove empty, and when we finally pass by Wolfe's office near the end of the corridor, the door is sealed shut.

My last hopes of being rescued fade away. I need to find an out myself. Because as painful as a lunch taken with King sounds, the thought of missing my only opportunity to search the bluecoats' quarters for weapons earmarked for the Mavericks hurts even more.

But once I'm ushered inside King's mammoth-sized office, I see that it won't exactly be just the two of us. A number of staff stand along the far wall of the office, including the head butler and King's faithful servant, Gerard. All of them stand with their hands behind their backs, staring resolutely at a pocket of space several feet in front of them. Another bundle of servants place out lunch items on one of the countless coffee tables set up around the room, while James sprawls across one of the wingchairs.

"Papa, you've been shopping, and you've come back with a shiny trinket!" he calls gaily when he spots me.

"This poor girl was positively famished," King replies, pushing me into the chair next to James and taking the other for himself. He rubs his hands together and makes a show of sniffing the air. "Lasagna," he exclaims.

Indeed, a massive dish of lasagna is placed in front of us, and the servants set to work dividing it into generous portions.

I clear my throat. "You know, sir, as kind as this is, I'm afraid that having something so filling would ruin my appetite for dinner." I stand, thanking him profusely as I spot an exit.

"Sit, sit!" he shouts. "Your wish is my command. Turnip," he continues, addressing the servant hovering at his right elbow, "bring this young lady high tea, hmm?"

She curtsies and vanishes before I can protest. Reluctantly I sit down. Why, now that I have to wait for my own food to be prepared, I've prolonged my visit even longer, and I bite the inside of my cheek. My palms sweat. But as I watch King and his son dig into their hearty lunch, it strikes me that I should make good use of this time.

"Are the two of you working on anything exciting?" I ask in a mild-mannered tone.

As I anticipated, James can't hide his glee. He rubs his hands together, much like his father, and laughs. "You might say as much," he says with his chest puffed.

"Oh? Concerning simply the palace, or all of Airo-Aurora?"

"Nation-wide, most definitely," James says, his head bobbing, "and absolutely riveting stuff. Here's a tip: keep your toes in line." He winks.

"That's enough of that," says King, swatting James and causing his fork to fall.

"My lady," comes a voice over my shoulder—the servant King referred to as Turnip. She places a three-tiered plate in front of me, overflowing with an assortment of minuscule sandwiches, fruit, and dessert.

"Was that really necessary, Papa?" James queries as I make quick work of devouring the sandwiches—an attempt to expedite things.

"If you're going to behave like a buffoon, it is. Now, tell me, dear Alex, how has palace life been treating you as of late?"

"Very well, sir," I reply swiftly. "And these sandwiches are delicious, by the way. They're really hitting the spot."

"Aces. It seems to me you've settled in well, at least compared to the first month or so. A rocky start, hmm?"

"Perhaps," I oblige. I take my dessert—a macaron—making sure he sees. "Certainly, I've had the pleasure of becoming familiar with everyone by now."

He sighs. "If only Dear Matthew could settle himself so."

"He never will, Papa," James advises. "He really is rather dramatic."

"And not much of a worker, either," adds King.

"Absolutely shameful," James continues, wiping his face clean using his sleeve. "A disgrace if I've ever—"

"What's this?" comes a new voice, and when I look over

my shoulder, I see Wolfe, his closely cropped hair skimming the doorframe, such is his height.

"King was kind enough to provide me with lunch," I explain in haste, wiping my face off with a napkin and standing. "I'm finished now," I continue hurriedly, "so you can have my seat."

I push around the furniture and slip past Wolfe before he or the others can suggest otherwise. And then I'm off, streaming down the servants' stairs, out the back door, and into the tree line. I run under branches and over overturned logs. I run until the ground is dropping beneath me, and then it's leveling out again, and I'm circling the white mammoth known as the Mainframe, my eyes peeled for bluecoats and for Jill, my pulse still unsteady from that most unwanted lunch.

"You're late," comes a gruff voice, and Jill steps out from the far corner of the building.

"King forced me to have lunch with him," I say, wiping my brow of sweat. "I'm sorry. I didn't have time to think up a good excuse, either."

"So let's hope nobody asks," she says, gesturing me forward.

She leads me to an unmarked door, then swipes her greencoat keycard, allowing us entry. Inside, the empty hallway is painted white, the fluorescent light overhead shudders and shakes, and it strikes me that this will be easier than I thought. No need to worry about my tardiness or my inability to formulate and follow through on a plan. No need to worry at all.

But then I hear someone coughing up ahead, and my hopefulness wanes. I look at Jill with wide eyes. "Reception is that way," she whispers, pointing in the direction of the cough. "Wait here."

She moves off and out of sight. I can hear her low voice reverberate, along with another voice, and more coughing.

And then her footsteps echo closer, and she appears in the corridor up ahead. She bends down, as if to lace her boot, though it looks perfectly fastened, and gestures at me to go outside and move toward the rear of the building.

Silently I do as she says, confused at first, but then I notice it. A garage door, elevated a few feet off the ground, the perfect height for truck deliveries. Whatever was delivered this morning, it came right here.

eleven

. . .

ONE MINUTE TURNS INTO TWO, to five, then ten.

I start to pace. Our time is dwindling—the bluecoats will be back from lunch shortly. I'm worried about Jill, too. Is she okay? Has she been caught red-handed, nosing her way through the bluecoat quarters?

It seems like more and more of a possibility as the minutes tick by, but finally, there's a sharp noise, and the garage door draws open in one swift motion. Jill stands there looking triumphant. "Climb up, princess. You don't have much time."

With Jill's help, I tumble inside, eyes on a series of crates in the middle of what looks like a small warehouse. The crates are wrapped several times over in plastic and housed in wood. Essentially impenetrable, at least if I want to be subtle, and my hopes are dashed. "Do you think that's the weapons?"

She shrugs. "Doesn't look like you're going to find out too easily, does it."

I shake my head.

"Let's close the door in case the bluecoats start showing up. There's a light switch over there." She shoves her chin in the direction of the door she must've used to access the warehouse. I go turn it on as she locks up the loading dock.

"What'd you tell reception?" I ask as I circle the crates.

"Basically that I'm bored with my shift at the Mainframe and want to look around to see what life's like for the bluecoats."

"That's it?"

"The receptionist looked even more bored than me. I could've asked to steal all the lightbulbs and she would've been on board. Anyway, I left her in the breakroom and told her I was heading back to my shift. She doesn't know we're here, so be quiet."

I nod. "Should we lock the door, just to be safe?"

"Already locked, princess. So, what's the plan?" and she considers the crates.

"I don't have one," I admit, then I point to the smallest crate. "If the big ones are full of guns, what do you think's in that one?"

She pulls down her mouth, then says, "Ammo?"

"That's my guess, too."

She takes a pocket knife from her pocket and hands it to me. "First things first. Make sure the weapons are actually in there. A clean slit won't look too suspicious," she adds.

Carefully I take the knife and cut through the plastic. Inside the crate are a series of pallets stacked on top of each other, and on each pallet are black metal objects.

I finger one through the slits, then peer at Jill. "I'm ninety percent sure."

She rolls her eyes, then crouches beside me, sticking her own fingers through the crate. "Yeah, okay, princess. I guess I'm ninety percent sure, too."

"That's pretty close to positive," I point out.

She grins. "Okay, fine. Let's say it is the guns. And the small crate is the ammunition. What do you want to do about it, keeping in mind that my shift starts up again in twenty minutes."

I pull at my lip. "I think we should switch out the ammo, like we discussed. Pack this crate full of the bluecoats' bullets. Using the wrong gauge will damage the gun," I add, citing the little I gleaned in the library.

"It could also hurt the shooter," she counters.

My mouth twists. "I think it's a risk worth taking," I finally say. "Do you think the bluecoats will notice it's the wrong ammo if they unpack and ready the weapons?"

"I think it's unlikely they'll bother to check, if that's what you mean. And as long as the bullet fits inside the chamber, I don't think it'll raise alarm bells."

I nod. "Where do you think the bluecoats store their ammo?"

She stares around at the crates stacked against the walls. "Here."

"Really?"

She shrugs. "We keep our surplus in a space like this." She shoves up her sleeve and looks at her watch. "I'll help you open the ammunition crate, but the rest is on you. I can't be late for my shift, or I'll get in shit."

"Okay. How do we open it? And, more importantly, how do I make it look like new once I'm done?"

"You're going to need a screwdriver and a lot of patience."

I groan.

"You go look for bullets. I'll open the lid." She pulls out her keys from her pocket and takes off one of the keychains. "I'll leave this with you once I'm done. Philips head. Always handy."

It only takes ten minutes for Jill to open up the top of the crate. "You'll need to tape up the plastic we've cut through," she reminds me as I shift boxes and crates around, sweating from the exertion. Finally, though, I find a bunch of white, unmarked boxes brimming with bullets.

"Found them," I say, bringing a box over.

She examines the contents, then pulls out a box from the crate she just cracked open, holding two of the bullets up in comparison.

"The bluecoat ones are smaller. I'd give it a fifty-fifty chance on the bluecoats noticing, if they even bother to load the Mavericks' guns in the first place." She hands me the screwdriver and turns for the garage door. "Good luck. If people start trying to get inside, you're going to have to make a run for it," she adds, gesturing to the loading dock door that she opens an inch. She gets down on her stomach, her ear placed next to it, then opens it several more inches. Finally, she sticks her head out, then glances at me over her shoulder. "See you on the front stoop," she says as she drops out of sight. The door rolls shut behind her, and for the first time since this lunchtime adventure began, nerves set in.

Yes, the adrenalin from escaping lunch with King has faded away, and without Jill's steady presence next to me, along with the authority gifted by her greencoat uniform, I feel exposed, vulnerable, and, if I'm being honest, foolish.

After all, this is crazy—a shot in the dark, little more. A risky one. And yet, if I can save a life, even one, it's a risk worth taking.

I roll up my sleeves, lifting out boxes of bullets from the ammunition crate destined for the Mavericks, and setting up a pile next to the bluecoats' collection. I run as I work, going as quickly as I can, pausing only when I hear the slamming of doors and the echo of voices.

Lunch hour must be over. The building will soon be swimming with men and women who have the authority to detain me while Doctor Lebwitski readies himself and his tools.

I shiver, but I keep working, even as my fingers shake. Finally, the entire crate is empty, and I begin the swap.

Once it's complete, the only thing left to do is screw the boards back in place and tape up the plastic wrap. But my hands are so unsteady that I fumble the screwdriver, and it rolls out of sight. Finally, I fish it out from under some garbage bins, then take a moment to breathe, to commit to the task at hand, and tackle each screw, one at a time.

I'm halfway done when I hear it.

The thud of the locked door. The handle swivels, the whole thing shudders as someone tries to gain entry.

I freeze, I swallow, I panic.

Then I'm stooping down and scooping up the remaining screws. I sprint to the loading dock door, shove it open a foot, and roll out, not bothering to see if anyone is nearby.

I can only hope I have luck on my side as I fly around the corner and out of sight.

I don't stop running until I'm behind the palace, tucked inside the tree line, and then I force my pace to slow to a laidback-looking saunter as I head to the front of the palace and up the steps, as if I've been doing nothing more exciting than checking on the chickens.

Jill spits over the banister and surveys me. "Well?"

I shrug, then hand her the screwdriver when the other guard isn't looking. "I had to leave early. Someone was trying to get inside."

Her eyes widen. "Did anyone see you?"

"I don't know. I didn't have time to look around. I just... I just ran." My fingers tremble worse than earlier, and I push them inside my pockets.

"It's okay," Jill says. "Relax—if someone saw you, they would've shouted something."

Slowly I nod, more at ease than before. "Thanks."

"What about the boxes? Did you get them all switched?"

"All of them," I confirm. "But I only got halfway securing

the crate. Hopefully nobody notices that some of the boards are loose."

"You didn't leave the extra screws on the floor, did you?"

I pat my pocket. "Somehow, I managed to remember that part."

"Hopefully they assume the manufacturer's packers got lazy."

I nod, my pulse still unsteady as I stare down at the Mainframe.

"You okay, princess?"

"I think so."

"You did good. No offense, but I thought the whole idea was crazy when you first mentioned it. Can't believe you actually pulled it off."

"We don't know if I pulled it off or not," I remind her.

"Come on. Pat yourself on the back already."

"Don't forget, I couldn't have done any of it without you."

"True," and she proceeds to pat herself generously on the back. A moment minute later, I enter Strath Glen, feeling agitated and concerned, but a little proud of myself too.

twelve

. . .

THAT EVENING, I sit in my usual seat as the party swirls around me. All of it is dizzying and, after the day I had, completely unwanted. In fact, it's all I can do to not put my head down and go promptly to sleep.

A loud thump draws me from my stupor, and I blink up at a smiling Evie.

"Sister, you look positively awful, my! What in heavens have you been up to to cause such dark lines under your eyes? And the roundness in your shoulders? And here we are, with a wedding to plan!"

I ignore her litany of questions and stare at the mammoth book dropped onto the table—the source of the thud. Upon closer examination, I see it's a binder six inches thick, bursting at its seams. "Evie, what is that?"

"Oh, that?" cries Evie, following my gaze. She taps the binder and drops into the seat next to me. "The wedding ideas book I've developed, naturally. It has all my absolute favorite things in it, isn't that spectacular? The time has come, sister—absolutely it has. We must decide on every last detail and in haste, my!"

Inwardly I groan, though I'm careful not to let the dread

show on my face. Not when Evie's been so helpful through the whole process. Indeed, I sit straighter, tamp down the angst I continue to carry from my mad dash from earlier, and ask, "What's first?"

"I love your enthusiasm, sister—truly I do! Let's review, shall we? The theme is bohemian, so the wedding, which will naturally take place in the ballroom, will be brimming with beautiful blooms. Exquisite? There will be an extra abundance of baby's breath, to honor your mother, and tulips of the parrot variety. Correct?"

I nod.

"Your wedding dress is already picked out—hurrah. Now, since you want it to be such a simple affair, I assume you'll skip the tradition of bridesmaids and groomsmen?"

"Please."

"Consider it done. Moving on. Now, while napkins and table linens will be white, I think we ought to choose napkin rings and centerpieces that will soften that austere palette to bring it more on-theme. Thoughts?"

"Er, sure." After several more minutes, and the flipping of the binder pages back and forth several times, we decide on beaded napkin rings, and mason jar arrangements for the centerpieces. "I really did like the fairy lights that Agnes used at her wedding," I add.

"Not a problem whatsoever!" trills Evie, making a note in the binder and smiling widely at me.

"What is it?" I ask when I notice she beams at me.

"Why, it's the first time you've made an actual request, sister. Could it be you're actually starting to look forward to the big event?"

"What? No—I simply thought it was festive, those lights. That's all."

"Why is it," comes a voice from up high, "that you were taking high tea with my uncle and cousin today? And where on earth did you vanish to following?"

I shoot a look at Wolfe, trying to urge him to drop the subject with Evie looking on, but already he has rounded the table and taken up his usual seat, a newspaper clasped under his arm.

"Well, Alexandra?" he continues once he settles himself.

"Brother, how terribly rude!" shouts Evie. "One look at sister should tell you she's absolutely spent, not to mention that we're clearly in the midst of something." She taps the binder pointedly.

His dark eyes shift to me. "Spent from what?"

Somehow I manage not to roll my eyes. For being as astute as he is, he really can be obtuse at times. "Perhaps I'm a little under the weather."

"A common infliction for you," he murmurs in a disbelieving way as he opens his newspaper.

"Now, appetizers, sister!" and she proceeds to list off two dozen different options.

"Perhaps the groom would like to decide."

"Brother?"

"Let's go with options 3, 9, and 11," he says, not breaking from his paper.

Evie scans the list. "Zucchini fritters, ceviche, and—"

"It's decided, then," he says crisply before she can finish.

"Even for you, Wolfe, that's rude," I hear myself say.

My own surprise is dwarfed by his. The paper lowers all the way down to his lap, he gazes at me with widened eyes. Evie gazes at me with the same expression, and I'm reminded that it's typically her scolding him like this.

I decide to hold my ground. "Your sister is going out of her way planning our wedding since neither one of us can be bothered. I'd say some appreciation is in order."

Evie sits straighter and turns to her brother expectantly.

Wolfe, for his part, shifts in his seat. He grumbles an apology to Evie, then returns to his paper. Evie winks at me as we discuss the third appetizer.

Inwardly, though, part of me reels, and the rest surges with something distantly resembling excitement. I kissed this man, and I scolded him just now, too—as though he's my true partner. So, am I just growing accustomed to the idea that this man will be my spouse, or have I truly warmed up to the notion?

The latter seems unlikely, and yet I can't say I detest him the way I used to. In fact, I don't think I harbor any negative feelings toward him anymore—not really. And, more pressing, how did all those negative feelings vanish like a lick of smoke, and without me even noticing?

Suddenly he looks up at me, and I realize I've been staring. I drop my gaze, somehow managing to knock my water glass over in the process. Well, that settles it. I really must be under the weather.

———

BY THE TIME Sunday evening rolls around, with my meeting with the others merely an hour away, I'm on pins and needles. I can barely muster the will to eat, and sleeping is completely off the table. Twice more, Wolfe had woken me from my nightmares, and Evie is now terrified in her own right, though her fear is that the wedding gown will drape off my frame in three weeks when the wedding takes place.

I feel so terrible that part of me wonders if I really am battling a spring virus, but mostly, I'm sure it's nerves. Yes, serving at the epicenter of my near-nervous-breakdown is King's national address scheduled for the following evening.

Tomorrow.

The time is practically upon us, and whenever that thought flits through my head, my stomach drops like I've just been punched.

Are we ready? Did Timothee perfect the computer

program? Is Jill ready to risk her job all over again tomorrow evening at the Mainframe? Is Neo still willing to risk his? So many unknowns—it makes me woozy. But it's surreal, too. Surreal to think that after all this time, all the suffering, all the tormented thoughts—the time is upon us.

The time for change.

It doesn't help matters that tensions are so high around the palace. Morocco had heard all about the kiss that James had stuck on me, and she now takes every opportunity to hiss at me whenever I'm within earshot. Matthew has gone missing yet again, which has wiped King's face of his usual beguiling grin, and Aubrey has been banished from festivities at her father's orders for her continued antics with Butch. Barred from the mayhem of palace life, though, she has found her own peculiar way of adding to it, standing outside the doors of Carnegie and issuing deep-bellied screams at various points throughout each evening. To make matters even worse, the servants have been tasked with helping King memorize his national address, meaning a large entourage follows him around the palace reciting the speech and hushing others.

As for Wolfe, I've barely seen him, so busy has he been with work. It seems that since being demoted from King's number two slot, the one now held by James, Wolfe has had his hands full, probably making up for lost time spent working on King's secret dossiers.

It's better this way. Not only would Wolfe pick up on my building excitement, nervousness, and apprehension concerning tomorrow night's address, but, well, the closer the wedding draws, the more awkward things between us become.

Then there's the question of whether the wedding will even happen, considering the bomb, so to speak, that will drop on Airo-Aurora tomorrow evening. Will King immediately step down? Will the override chip program be abandoned at once? Will people take to the streets in anger?

And, if any of those things come to fruition, will the entire system collapse? What will things with Wolfe look like? What will the future hold? And then I remember what he had said after Agnes' wedding, and I have to clutch my stomach.

It had been right before I kissed him—no wonder I haven't given it a thought until now. He had said that he had feelings for me. Him—the ice-cold viscount who rarely smiles or shows any semblance of human emotions whatsoever.

It feels overwhelming, replaying that moment in my mind, like I'm being slammed against a wall, but for some reason, I do it again and again.

I let out a long exhale and steady myself. It wasn't supposed to happen this way. We were marrying each other because the Mainframe mandated it, plain and simple. Feelings...feelings complicate matters. Especially when I've put a plan in motion that might undo everything.

Then the door swings open, and Wolfe strides inside, pausing when he spots me. "What's wrong?" he asks at once.

I shake my head as my face fills with heat. "I'm tired, that's all."

He nods, then carries on, placing some books onto the table near the bed. "Don't bother opening the window tonight," he says after a while, "if it interferes with your sleep."

"It doesn't," I assure him as I begin making up the couch with bedsheets. I switch off the lights and crack the window enough that the wind whistles in. Finally, I climb under the animal pelt and watch the minutes tick closer and closer to my meeting time. Wolfe, after putting in so many hours, must surely be exhausted, and sure enough—when I finally lift my head from the pillow and peer around the room—I find him motionless, breathing in and out deeply and rhythmically.

Relieved, I tiptoe across the room and out the door.

"Aye, where are you goin', miss?"

I stumble when I see Rebecca where Monsieur typically stands, gazing down at the darkened city below. "Uh—"

"Monsieur asked me to act the watchman tonight, like," she continues, sensing my confusion. "Don't worry, I'll get you in safe n sound."

"Oh, yes—yes, of course. Thank you. I won't be long."

"Where're you goin', like?"

"Just to have a drink with a couple friends, that's all," I lie.

"And does your mister know?"

"Uh, well, not exactly—"

"I won't go on and tell. Now get movin', or you'll be all kinds of late."

I wave goodbye and head down the servants' stairs, a sense of unease heavy in my stomach. Rebecca isn't trustworthy, I know that. In fact, she's the last person I'd want caught up in my rule-breaking. But it's too late to change my plans now—the others are expecting me, and, besides, I can't stand not knowing whether things are in place for tomorrow night or not. I have to take the risk, so I grab a cloak and push into the night.

A fine mist falls, gentle against my cheek. But the ground is sopping, and traversing the backyard to the tree line takes more effort and noisy squelching than I'd like. Gazing skyward, I realize that clouds sit low, blocking out light from the moon and the stars, and all around me is velvety darkness.

I walk, and shiver, and shake. Nerves grow worse with every step, and by the time I reach street level, my throat has gone dry. What if, what if, what if.

What if the program isn't ready. What if access to the Mainframe is impossible. What if we came this far for nothing.

I draw the hood of the cloak down low over my eyes and cross the boulevard, scanning Skelton Park for any sign of movement, any sign of life, knowing that once I'm inside, the eerie and all-encompassing darkness will return.

I head directly to the same spot as last time, and sure enough, the others have already congregated, the whisps of their fluttering outlines just visible.

"Sorry—have you guys been waiting long?"

"Just got here," grunts Jill. "You better give everyone a little update on what you've been up to."

I smile, more at ease than before, and once again, I feel a rush of gratitude toward my friends. "Well, with her help," I say, pointing at Jill, "I found the weapons destined for the Mavericks. I switched out the ammunition with bullets the wrong size. It's possible the bluecoats will notice and find the proper ammo—and it's also possible one of them spotted me when I was leaving, I don't know."

"It's *also* possible," says Jill, "that none of that happened, and the switched-out ammo will jam the Mavericks' weapons, saving how many lives?"

"That's the hope," I say. "So, is everything ready for tomorrow night?"

Timothee nods. "As ready as it'll ever be. Anyone else getting cold feet over all this? I'm so nervous, I can barely eat."

"It's our only way to expose King," I remind him. "It could change everything."

"I know. I've just been so busy running lines all week that I haven't stopped to think about what's actually happening. And now it's time."

"I foresee a sleepless night ahead," agrees Neo.

The rest of us murmur our agreement.

"Did you spread word to your White Ribbon members, Agnes?"

"Everyone will be watching tomorrow night's address like a hawk. They're practically looking for an excuse to take to the streets and make some noise."

"What time does it start?" Jill asks.

"Eight," says Neo. "Which means we should plan to meet outside the Mainframe at 7:30 sharp."

"Yeah, that works for me," says Jill. I hear rather than see her spit.

"Me, too," adds Timothee.

"Is there anything I can do to help?" I say. "Should I meet up with you guys, too?"

"No, don't," says Neo promptly. "It would raise too many red flags if you're missing during all this. In fact, you should make sure you're visible inside the palace when the address happens."

"Good advice," Timothee adds. "Especially if you think you were spotted moving those weapons around."

"Okay. We should plan to meet again after the address."

"It'll be too dangerous tomorrow night. Not only will people be mad, but the authorities will be everywhere, too."

"Do you think the following night will be any better?" I ask.

"Hard to say. We can plan to meet, but people should only come if it feels safe."

I nod as my stomach flips. "So, this is it." I clear my throat. "Good luck tomorrow night."

"Yeah," adds Agnes. "Good luck, guys."

"Let's all try to get some sleep tonight," adds Neo.

Then, with nothing left to say, we break apart and vanish into the night.

thirteen

. . .

THE NEXT MORNING, after a long night with short, fitful bouts of sleep, I lift myself so I can look out the window that runs over the couch. A few cars go by, up and down the avenue, but mostly the streets are quiet, people still tucked inside their homes. Yes, Airo-Aurora looks peaceful, cast in dusty yellow and pink hues crafted by early morning. Nothing like the inner turmoil inside my head, chest, and stomach that make my palms slick and my fingers shake.

Peaceful at dawn, but what about this evening, at dusk? I picture the calm streets below, flooded with outraged citizens demanding better, and my heart swells with hopefulness, with anticipation.

But I'll erupt with nerves if I keep this up all day. That or I'll exhaust myself from the constant flood of endorphins that hit me every time I wonder what's to come. No, I need to set it aside, put it out of my mind, and carry on like usual. Besides, I can't afford to have anyone be suspicious of me during such dangerous times.

With exactitude, I begin readying myself for the day. I pull on a strappy gown of silk first, then several sweaters over that. I pull on the riding boots that Wolfe had returned to me despite his mother's orders, and then head out the door with the intention of grabbing a bacon roll from the kitchen and heading to the library for some cataloging work, just like any other day.

"When does the miss want to nip out for another night-cap, like?" comes Rebecca's voice once I reach the basement.

"Good morning," I say pleasantly, reminding myself that she'd been perfectly agreeable last night when I'd returned to the palace, wasting no time opening the back door for me just like Monsieur Sawyer does. "I don't have any plans," I assure her—a lie, "but I'm happy to return the favor whenever you'd like."

"Aye—how 'bout tonight, miss?"

I stumble. "You mean—oh, but isn't tonight King's national address?"

"It never takes past the hour, like. Makes no difference, does it?"

"Of course not," I say. After all, I can't exactly tell her the streets will be full, or that it will be dangerous to be out and about. With any luck though, it will be self-evident.

"So, it's a plan?"

"It's a plan," I agree, carrying on to the kitchen and helping myself to a bacon roll from the large platter destined for the top floor.

I force myself to take a bite as I wind my way to the main floor, feeling unexpectedly comforted by the combination of fat and carbs. I take another bite and think that maybe this will be okay.

"Even with all those layers, you're as minuscule as a thimble!" shouts a jovial voice from overhead. I turn and see James descending the imperial staircase with great fanfare. He's dressed to the nines and holds what looks like a baton, as a number of tumblers descend the stairs with impressive contortionist skills. "Did you hear the big news?" he asks once he reaches the bottom. His eyebrows wiggle.

"Big news?"

"Indeed. Given my new position as Papa's number two, he thinks it should be me to join him during tonight's national address. Isn't that a feather in your cap?"

Immediately the bacon roll slips between my fingers to the floor below.

He claps his hands together in surprise. "Whatever's wrong?"

"N—nothing." I force myself to pick up the dropped sandwich and stand tall. "That's quite an honor," I manage to say.

"Of course, it isn't official, not yet, but I don't see what should stop me!"

"It's not yet official?" I echo, forming words on auto-pilot. "That's rather serendipitous as I was hoping to speak with you in private, and I was thinking this evening might be the perfect opportunity. You know, with everyone caught up in the address and all."

His brow lifts to his hairline, and he goes still, the acrobats forgotten about. "Is that so?"

"Only if that's alright with you. It would mean your mother would once again have to appear in the address tonight—"

"What's the rush, that's what I say. Why, I have many years—nay, decades—of appearing in the addresses, isn't that so? And not simply fading into the background, no, no. It won't be long until the throne is mine and it's me that's delivering the update on our beautiful nation-state, hmm?"

"Yes, indeed. That's just what I was thinking."

"Then it's settled. Consider me tickled!"

"Should we meet—"

"In Papa's office, of course. It's customary for the whole family to gather there to watch the address in person. But it won't hardly be noticeable at all for the two of us to slip out, I promise."

"It's a plan." With that, I walk on legs filled with jelly to Counterdown and disappear inside. I find a dusty and forgotten-about spot between two rows of books and sink to the floor. My hands shake, I realize, as I place my head in them. My heart hammers.

But I had come up with an out, a way to ensure Queen will be in tonight's frame, saving the plan shared with Neo, Timothee, Jill, and Agnes from unraveling. Still, it was a close call.

James could still have a change of heart. God knows he's easy to manipulate. Just how badly does King want him on camera? And, more pressing, why?

Is there any possible way that King's been tipped off about tonight's plan? That he suspects something is afoot?

It's enough to make my stomach heave, and I have to work hard to keep the half bacon roll situated where it is.

Then there's the private matter I apparently wish to discuss with the prince. Just what can I come up with that won't make him feel as though I've concocted the whole story? Assuming things work as planned with the Queen, it will look awfully suspicious if it appears I drew James away for nothing.

Before I can draw up a list of ideas, there comes a commotion out in the hall, and my worries are momentarily suspended. I move toward the door, intent on listening unseen.

But the voices are too numerous, they're speaking over and around each other. Finally, I push out of the library and stumble into an array of colorfully dressed royals. Princess Aubrey is the most distinctive, her taffeta dress a canary yellow and resplendent in its countless folds and satin embellishments. Her eyeshadow is the same shade, her lips are painted a bubblegum pink, and right now, they shout incessantly.

It doesn't take long to figure out why.

Both Butch and Dear Matthew stand amongst the Ming vases, sparring with their words. But no, that can't be right, because Butch has an override chip implanted in his brain, so such unsavory behavior isn't possible. And yet here he is, declaring his love for Aubrey and the unborn baby.

It takes a minute to register that it's Dear Matthew whose voice doesn't rise above Butch's or Aubrey's, or even her colorful entourage. In fact, as I gaze at him, I notice there's something different. Something…empty.

The realization hits me like a bus. Dear Matthew didn't go missing again. He was taken, by Lebwitski and the bluecoats.

In time, Aubrey and Butch notice that Dear Matthew lacks their vigor, their passion, and their anger. They stop shouting, and with one swoosh of a hand laden with jewels, Aubrey silences her admirers.

"I don't mean to cause offense, dear sir and dear gentle-woman, but I was hoping to head to my quarters for a hot soak. Might I squeeze through?"

Everyone stares at him. Aubrey is the first to move, ruffling the taffeta as she places her hands on her hips. "You mean to say you don't take offense to my, ahem, male suitor —I mean 'friend'—sharing our company?"

"Alas, my dear wife—the more, the merrier." He tips his hat to her and to Butch, then glides across the polished floor toward the staircase.

"Well then," murmurs Aubrey. She glances at Butch and smooths her dress. "I suppose that is that, hmm?"

"Perhaps his sudden agreeability can be shared with your father next?"

Aubrey's face breaks into a charmed smile. "You devil,

you," she scolds, swatting him. This kicks off a round of chasing and giggling, and I slip back inside the library.

I scratch my head. Is it possible I'd been wrong about Butch's override chip all along? And yet...he *was* taken. And he was altered. Initially.

Well, regardless of what really happened to Butch, it's a shame what happened to Dear Matthew. But one other thing becomes clear—this newest development, with Butch's triumphant return to Strath Glen alongside Dear Matthew's lack of objection, spells trouble for King. He won't be happy about this, not in the slightest.

I shiver to think what his reaction will be this evening, assuming things go according to plan during the address. I know from experience that when King's back is pressed against a wall, he's at his most volatile. He's at his most dangerous, too, and for the rest of the day, I just sit there, unable to do an ounce of cataloging work, unable to do anything but shake in anticipation.

———

DINNER IS A DULL AFFAIR, compared with the normal spectacle. The palace is roped off to visitors and guests, and instead of a formal meal with candlelight and a multitude of forks, all that is offered is finger food served à la buffet. King's not in attendance—I'm told some sandwiches have been sent up to his office where he rehearses his speech, but James is here, whispering in my ear about how much he's looking forward to our 'special' meeting.

I swallow—doubly so when I notice that Wolfe watches us.

And then there's Aubrey, no longer banished, who now seems fixated on Dear Matthew. Is that genuine concern that lights her eyes?

Evie, too, is melancholy, and when I ask her why, she

echoes the same worries that have long been plaguing her, surrounding her upcoming Selection and the unknown future she's powerless to control.

I reassure her that all will work out, and somehow, I believe it too.

fourteen

. . .

BY THE TIME dinner is over with, and all of us jam inside King's already cramped office to watch his address, most of the clan is in a sour mood, nerves fraying from all angles—though none of course worse than mine. James is the only one who seems chipper, and, to make matters worse, his eyes keep darting toward me—a reminder, I suppose, that soon we will slip out unnoticed.

Part of me feels badly for doing this to him. For playing games, although, if I'm being honest, it won't exactly make me lose sleep.

What *will* make me lose sleep, however, is if anything happens to Timothee and Neo. There's much riding on their shoulders right now—Jill too, and here I am being offered a macaron from a servant. I decline politely—my stomach twisting—as Aubrey scoops up a handful. She munches on them, looking more content than I've seen her look in days.

"Kssssssskkk." I pretend not to notice Morocco, who stands a few feet away, staring at me. "Kssssssssssssssssskkkkk."

Wolfe lifts his eyes from the paper he holds under his

uncle's nose and stares briefly at the small drama before returning to his notes. He points out several things to King, who is currently having his face powdered. Behind him, the Queen holds still while a servant removes her hair curlers. Another servant polishes the desk that already sparkles, and a team of men unfamiliar to me and dressed in black hook up the camera.

Much of my tension from earlier melts away. It's official. Queen will be on camera, as per usual, and James won't be. We are, as of now, primed and ready for success.

As King warms up his voice with the practice of scales, Wolfe maneuvers around the furniture to the back of the room where the rest of us stand. He situates himself beside James, at the very end. His parents stand behind him while Evie brushes past everyone in the midst of filing her nails so she can stand beside me.

"Sister, these broadcasts are an absolute bore. I should have advised you to bring something to occupy yourself." She puffs at her nails.

"Uh—yes, good thinking. I'll slip out shortly to do just that."

"Cufflinks. Have you tried cufflinks?" Morocco asks Aubrey.

The princess sniffs. "Why on earth would I give Dear Matthew gifts?"

"Because as far as *they* are concerned, *he* is your loving husband—"

"You sound just like Papa," she declares. "He's no Butch," she adds as she pushes the macaron completely into her mouth. "Besides, Dear Matthew has changed his position completely. He's totally fine with it!"

Morocco crosses her arms. "Totally fine. Is that so. Well, I'll tell you what *isn't* totally fine. A plain little whore exchanging saliva with my husband, and right under my nose!"

At this, James winks at me, then angles his head suggestively toward the door.

I sigh. "I'm going to go grab a book," I whisper to Evie.

Wolfe stares at me as I inch around the others, but I avoid eye contact. King, meanwhile, claps his hands together. He points to each of us in turn and holds his thick finger up to his lips to indicate silence, and I tiptoe faster toward the door.

Still, out of the corner of my eye, I watch him as he walks behind his desk with his arms spread wide. He sits on his throne with a flourish, has one last haul of a cigar held out to him from the butler, and stares into the camera with his head tilted, a toothy smile contorting his face. The Queen glides with her usual fluidity to her spot behind him and just off to the side, her smile set as it always is.

My pulse races.

Three lights are turned on, they illuminate King's jovial face and make each curl on the Queen's head shine like a dazzling diamond. The man behind the camera initiates a countdown. "Ten...nine...eight..."

At that moment, Aubrey spits out her macaron and says in a furious little voice, "I love Butch, Papa!"

"six...five..."

"OUT!" King screams from his perch.

A greencoat clasps Aubrey around the arm and drags her past me as she wails, while a hand lands firmly on my back and propels me after her.

"two...one..."

The door is sealed shut in my face. From the other side, I hear the cameraman shout, "Action!"

James grins as he peers down at me. "Shall we—"

I shush him, desperate to know what's happening in there.

"Good evening, beautiful citizens of Airo-Aurora," I hear, King's voice muffled yet jovial enough to claw through the walls. "I want to start this evening's broadcast with my thanks to each and every one of you. Thank you for being you. Thank you for being the best version of yourself, and making our nation-state the best version of itself too. Thank you for tuning in tonight, to boot!"

In my peripheral vision, I see James cross his arms, and I'm reminded that I deprived him of his opportunity to be on camera. I'm reminded that if I don't make this convincing, he may very well insist the broadcast be paused, that he may take his mother's spot. And who knows how long it will take for Timothee to unleash the program targeting the override chips.

"I have a stone in my boot," I whisper to him. "One moment, and then we can carry on to your, er, office." I bend over and rummage around in my boot, my ears continuing to strain to hear what is happening on the other side of the door.

"I also want to take this moment to share some personal news. It isn't often I take time to discuss the Rocksavage clan that works so hard to keep this sparkling gem of a nation running along so smoothly, but here I go! First off, my glowing daughter, the Princess, and her husband, Matthew, are pregnant with their first child, something I believe many of you already know from the Winter's End parade just last month. You can only imagine the happy flurry of activity here as Strath Glen readies itself for a babe!"

Somewhere off in the palace comes the princess' blood-curdling scream.

"Also, my nephew, the Viscount, is to be wed in just three weeks, only adding to the festivities. If only, dear viewers, I could turn this camera around and hear about all the exciting developments in your own lives! Will you write to me?"

"Better?" asks James as I finally straighten.

I nod.

"Delightful! Come, little one," he takes my hand and turns on his heel.

"Now, to business," echoes King's voice. "Airo-Aurora has been the center of many exciting developments in regional trade, meaning a stronger bottom line for our nation and, by extension, a deeper pocket for each of you. Yes, you heard right—"

I'm pulled along Bishop's Aisle, my mind racing. At any second, will the Queen erupt into an unexpected dance? The thought seems downright outlandish right now. It seems completely unfathomable. The whole thing is one big act so finely orchestrated that how could I be so arrogant to think that I, a lowly girl from Quire, could meddle with this mighty machine?

My palms aren't simply clammy anymore, they openly perspire. My mouth is dry and minuscule pops of light pepper my vision as I'm dragged behind James and past all the floating heads. Did Neo open the channel as he promised? Did Jill subdue the greencoats on duty? Is Timothee installing the program this very minute?

As James ushers me inside his office, I remember the precarious position I'll be in, alone with James, so I stand back and say, "After you."

He does a doubletake, then carries forward to his seat behind a desk almost as grandiose as his father's. I breathe a sigh of relief, for this way, I can keep the door open. A servant walks by at that moment, whistling a jingle, making me feel even more at ease.

Carefully I sit across from James and smooth my dress, observing—without appearing to—the state of his office. Sloppy, yes, but not with the items I'd typically expect to see in the office of the nation's second-in-command. Instead of the room being awash in paperwork, for instance, this one is cluttered with what looks like gym clothes, dirty socks, and rolled-up posters.

He places his chin in his hands and gazes at me in a hungry way. "My darling little mouse, you've requested a private meeting with me, and here we are."

"Er, yes—"

Another passing servant coughs at that moment, and James considers the open door, then stands.

"Allow me," I say, maneuvering quickly toward the door and motioning for him to sit. "You've already been so kind as to accommodate my request." But when I reach the door, I stick my head out of it and stare down the hall at King's office. Nothing looks different in the slightest. What are Timothee and Neo doing? Did the plan fail?

"Mouse?"

"Er, yes," I refocus on James and my current predicament. I make a show of closing the door, then abruptly swing it back open. "On second thought," I declare, returning to my seat, "given the sensitive nature of what I'd like to discuss, I think it's more prudent to keep the door open."

"Oh?" He leans forward with interest.

"You see, I wanted to discuss that..." I clear my throat, "...kiss."

"Kiss?" More theatrical blinking.

"Yes. When your father was looking to punish me."

"Ah, yes—I remember now," he says falsely. "Wasn't it divine?"

I force myself to nod. "It's just that I believe word has gotten back to your wife, and—"

"Shhhhh," he interrupts. He lays a finger to his lips, then proceeds to kiss it gently. Next, he begins to suck it.

"Uh, yes, well—anyway. She doesn't seem very happy about it, and I was hoping—"

"She can't stop true love," he says between slurps. "Nobody can."

And then, before I can gag, there comes the most beautiful sound in all the world. The sound of commotion.

Immediately I'm on my feet, sprinting past floating heads, and at the end of the hall, King's office door flies open. From inside, I hear the Queen blowing a series of raspberries.

My heart thumps furiously in my chest and my throat and just behind my eyes. Over my shoulder comes the sound of James' hammering footsteps, and inside the office, I see the other royals looking around at each other, confused. King, too, looks unsure, his mouth hanging open, his speech forgotten about.

A series of sounds issue next from the Queen, all an even cadence and pitch, and she bends down so that her body is bent at a ninety-degree angle, then back up again. The sounds and the bends continue, robotic-like, again and again, then suddenly she is rotating, her arms are held at awkward and unmoving angles, and the effect is complete.

"Christ!" shouts James, and when I glance at him, I notice that Dear Matthew is carrying out the same dance in the corner, blocked mostly by the other royals.

He and the Queen are being controlled from afar. Controlled by a computer, no less. It's impossible to think otherwise, and every cell in my body surges with triumph.

King stands, he motions to the greencoat, and together they lift the Queen to the side of the room where she's no longer on camera. Though the greencoat tries to reason with her, King doesn't bother. "Call Doctor Lebwitski," he orders Gerard as the giant mic is lowered and the camera is switched off.

A minute later, the butler hands the telephone to King. "He's on the line, sir," he says with a deep bow.

King snatches up the receiver. "Did you see?"

Whatever it is that Doctor Lebwitski says, it must be quite a mouthful, for King is silent for a stretch of time, looking more somber yet also more irate with every passing second.

The royals around me exchange nervous glances, muttering to each other, wondering aloud what on earth just happened.

"It's not just Mama," James says. "Look at this fool!" and he jams his thumb in the direction of Dear Matthew.

It's clear the others haven't noticed him, so focused on the Queen as they were. The duchess mutters a curse word under her breath, and Evie throws her hands over her mouth, stifling an audible gasp.

"My Matthew!" exclaims Aubrey.

"What in Jesus' name is going on here?" shouts Morocco.

It's only Wolfe that stands stalk-still, staring at me with an expression so hard I think he may be carved from stone. The stillness, I see, when I finally dare to meet his eye line, doesn't reach his eyes. They spoil the illusion. For they are raging with fury.

"Everyone, you say? The same exact motions?" King's eyes dart to Dear Matthew, and they narrow. Finally, though, both him and the Queen go still.

She blinks at the greencoat and smiles vapidly.

"Uh-huh. Uh-huh. It's over now. The rest, too? Uh-huh." After several more minutes of this, King hangs up the telephone with a loud crash. He gestures to the cameraman to start up the broadcast and repositions himself behind his large desk. This time the theatrics are gone. No smiles, no silly little stories. My skin prickles with electricity, with success, but also with nerves. After all, what now?

"For those of you who may be wondering what happened just now," booms King, "know that you are not alone. Interference with my wife and the people of my nation is not something I take lightly. I consider it to be an extreme act of terrorism, of war, and know that I will have the perpetrator before you at first instance for a most public execution. Justice will be served."

With that, he stands and stalks out of the office, looking far scarier than I've ever seen him. The cameraman hastily turns off the equipment. The Queen floats after her husband with an expression of serenity. Gerard takes up the tail with King's cigars.

As the others stand around staring at each other and eyeing Dear Matthew with a mixture of concern and suspicion, I wonder just how many in Airo-Aurora watched not only the Queen's bizarre behavior, but also a loved one sitting nearby. I wonder how concerned and suspicious they must be.

But what if they believe what King said just now? What if they believe that whatever force is at work isn't their ruler? The possibility hadn't even crossed my mind. Neither had King's swift performance that positioned himself not just as innocent, but as an angry guardian of justice determined to right the flagrant wrong.

This is what plagues me the most as I teeter to the nearest window, light-headed from all the excitement. I look through three panes of glass and intricate black latticework at the glittering city below. It's hard not to wonder what's happening all the way down there...

"So, that is the plan you have been hatching, Alexandra," says an undertone in my ear. "I suspected you were up to something, though never something of this magnitude."

I startle, then glance at him over my shoulder. The others are completely consumed with gossip. "Something you don't look all that happy about," I acknowledge.

"What you have done is neither subtle nor reversible," he hisses. "Indeed, it is fraught with risk. The consequences, I imagine, will be dire. My uncle's iron grip around the nation will only tighten if he is provoked by an uprising likely to follow this exposure. Why did you not think to come to me before pulling the trigger? You proclaim me an ally, do you not?" At these last words, he shoves his long nose right up to mine, then adds, "And what in hell did you and James leave for?"

I swallow. I knew Wolfe wouldn't be happy about tonight's intervention, but I never expected this level of derision. "With James, it was looking like he'd be taking his mother's place on camera, so I concocted a reason to speak to him to prevent that from coming to fruition. As for the rest of it," I say, under my breath, "I do count you an ally, of course I do. But I knew very well you would have called the whole thing off, given your desire to…"

"Yes?"

I turn back to the window rather than complete the sentence.

"With whose collusion did you manage this?" Wolfe continues, stepping closer so that his body is only an inch from mine. Behind us, the royals continue to trade theories.

"Timothee wrote the program," I admit, "and Neo, the technician at the Mainframe, opened the channel to the override chips."

"Could a self-destructing program not be used, considering you've secured yourself access to the chips in the first place?" he asks unexpectedly, and once again, I'm reminded we're on the same team.

"Apparently, that's more difficult than it sounds. Risky, too."

He nods. "Were you mindful of the recording chips in your brains when these plans were devised?"

"Of course," I say, fidgeting with the cuff of my cardigan. "What did you think of King's reaction? It was swift."

He frowns. "You didn't anticipate that?"

"I didn't," I admit.

He rubs his head around the temple and then reaches past me so that he grips the windowpane. "I suppose I should have shared with you my own intentions," he mutters. "This is my fault as much as yours."

I don't dare look at him—not when we stand in such close proximity. Instead, I address Wolfe's shirt buttons. "Your intentions? It looks like we could have both been more forthcoming," I admit. "Will you share them with me now?"

"Likely, it is too late to act upon them. My uncle will be too distracted by this turn of affairs to have my own chips dismantled."

Now I do point my face skyward, right up to his. "You were going to have your chips dismantled, like King and Doctor Lebwitski?"

"How do you know about that?"

"Neo."

He nods, returning his gaze to the city. "It would be done already if my uncle hadn't been so angry with the weapons delay." He sighs. "But now that I've cleaned that up, I think he will bring me back to his special dossiers."

"You've cleaned that up?"

"The weapons have been delivered," he says in a somber tone.

"The ammunition, too?"

His gaze narrows. "Of course."

"I should tell you, I suppose, that before it was delivered to the Mavericks, I switched theirs out with the ammo the bluecoats use."

He looks as though he's swallowed a lemon. "You did what now?"

"They were first delivered to the bluecoats' office," I explain. "I spotted the armored car. Was I really supposed to sit tight and do nothing?"

He sighs deeply, his lips pressed together to form a thin line.

I clear my throat. "So, after your own chips were dismantled, what were you intending to do?"

Before he can answer, the door to the office bangs open. Sedaris stands there, his face flushed with exertion. "There's been another security breach," he shouts. "Everyone down to the parking garage!"

fifteen

. . .

WHAT MIGHT HAVE BEEN a mad panic is met instead with an eye roll.

"Not again," groans Evie.

"For god's sake," shouts Morocco. "I need my beauty rest, you know."

"I'm going back to my quarters," says James, sounding annoyed.

Sedaris blocks the doorway. "Sir, palace policy right here. A security breach is a serious—"

"It's my blasted sister sneaking in her lover, nothing more." He makes to move around Sedaris, but the greencoat calls for someone over his shoulder, and suddenly Jill appears, blocking the exit and looking more disheveled than usual.

With one look at her thick muscles and the merciless glint in her eye, he falls silent.

"Now then," continues Sedaris, looking triumphant, "everyone, follow me. Absolutely no speaking, no sound whatsoever. The others in the palace are being rounded up as we speak and will join us in the garage."

I try to catch Jill's eye, but she's busy muttering something to Sedaris at the front of the pack. I tug on Wolfe's sleeve instead. "Maybe it isn't Butch, after all. Maybe the intruder has something to do with the—"

"Naughty, naughty. For looking so sweet and innocent, you really do like to bend the rules," Sedaris scolds. When he catches sight of the expression on Wolfe's face, though, he immediately blanches. "No talking, didn't I say?" he adds, in a less familiar tone. "You've got your hands full with this one," he mutters to Wolfe.

"Perhaps you should be following your own advice where your mouth is concerned," Wolfe counters. Then he pushes me ahead, alongside Evie. We trudge along Bishop's Aisle, past the floating heads, and then down the staircase typically reserved for servants. At the second floor comes the sound of flurried footsteps and breathlessness. "Move!" screeches Aubrey as she shoves past us, descending to the basement far quicker than the rest of our group.

We look at each other.

"So...it's not her forbidden fruit?" James queries, his voice wavering.

Evie gasps, her fingers suddenly trembling so profoundly that she drops her nail file.

"So, it's a *real* security breach, then?" asks Morocco.

"Quiet," Jill reminds us, from the front of the pack.

Now the chatter is gone, nerves are spiking. We descend lower, to the main floor, when Jill suddenly goes still.

A voice emanates from somewhere in the corridors—a woman, an older one—and for a heart-stopping moment in time, I think it might be Aunt Jo. As Jill pushes out of the stairwell to investigate, I dart around the royals after her.

The viscount tumbles out next, then all the others. King and Queen are there, too, having been cajoled into the servants' stairs with the rest of us, and our mighty group freezes, coming face-to-face with Strath Glen's intruder.

The petite, elderly woman, dressed in a polyester night

robe and with an umbrella as a makeshift cane, stares at us. Then she points the umbrella at King. "You, young man, have some explaining to do."

Seeing as how Jill shows no inclination to tackle this frail intruder, King pushes to the front of the crowd and approaches her with that familiar Cheshire grin. "What is it you speak of, fine mademoiselle?"

"Cut the crap," she says. "My husband spent the last ten minutes behaving like a total arse, that's what. An improvement over his usual dazed state, mind you. Oh sure, he had a temper before, tiring as it was, but anything's better than the braindead version you've left in his place. I'd think an explanation is warranted."

"I know not what you speak of, madam, but rest assured, and just as I told all of Airo-Aurora, I will find the person responsible for, er, this."

"See, where I'm from, it's the chief who has to answer for the crimes. So, whether it was you or one of your lackeys doesn't make a difference to me."

King chuckles, but he looks far less comfortable than a moment ago, and something surges inside of me.

Then there comes a pounding at the front door, an unexpected one, and King's slick nonchalance falls away, along with the remnants of his Cheshire grin.

"Everyone, downstairs!" Sedaris shouts to our group. "The blackcoats are on their way," he adds to King as their sirens scream off in the distance. Before I can determine who is pounding at the front door or what happens to the old lady, I'm shoved into the stairwell with Wolfe behind me.

Down we go, until finally we emerge into the parking garage, one that's cool, empty, and exceptionally damp.

I pat Evie on the shoulder to reassure her, but Wolfe wastes no time corralling me away from her and the others, parking me around the other side of Monsieur's limousine.

"Off to the gallows for that old bird," he hisses into my ear. "That or an override chip implanted in her. That's her fate and whoever else rises up, and all that—that's on you."

The surge of hope I felt a minute ago withers. A tide of defensiveness rides in in its place. "Well—you said yourself this was as much your fault as it was mine."

He gives me a sour look.

"Better action be taken rather than your self-serving plan," I throw at him next.

"Self-serving?"

"Freeing yourself of the Mainframe's watchful eye assists only yourself," I say in an undertone.

"That wasn't the whole of the plan, you fool," he seethes.

"So elaborate, then."

"With the watchful eye, as you call it, gone, I intended to take my uncle into the woods where I would eliminate him. James, who would take over the throne, is stupid enough to be easily manipulated. Either through trickery or persuasion, I intended to have him abandon both the override program *and* the Maverick army."

I go still. "What do you mean, *eliminate* him?"

He looks at me as if I'm unfathomably stupid. "Kill him, of course," he breathes into my ear.

Before I can react to what should surely be a startling admission, the door to the parking garage is banged upon with the sound of shrieking coming from the other side. Sedaris and Jill exchange a dark look, pull their weapons, and start forward. When the door is finally inched open, Rebecca stands there, white as a ghost.

"It's the duke!" she shouts. After a sob chokes her, she adds, "He's dead!"

sixteen

. . .

THE NEXT MORNING I wake early with a sinking feeling in my stomach. A sinking feeling that comes from far too much stress, far too much bad news. As for Wolfe, he hadn't come to bed until very late the night before, insisting upon closing himself in his office instead. Despite doing my best to offer condolences, they had tumbled from my mouth in a clumsy way, and he had been disinterested in them all the same. Quiet was what he wanted, so quiet I had given him.

Now I pull on a grey satin dress reaching to my knees and a cashmere sweater over that. I brush my hair into a loose plait that coils around my shoulder, then slip downstairs in a palace that has a different feel than yesterday. The cloud of humiliation and rage emanating from the national address intermingles with death, leaving an oppressive atmosphere that's thick—almost sticky—to pad through. Down in the kitchen, I pick up Wolfe's breakfast and chat with the servants, gleaning from them what I did not know: that the duke, a long-time alcoholic, had died of heart failure shortly after the rest of us filed out of King's office.

The most tragic part is that if any of us had bothered to

scan the room prior to leaving, we may have spotted him, may have been able to alert the medics in time to save his life. My chest squeezes for Evie and Wolfe.

Upstairs, I drag the heavy breakfast tray from the dumbwaiter into my chambers, thinking yet again of my soon-to-be sister-in-law along the way. She had been devastated upon learning the news, and it had been excruciating to listen to her weep. It brought up other feelings, too. Memories, painful ones, from when I learned that my own parents were no longer...

I set the tray not in the entrance hall, but inside our suite on a side table. When I see that the bed is empty, I call, "Wolfe?"

"In here," comes a weary voice from the closets. He walks out a moment later, wearing a black suit. By the looks of him—his crumpled hair and the pronounced bags under his eyes, very little sleep had been managed.

"You should try to eat something," I murmur, suddenly unable to meet his gaze. The unbearable sadness of the situation has robbed me of my steadiness. "At the very least, some coffee might help."

He nods in a distracted way, and I turn for the door, intent on spending the day in the library, where I can both give the family space to grieve and also observe the glittering city down below. Did protests grip the city last night unbeknownst to me? Will today be marked by anger? By demands for justice?

But as I descend the imperial staircase, I see with a quickening in my pulse that avoiding the royal family and allowing them to grieve privately isn't really possible. Not when the duke's body has been placed on display in a casket in the center of the long entrance hall. Long-stemmed roses are scattered around it, looking eerily like drops of blood on the black polished floor. The women of the palace gather in a circle, Evie shaking with tears, the duchess ashen-faced,

Morocco and Aubrey applying lip gloss. James and King stand off to the side, saying nothing.

It isn't my first choice to pass by them, but turning around would be rude. With no other choice, I draw up alongside Evie. She spots me through her tears, and we embrace like sisters.

For a while, I do nothing but hold her, but eventually, she wipes her eyes and looks me square in the face. "How did you ever cope when you were robbed of both your parents?" she wails.

I nod solemnly—it's a fair question. "Much the same as you're doing right now," I say after considering it. "Grieving, and I don't think there's any other way about it, unfortunately. But know, at the very least, that eventually, it will hurt less. Far, far less."

"But the pain never goes away completely, does it. I'll never be the same, I'm sure of it!"

"The pain never goes away completely, of that you're right. But it doesn't hurt the same way after a while, I promise you. And no, you'll never be the same. You'll be far stronger." With one last hug and murmured thanks into my ear, she returns to her mother, who now looks to be fighting back tears herself. The Queen, who passes out bacon rolls, pats her idly on the back.

I nod respectfully to King as I pass by, a nod he returns. The day's most somber of occasions equalizes us, for now.

And then the palace doors swing open, and a great swarm of people appear, and for one passing moment in time, I think the citizens of Airo-Aurora are here, rising up and rushing the palace...

But no—these are guests currently pushing inside, all dressed in black with elaborate veils, fans, and fascinators. Suffering, I note as I watch them, seems to be a performance —perhaps even an artform. Eventually, when nobody is watching, I slip into the library, then tuck myself into the back corner.

Work, as I suspected, is a lost cause. I'm too distracted by it all. The death of a senior member of the Rocksavage clan. What happened last night during the broadcast. Its potential ramifications. My meeting tonight with the others. I think too about Wolfe's admission from the night prior, that he had planned to kill the King of Airo-Aurora *himself*.

I shiver at that last thought, then go to a nearby window so I can watch the streets down below. Nothing. Nothing looks out of place. Nothing looks different. Where are the protesters? The White Ribboners? The anger?

I sigh, then turn my attention so I can watch the endless stream of the city's finest coming and going from the palace. Wolfe, I imagine, stands in the hall with the others by now, making small talk and exchanging unpleasant pleasantries. I'm surprised to spot him a while later through the books, pacing back and forth between the library's dustiest collection. For a while, I just watch him—that brow pulled taught, his mouth pressed into a hard and unforgiving line, the way his fingers jump at his sides.

This is a man not unfamiliar with suffering. His wife, his child... Does this most recent blow conjure up past pain, as it does for myself? Of course, I realize, and instead of ruminating any longer, I slip out the door, returning a few minutes later with hot tea.

"Wolfe," I say quietly, stepping in front of him. He doesn't hear, so I say his name again, louder this time. Finally, his gaze clicks onto mine. "This will help. Will you sit?" I motion in the direction of the chairs set out around the hearth.

As though it pains him somewhat, he takes the tea from my hands, moving robotically, then settles awkwardly into a chair. I sit across from him and, sensing that conversation isn't what he wants, busy myself with a stack of books perched nearby. After a while, he sips the tea, and his twitching fingers begin to settle. He sets the empty cup and saucer down on the table, murmurs his thanks, and disappears back into the hall that still bustles with activity.

All in all, it wasn't one of our worst interactions.

After another hour passes with little to occupy me besides my racing thoughts, the doors to the library bounce open. I look up from the titles to see James stride inside, his gaze swiveling until it lands on mine.

"Thought I'd find you here—consider me charmed. And amidst such a travesty, too."

"Heartbreaking," I agree. "Especially for his immediate family."

"What, that?" He waves his hand dismissively. "I was referring to last night."

I frown. "You mean the issue with the Queen."

"She's acting like the most splendid breath of spring theater," he calls to nobody in particular. "Why, I'm talking about our special chitchat that was forced to end far too early, but you already know that."

That had been the last thing on my mind, but I don't bother to mention it.

"I was thinking," he says, "we could continue our chat off palace grounds, perhaps over champagne?"

"Uh—I'm not permitted to leave the grounds, but thank you for the offer—"

"I shall speak to Papa. It won't be an issue to whisk you from these old palace walls—I promise!" and he turns on his heel, leaving the library before I can protest.

I swallow. Abducted by James—wouldn't that be something. At least the chauffeur is someone I trust.

By mid-afternoon, the steady stream of visitors has slowed, and things in the hall have quieted. With my stomach growling, I step outside, noticing that even though the visitors have gone, the Rocksavage clan remain in place, standing around the now-closed casket looking considerably fatigued.

"Sister," Evie gulps, looking every bit as strained as earlier. "I really must discuss something with you."

I edge toward her. "What is it?"

"Your wedding. I don't think I'll be able to devote myself to it the way you deserve, given..." Another gulp.

I shake my head. Of all the things to worry herself over, my wedding is the last thing that should weigh on her mind. I tell her so.

"Perhaps a new date should be set," suggests the duchess as she wipes her eyes. "I don't think anyone feels in the mood for a party," and she gazes around at the others, looking for confirmation.

Murmurs of acquiescence arise from all corners of the sparkling hallway. Even the servants chime in, agreeing that the time for festivity isn't now. I begin to nod along, too, when Wolfe steps forward.

"Our plans will remain the same," he announces.

Morocco looks faintly intrigued. James scowls. The rest of the family glance at each other, perplexed. Then the duchess turns to Aubrey. "Would you be a savior to us all and put the final details in place? Evie's already organized the bulk of—"

Aubrey squeals, tempering her enthusiasm only at the last second as she remembers the dead body situated just a few feet to the left. "Of course I shall, dear Aunt. Evie, darling," she adds, turning to her, "do you have that rather ridiculous, swollen, album-like book handy, the one you drag around with you that has all the wedding details sealed inside, hmm? I'll be needing it at once. Of course, a few changes may indeed be in order," she adds pointedly.

Evie shoots a nervous glance at me, then tasks a servant with fetching it and placing it in Aubrey's quarters. The conversation shifts to burial details, and I back away from the others, once more keen to give them their space. But just as I near the imperial staircase, the sound of high heels draws up behind me.

"Madam," I cry as I'm caught around the arm.

"You have been a comfort today to both of my children, and for that, I am grateful." The duchess bows her head solemnly as a gust of wind wraps around my ankles.

"I haven't done much, madam."

"I heard the words of comfort you offered Evie. I saw the tea you prepared for my son."

"It is a tremendously hard thing, to lose a parent," I concede.

"Indeed, it is. And I'm given to believe you've lost not just one but both of yours."

"A few years ago, yes."

"A terrible tragedy."

"And for you too, madam. To lose one's spouse, I can't imagine."

For a second, I think the statement that popped so easily from my mouth might be met with resistance. Instead, the woman seems to deflate somewhat. "My parents are both long gone, and now my husband. I feel like you must have, and perhaps still do. Completely on my own. I've underestimated you, child."

seventeen

. . .

"DO you see what I do for you?" Monsieur hisses at me.

"A prior commitment obligates me to go," I explain. "This isn't my first choice, not with all that's happened over the past twenty-four hours. And besides, Rebecca's already gone."

"Yes, she's gone because you found an out from playing watchman last night."

I fix him with a look. "I don't think the duke's unexpected death counts as me 'finding an out.'"

"Call it whatever you like. If you're caught by one of those guards roaming the grounds, it's your ass and not mine. Not a word of our arrangement, agreed?"

"Of course, Monsieur."

"Good. Be gone with you then, and mind to be quick. Count me exhausted."

He isn't the only one. The entire palace had retired to bed far earlier than normal, the drama of the day and the sleeplessness of the night prior no doubt to blame. Even the viscount's breathing had been slow and level when I tiptoed from the room.

As I walk toward the back door of Strath Glen, a sense of

intrigue intermixed with guilt washes over me. Sneaking around isn't what Wolfe wants right now from me, it isn't what he needs. So yes, there's guilt there. But the others—Jill, Timothee, Neo, and Agnes—they have been free to roam the city since the broadcast. They have contacts that aren't holed up at the palace. They will know what is going on down there, and that is information I desperately need to know, especially when I've gleaned absolutely nothing from way up here. The fact that King had ordered more green-coats to the palace does complicate things, however.

No sooner do I step outside am I forced to dive behind the garbage bins set out near the door. Peering around them, I watch a guard walking along the tree line, a dazzling-bright flashlight in hand that illuminates the stables and casts long shadows into the night. Only once he heads down the sloping hill at the far side of the property do I dart east, in the opposite direction. Seeing that another greencoat walks the hill in front of me, I side-step into the trees, hiding myself amongst the thick shrubbery that slices my face.

Finally, when I make it to the humming streets of the city, I allow myself to breathe. The anticipation of what I'm about to learn drives me forward, quickly now, along the sidewalks. My heart hammers as I forget about the turmoil at the palace, as I inch closer and closer to the truth.

Inside Skelton Park, I bump immediately into Timothee and Jill.

"Did you see it?" Timothee asks, and I can hear the excitement in his voice. "A beautiful work of art, wasn't it?"

"Indeed, it was," I whisper. "It was no problem gaining access to the override chips?"

"Not from inside the Mainframe. How's the King taking it?"

"Not well, although the palace has been distracted by the sudden death of the duke. Did you see what King said at the end of the broadcast? About finding the person responsible?"

"I'm not sure people are buying it," Timothee replies.

I lean forward, hopefulness surging. "People are upset, then?"

"More than that, even," he agrees, and a potent blend of triumph and relief floods my system. "Just about everyone I've spoken with knows someone directly or indirectly who did the robot dance last night."

"Yeah, it sure got people talking," Jill confirms. "Protests are being planned too, you know."

"They are?"

She nods. "I'm not sure what kind of numbers they'll get, though. People are confused and scared. For good reason."

"Do you think my friend is coming? I'm curious what the White Ribbon members think about this."

"Not sure where she is," Jill replies.

"Hey," Timothee interrupts, nudging me in the ribs, "is that our friend from the Mainframe over there?"

We squint through the darkness at a figure standing on the other side of the fir trees, where we typically meet. "It must be," I say, and we walk in his direction.

"Hey," I whisper once we're within earshot. He doesn't seem to hear, so I greet him louder.

He turns and smiles—I can make out his white teeth through the darkness. "Hi."

"So, last night worked out well. Any issues?"

"It was a mistake, what I did. I betrayed the Mainframe, and it isn't a mistake I will make again."

I gasp, and immediately my hands wrap around the arms of my friends. "*Run*," I yell to them.

In unison, we turn and plunge headfirst into the murky darkness, tumbling between trees, feet hammering the ground. The sound of my own heartbeat is thunderous in my ears.

"Go in different directions," Timothee shouts, so I dart right, away from the others, running furiously as saliva pools in my mouth, choking me. It can't be. *It can't be.*

But it is, and I have to blink back tears as I start up the hill toward the back of the palace. My entire body shudders and—

A hand grabs me by the shoulder. I scream.

"Jesus. What's with you?"

"Sedaris," I breathe when I see him staring at me under the moonlight, fitted smartly in his green uniform.

He shakes his head. "Why is it you're always up to something, anyway?"

"You know me well enough to know that I wouldn't harm a fly. I'm not an intruder here, at my own home. I was out for a walk, and now I've returned. Nothing more to it," I add in a voice that quivers.

"Nothing more to it," he echoes, laughing. "So why aren't you going through the front doors then?"

"Well...Typically I visit the stables and the chickens, so that's why I tend to use the back door. But if you insist..." I gesture to the front steps, and together we walk toward them.

"So, you went for a walk, eh?"

"That's right."

"You really think I believe that?"

"I'm not sure why you wouldn't," I say, but even I can hear how hollow my voice is right now. The shock and horror of Neo's fate has robbed me of my conviction.

"I've never seen you so jumpy."

"It's rather disconcerting being approached unexpectedly in the dark."

He smirks. "You certainly have a way about you. Enjoy your sleep," he adds as I step inside the palace. I head at once for the backdoor, catching up with Monsieur just as he nears it.

"I'm already in," I tell him. "Thank you, Monsieur." I turn and walk quickly in the opposite direction.

"Everything okay, Miss Alex?" he calls after me.

With tears prickling once more behind my eyes, I can't bear to turn to him. Instead, I say over my shoulder, "Sleep well, friend," then take the servants' stairs two at a time to the second floor.

Once I lock myself into my quarters, I lean against the door and hold a hand over my mouth. Neo. *Neo.* My ally inside the Mainframe. My friend.

And then there comes the nagging worry...If he has been interfered with, am I and the others next?

Agnes. Where was she? Why wasn't she at the meeting? Was it too dangerous for her to come, or was she *unable* to come?

I stare into the darkness and try to breathe. Breathe. It will be okay. The override chip program will be over soon, it *has* to be. Neo and all the other targeted citizens will be themselves again. Timothee, Jill, and I are safe. We've been careful—we'll continue to be careful. And as for Agnes, she forgot. That's all. I'll have Monsieur take me to the nursery tomorrow, just to be safe.

Breathing easier, I go inside the closets and change into my nightgown, a process that takes far longer than it should, given the trembling that remains in my bones. I can't stop thinking about Neo, and it seems so obvious now. There had been a pause, a too-long hesitation, when we discussed opening up the channel from inside the Mainframe. He knew the dangerous position he was putting himself in, yet he did it anyway. Because, *of course,* King wouldn't let the incident go uninvestigated. He would find which technician's computer left the system open to attack. He would have ordered a review of Neo's feed, he would have learned that it was done with a calm and deliberate mind...So why hadn't Neo been hauled away by the blackcoats, thrown into jail?

Because clearly, Neo wasn't working alone. Best to send a message, that's why. At the very least, though, it must mean—surely—that there's no footage capturing Timothee's face, or Jill's, during their mission at the Mainframe. Neo was careful, as he always is. Was.

Stepping from the closet, my gaze moves immediately to the bed, to the long bulge under the covers. Perfectly still, aside from the rhythmic breathing that suggests he's sound asleep, still. Waking him would be downright rude—I wouldn't dare, especially given what he's going through. I won't be so needy, not a chance. But as I step toward my makeshift bed on the couch, the weight on my shoulders becomes downright unbearable. The terror that had encompassed me when I discovered that Neo was gone overwhelms me, and I find myself tiptoeing past the couch, toward the massive bed.

Sound asleep, just as I thought.

I'll leave him be, of course I will, and yet my hand reaches out—my body disobeying my brain.

He wakes as only Wolfe would. Suddenly completely lucid, sitting upright and peering at me through the darkness with his signature frown. "What is it, Alexandra?" he demands. "What's wrong?"

The dam breaks, I throw my arms around his neck, and all the emotion from the past hour is unleashed.

Wolfe's entire body, meanwhile, goes rigid. He takes a deep breath in, I can feel his ribs expanding near mine, then, as he exhales, he clasps his long arms around me, both of them, bringing me tightly to his chest so that no air separates us.

"I need to tell you something," I say, my voice cracking.

"Yes...Yes, I figured." He sounds awkward and unsure, not like his usual self at all.

"But I don't wish you to be angry."

"Is it another man?"

I pull back and gaze at him, almost laughing at the absurdity of the question in this instance. "Another man? Why is it your mind always goes in that direction?"

"You'll notice how my cousins conduct themselves, you see."

"Yes, well, that isn't how I conduct myself."

"Noted. I take it, if it's not that, it's something that requires our utmost discretion?"

I nod, wiping away my tears and putting some space between the two of us, realizing how gravely I breached our unspoken rule to avoid physical contact at all costs.

"You have my word that I won't be mad. Now, as you're shivering, will you consider making yourself comfortable on your side of the bed? I promise I won't...do whatever it is you fear I will."

"I know...you won't," I say quickly, clearing my throat.

"It really is far more comfortable than the couch."

So carefully, on unsteady legs, I walk around the bed and slip under the covers. The sheets are exceptionally cold, and Wolfe's exceptionally far. The bed really is absurdly wide, and I realize how foolish we've been, utilizing the couch all this time.

For right now, though, I nudge myself over, closer and closer to the middle of the bed. "As we need to be in close proximity," I begin, "I—"

"Aren't we passed that point?" He moves himself with efficiency toward me until we meet under the covers, lying side by side with our sleeves touching.

For a minute, we're both silent, frozen in place. Then, as the evening's events rush back to me, I say, "I'm sorry for troubling you with all this right now, when you're grieving. The timing really couldn't be worse."

"It's fine, Alex," he says. His voice is without its usual edge. "Tell me now, please."

I lower my voice until it's barely audible. "Timothee, Jill, Agnes, Neo, and I had plans to meet this evening, to discuss the national address. I snuck out about an hour ago." Feeling his body tense up next to me, I add, "You promised not to get mad."

"I'm not mad. Continue."

I have to bite my lip to stop myself from crying all over again.

"What is it?" he prods. He glances at me, and I'm struck to see not anger cut through his eyes, but concern.

"Well, first of all, Agnes didn't show up, and I don't know why—"

"Why is Agnes wrapped up in all this?"

"I didn't tell you?"

"No."

"She's the one behind the White Ribbon Campaign."

His brow lifts with surprise. "And you fear she is now in trouble."

I nod. "And that's not all..." Once again, I feel that wave of terror crashing into me.

"Yes?"

"Neo. He's been turned," I whisper. "King must've discovered his role in interfering with the override chips. How much longer until me and the others are caught, too?"

"I won't let that happen," he says evenly.

"Pardon?"

"I know I haven't been a very good fiancé. I haven't done anything to ease you into palace life, or to make you feel wanted or at home here. But rest assured, if my uncle comes for you, he'll pay with his life."

eighteen

. . .

IT'S A RESTLESS NIGHT, with barely any sleep managed until the early hours of the morning. By the time I wake, the day has begun, and Wolfe's side of the bed is empty. It's foolish to feel disappointed by this—Wolfe has a busy job and, now, a funeral to plan. And yet the comfort he had offered in the middle of the night had been helpful, sweet, and therapeutic. Even his presence next to me as I struggled to sleep brought me solace.

Funny how drastically things have changed since I first arrived at the palace. As determined as both Wolfe and I were to keep our distance from one another, closeness has emerged. Is it the fact of being betrothed to one another that tethers us? I suppose that it is. That and knowing all we do —the truth.

I pull on my stockings and think about that kiss I placed on him in my drunken haze. The meaning to that, I still can't ascertain. But thinking of the kiss makes me think of Agnes' wedding, and that makes me think of my friend. With Neo already gone, I simply can't stomach something happening to her. I need to track her down, quickly, no matter the risk.

With that intention in mind, I slip downstairs, finding that the duke's casket has been moved and that the palace buzzes with preparations for the funeral scheduled that evening. White roses by the dozen are carted to the ballroom, and a number of cellists stand near the doorway, gesticulating with their bows. It's eerie to think that soon a similar bustle will be underway, but instead of a funeral, it's for a wedding—

Aubrey bursts out of Devonshire Commons at that moment, wearing a neon green dress dusted with gold, ushering out a large team of poshly dressed women holding clipboards. "My party planning entourage," she explains to me. "Selected by this delicate hand" —and she waves her fingers, all ladled with diamonds—"to plan you the most scrumptious wedding known to humankind!"

My mouth opens and closes, but before I can protest—or kindly ask her to keep things simple as they were before—she sweeps past me, citing the need to ready herself for the funeral.

"Miss Alex," comes a voice from behind me.

I turn and manage a small smile. "Monsieur," I reply.

"You look significantly happier than last night."

I do? Nothing of great significance had changed between then and now. Neo is still gone, my own fate still hangs in the balance—and Agnes', and the effectiveness of hacking into the override program remains unknown. And yet something approaching contentedness does harbor itself inside my chest, even amongst all the worry and concern, not to mention the unwanted changes to my wedding coming fast and furious.

"I apologize for last night's demeanor, then," I reply as he considers me. "And for being corralled to the front doors at the last second by a greencoat I happened to know. Your services were greatly appreciated, all the same. I trust Rebecca made it safely back?"

"Indeed. Where do you keep going, anyhow?"

"To meet friends, Monsieur."

His eyes crinkle. "Is that the truth?"

"It is," I reply, surprised. "Why do you ask?"

"What did you make of the Queen during the broadcast the other night?" he asks, ignoring my query. Servants shout about refreshments down the hall, and potted roses are carried past us by half a dozen men wearing kilts.

I eye him, surprised to see him eyeing me just the same. "Peculiar," I say after a while. "I found her behavior to be peculiar. What did you make of it?"

"I heard Dear Matthew suffered the same affliction."

"Indeed."

"I was speaking with Rosa this morning, you remember her?"

"Of course."

"She and your friend Worthers were close back in the day, don't ask me why. She had some interesting theories—"

"Monsieur, I feel like some music, don't you?" I walk past him, into Devonshire, and over to the record player. A moment later, the room fills with an operatic melody. I sit on the window seat and motion him over. "Best to mask such scandalous conversations from the chips in our heads," I explain pointedly.

For a while, he just contemplates me. Then his gaze slips over my head, it tilts all the way down to the low-slung building of white known as the Mainframe. "Word is, the Queen and Matthew weren't the only ones in our beautiful city to behave so, as you say, peculiar. Rosa suspects that Worthers was performing that same dance. Do you concur, Miss Alex?"

I swallow deeply. Then I murmur in an undertone, "The thought had crossed my mind."

"Mmm, indeed it had. That was the real reason you wanted to see that old man in the first place, wasn't it? I remember you asking then and there about our lady the Queen."

"Best to keep your shadowy suspicions to yourself, Monsieur," I advise.

"Just what secrets do you know?" he continues, leaning toward me.

"The same ones you're beginning to suspect. But, to make your suspicions known at large, would be to risk befalling the same fate as those just listed."

After a long pause, he nods. "I shall heed your warning, but don't think I'll stop pondering, just the same."

"I'd expect nothing less. On that note, one of those friends I was supposed to meet with last night didn't show, and I must say I'm worried about her. Could I convince you to cart me to Quire, Monsieur?"

He rolls his eyes. "I daresay I'll first need to check my schedule. It's rather a busy day at the palace, haven't you noticed?"

"I understand."

"Hard to believe your wedding is just a few weeks off, isn't it?"

"That's an understatement. To make matters worse, I'm afraid Aubrey has taken over the preparations, meaning my simple affair will now be turned into a spectacle."

"Ah, that would explain the arrival of all that acrobatic equipment this morning, then," he says knowingly. "Doesn't the bride herself get a say?"

"You think me so bold as to go up against the likes of Aubrey?"

He chuckles. "I wouldn't be so surprised, Miss Alex. I'm sure whatever the spectacle, it will be a marvelous occasion."

"You're too kind. Best to bring your dancing shoes—it's sure to be a long affair."

"And I'll be in the limousine for most of it," he adds.

"What?"

He looks confused. "Pardon?"

"Oh," I say, crestfallen. "I had rather hoped you would be in attendance."

Wolfe walks into the room at that moment. I sit straighter at seeing him. Monsieur dives into a deep bow.

"Monsieur Sawyer," Wolfe mutters with a nod of his head. "Alex," he adds, motioning in my direction. "I'm not interrupting anything important, I take it?"

"Not at all—" begins Monsieur.

"Actually, yes," I insist. I slip off the window seat and tuck my hands behind my back. "Talk of the wedding, in fact. I do hope my friend Monsieur will be in attendance, and not simply in a professional capacity."

"I—Yes, I think that can be arranged," Wolfe concedes.

Monsieur coughs. "I'll go check today's schedule," he tells me, disappearing toward the garage a second later.

I return to the window seat and make room for Wolfe.

"I thought you'd be in the library—I just checked there, in fact," he says as he joins me.

"I'm afraid I didn't manage much rest last night. I've only now just managed to start my day."

"Ah." He pauses, then fixes me with a stern look. "I come bearing news."

"Oh?"

He leans forward so that his elbows rest on his knees. Then he says quietly, "My uncle has called in the army."

I gasp. "Are you sure?"

He nods, looking grim.

"But—for what purpose? Already the greencoats are giving the palace added security—"

"Protests, evidently, are being planned around the city. People are very upset by the development during the national address, just as you predicted, and desired."

Panic immediately dissolves to relief, and I realize how

deeply the lack of public outcry has bothered me. This is something Neo risked his life for, after all. Something he lost his life for, too—at least for now. So yes, I *do* want citizens to be riled up by what we worked so hard to show them.

Of course, the army...I don't want that.

"Alex?"

"Huh? Oh, yes—and King? He must feel like his back is up against the wall if he's bringing in the Mavericks."

"That's a fair assessment," he agrees, then he leans closer. "I know from experience that I can't dictate what you do or where you go, but I really must caution you against sneaking from the palace again. Once they arrive, there will be members of the army at every door and around the perimeter of the property—members unable to reason or show mercy. Frankly, I'm not sure how you managed to make your way out of the palace last night and in again without being detected, given the added security measures. I assume you don't use the front door after the last punishment imposed by my uncle?"

"The back door," I confirm. "And, actually, I was detected, but luckily it was Sedaris who caught me." Seeing the questioning look in his eye, I add, "The same guard you had tail me after that business with Mr. Worthers."

"He caught you sneaking about the property and allowed it to go unsaid? It seems to me, Alexandra, that you have a mysterious way of endearing yourself to the most unlikely of suspects. This Sedaris fellow, for instance, who seems like a hulking monolith to me and little more. Monsieur Sawyer, for another, not exactly known for his amiable charm. At any rate, in exchange for your word on this matter, I shall arrange to have Monsieur Sawyer himself take you to your friends whenever you see fit."

"A generous compromise," I say, with a bow of my head. "One I intend to take you up on today, if Monsieur's schedule permits it."

"You will be present for the funeral this evening, I assume?"

"Of course," I say at once.

He looks solemn for a moment, then his gaze sharpens, and he moves closer. "I have a number of servants and guards who are, I believe, somewhat allied to me, just as you have some of your own allied to you. Should Doctor Lebwitski step onto these premises, I will be alerted to it at once. I will also do my best to monitor my uncle's movements and pry him for information concerning the override chip scandal to better gauge whether you are suspected of playing a role. Does all that bring you any peace of mind?"

Half my mouth twists into a smile. "Thank you."

He stands and stares down at me for a long while. But, "You're welcome," is all he says, and he walks quickly from the room.

I stop the record player, then, seeing as how Monsieur has yet to return from the garage, I head for the towering front doors.

"I get the feeling you've complicated my life since we first met," Jill says.

"Considerably," I agree.

"Think we'll be next?" There's no need for her to say anymore—I know she references Neo and the override chip implanted in his brain.

I shake my head, even though I'm far from certain. "He never laid eyes on us in the light of day, and the scrolls were written and delivered in the dark, too. If someone has been tasked with reviewing his feed, they would have to do an exceptionally skilled reading to find us."

"I guess."

"Did he look at you at the Mainframe?"

"No, he had on a low hat. He was careful," she adds.

"Good. Well, if it gives you any relief, if anyone's in danger, it's me. King has long been suspicious of me, and the Mainframe would have captured Neo, at the very least, turning in the direction of the palace to deliver the scrolls. On that note, I have a favor to ask."

She spits over the banister. "Aren't you tapped out, princess?"

"Probably. Still, if you see an older man with white hair and the look of a doctor enter the palace, please let me know. Wolfe too."

"Howcome?"

"Because it's Doctor Lebwitski—the one who does the operations."

She nods knowingly. "So, what now?"

"Evidently protests are being planned throughout the city—that's what Wolfe heard. Perhaps King will capitulate to the pressure and abandon the program."

"So, we sit back and wait with our fingers crossed?"

"Toes, too. Apparently the Mavericks have been called in."

"Oh, terrific," she says, her voice heavy with sarcasm. "This is turning into a full-blown war."

"Let's hope our work in the bluecoats' warehouse will stop any bloodshed."

"No kidding. Hey—I got my invite to the wedding."

"The wedding?"

She rolls her eyes. "*Your* wedding."

"Ah, I didn't realize Evie had sent them out. Are you coming?"

"Free food and booze? Ask a stupid question."

I grin. "Your fiancé, too, I hope."

"About time the two of you met."

"I look forward to it. In the meantime, I'm going to see if I can track down Agnes. Just, you know, to make sure she's okay."

"Probably a good idea."

"I mean, I'm sure she's fine…"

"Yeah. Definitely."

I nod, then I wave goodbye, keen to track down Monsieur Sawyer that very moment. Inside the palace, however, I run headfirst into King.

He stomps his walking stick in frustration, then lets out a laugh intended to sound jovial. "You frightened me, wee fawn," he exclaims. "What in heavens were you doing out front?"

"Admiring the view of the city and enjoying the fresh air," I say promptly, without any hesitation. "Are you heading out to do the same?"

"Uh, yes. Yes—exactly." He turns and swings open the door, our conversation apparently complete, and I exhale. King is distracted right now; I am no longer in his crosshairs. All I must do is stay there.

"Always a killer," shouts the parrot as soon as I turn the corner into Devonshire.

Instead of heading down to the garage as intended, though, I stare out the window, trying to see what's happening on the balcony.

Several minutes later, as I hear the towering front door groan open and the echoing of the walking stick along the corridor, I slip outside in his place.

"You're back?" asks Jill, checking her watch. "You already check on Agnes?"

I smile, then edge closer. "What did King want?"

She checks to make sure the other greencoat isn't listening. "Quizzing us about any unusual activity on the grounds and making us promise to immediately report anything resembling a protest down there."

"He's worried, then."

"I'd say so. Maybe even paranoid. Not typical for him to come out here and talk to us lowly servants, so that says something."

It certainly does. Better yet, there's nothing to suggest King suspects me or Jill. At least not yet.

MONSIEUR GRUMBLES in the front seat. I sit on the edge of mine, my nose pressed to the window as we wind our way through Airo-Aurora's streets, en route to the Quire nursery.

But there are no people milling about, no open hostility, no signs of unrest anywhere, and I sink deeper into my seat, undeniably disappointed. Finally, though, I notice something. Posters, tacked up to every available surface. Posters with a familiar logo at the bottom—a white ribbon.

My heart leaps to my throat, and I shout at Monsieur to stop the limo.

It comes screeching to a halt, and Monsieur swings his head around. "What in holy hell is the problem?" he shouts.

"Sorry, truly, I am. I just need to check something," and with that, I swing open the door. Marching to the nearest streetlamp, I rip one of the posters from its tacks and return to the behemoth.

"Is your highness ready to carry on?"

"Indeed, Monsieur. Thank you for being so accommodating," I add as I smooth the sheet of paper over my knee. I gasp at the headline. *DOWN WITH THE KING,* it screams, and the sensation of pins and needles spreads to my extremities.

Has your loved one been targeted by the King? Do you fear you might be next? Now is the time to demand justice. Take to the streets and STAND YOUR GROUND!

This is dangerous. It's inflammatory. It's also brilliant. And clearly, Agnes has plenty of volunteers working with her, given the number of posters smothering every surface of every block. Yes, down with the King, indeed.

It has a nice ring to it, too. And it's certainly more concise than demanding the reversal of the override chip program.

More importantly, there's little King and the bluecoats can do if enough people take to the streets. The army, however, is a different story, and I shudder at the prospect of violence. Good thing they haven't yet arrived. In fact, I suddenly realize, covering a hundred miles would take days by foot. It would result in an army in need of sleep, too—not something the override chips can eliminate. And, given the density of the forest, landing a plane there or even at Ashville Range is out of the question. A helicopter would work, but transporting an entire army a few members at a time wouldn't exactly be economical or efficient.

So long as the first round of protests start soon, there should be little resistance—

"The Quire nursery," Monsieur Sawyer announces, lifting me out of my spiraling thoughts.

I blink at the little building, with its daffodils and children's toys stacked along the windowsill. Somehow I'd missed the entire passage through my beloved Quire. I fold up the poster and put it in my pocket, eager to speak to Agnes about it, then knock on the door.

A short woman with curly hair pulls it open, holding a baby in one hand and a soiled diaper in the other. "Yes?"

"Uh—yes, hello. Can I speak with Agnes, please?"

She shakes her head, and my stomach dives. "Haven't seen her in at least a week—"

Whatever else she says is lost on me as I sprint back to the behemoth at once. "West 24th Street," I pant. "Quickly, please, Monsieur."

So off the behemoth lurches, with me shouting directions from the backseat to a confused-looking Monsieur.

"Is everything alright?" he finally asks once we pull up to Agnes' family home.

"Everything's fine," I shout as I head for the front door and bang my fist upon it.

Movement, upstairs. In my peripheral vision, I see curtains shift, and, finally, the sound of footsteps. The front door opens an inch. "Alex?" comes her voice—her *regular* voice.

"Agnes," I breathe. "Why aren't you at—"

"Are you alone?" she interrupts.

"What? Yes—I mean, aside from the chauffeur, in there," and I gesture to the limousine waiting smartly along the street.

She shoves the door open a foot and pulls me inside, then locks it after me. Next, she peers out the window through the gap left between the closed curtains.

"Is everything okay?"

"Uh-huh," she mutters as she double-checks the lock on the front door.

"You missed the last meeting," I say cautiously, keenly aware that although Agnes hasn't been taken by Lebwitski as I feared, she's not herself, either. "And you haven't been at work."

"Phoned in sick," she says, sounding distracted.

"Are you sick?"

"Not exactly."

"Agnes—the closed drapes, the locked door, skipping work—what's going on?"

"What's going on? I'm being cautious, that's what's going on. Just like you said, remember?"

"Yes, I mean, I know—"

"Look, I saw the broadcast, just like everyone else. That's some messed up shit. No way that's happening to me."

Slowly I nod. I nod and wonder if I've made a huge mistake. If instead of stoking anger, I've created a city seeped in paranoia, governed by fear. "But I saw this," I say eventually, holding up the poster I pulled from the street-lamp downtown. "This is your work, isn't it?"

"Yeah, meaning I'm in more danger than everyone else." She shifts the drapes and peers outside once more.

"So the meeting the other night—"

"Too risky. Way too risky."

"Okay," I say, unable to think of anything else. After all, it *is* risky. And she is in more danger than the rest of the population, given that she's behind the White Ribbon Campaign.

"How are the others?"

I hesitate, and she picks up on it at once.

"What happened?"

"Neo—" I stop myself.

"Neo, what?"

I scratch the back of my head. "He was caught. He was...turned."

"Turned like the Queen?"

I nod.

"Holy *shit*," she shouts, finally staring at me instead of out the window. "What the hell? Like, what the serious hell. I had no idea when I started the campaign what I'd be up against. This is intense, Alex, and really, really scary."

I bite my nail. It is scary. It is dangerous. But didn't she know that revolution came with risks? "Agnes," I say carefully, "if this happens," and I wave her own headline under her nose—"if King is toppled, there's a very good chance you won't have to stay with Miller, and you won't have to work at the nursery anymore, either."

She looks glum, but slowly she nods. "I know I'm being a chicken. But I didn't know what I was getting into when I started the campaign, and now I'm in too deep. I mean, it's considered a *terrorist* organization."

"You were brave enough to circulate these posters," I

remind her. "That means you're brave enough to keep living your life. And fighting for what's right."

"Yeah...I guess."

I give her a hug and leave it at that.

But the ride back to Strath Glen passes slowly. I feel unsettled. If people like Agnes are hiding inside their homes, will anyone take to the streets? Is scaring people into total submission by exposing the override chips all we did? And...what will happen once the Mavericks arrive? The city will be a far scarier, far more intimidating place. How will change happen then if it's not happening now?

nineteen

. . .

DINNER IS TAKEN EARLY, given the funeral proceedings scheduled for this evening, and few guests are in attendance, presumably because they're busy readying themselves for what promises to be a fashionable affair. I haven't seen such bustle and so many stylists since the Rose Ceremony—that dreaded event where I was supposed to honor my soon-to-be in-laws with a hundred long-stemmed roses, but, thanks to Rebecca, handed them a hundred mutilated roses instead.

The décor inside Carnegie is somber. Mourning remains in season, and the dozen or so guests who have gathered are draped in black lace and feather boas. The duke's immediate family are in attendance, unlike last night, but none of them look in the mood to socialize—a normality for Wolfe and a rarity for the duchess and Evie.

It's well and fine for me, as I don't feel all that social myself. My visit with Agnes continues to weigh on me, even though she's alive and technically well. But I'm buoyed, too —or at least I should be—as the posters that are plastered all across the city rightfully cast King as the culprit—much-needed, considering his immediate claims of innocence.

Just as I turn my thoughts to our ruler, he sticks his nose through the doorway, halfway through the prelude to dinner, when gossip, appetizers, and drinks are indulged in.

At the same time, Aubrey descends on me with the wedding book that Evie had painstakingly compiled. She tasks Dear Matthew with holding it for her, who does so mindlessly, then proceeds to tear the bulk of the pages to shreds.

"Wrong, wrong, wrong," the princess declares. "That hippie nonsense is nothing but a bore," she pouts. "Instead, we're going with a pink bubble-gum fairyland theme that will dazzle the eye and ensnare the senses! Do you see my wig?" Aubrey has to ask the same question twice as my attention is now fixed to King, currently circling the perimeter of the room, until he manages to flag down Wolfe. He speaks to him in what looks like a terse voice, then seats himself in his usual spot, spurning all those who dare approach him. Beady eyes shoot around the hall, his face is pallid, he bites at his nails. A man come undone?

Paranoid, to say the least, and any feeling of satisfaction this gives me is negated by my worry over Agnes.

"Hell-*oh?*" Aubrey barks at me.

"My apologies. Your wig, er—" I glance up at a towering ordeal resembling the top of a cupcake, coiled tightly and dusted with sparkles. "Yes. I do see it."

"The quality is unparalleled. It was constructed entirely of hair taken from an orphanage beneath the equator. Of course, it had to be bleached, then dyed this dazzling purple, but aside from that, it's one hundred percent au naturel. And the best part for you, ditch-piggy? I'll procure you the very same for the wedding. Isn't that absolutely splendid and terribly generous?"

A stone sinks in my stomach at the thought. Already the marriage is a sham. Do I really need to underscore the fact by dressing in such a ridiculous getup? Like a woman Wolfe seems to loathe, no less? "Actually, Princess Aubrey," I begin tactfully, "I'd really rather—"

"Consider it settled." She smooches me on the lips and drags a bored-looking Matthew behind her.

"What was that about?" comes a level voice behind me.

I turn and look up at Wolfe. "Wedding planning. It would seem your cousin is making a number of changes to the day. Apparently, I'll be wearing a wig."

"It's meaningless, I wouldn't take it personally." Then he smooths his suit jacket and adds, "I mean to say, you don't care about such things as weddings, isn't that correct?"

"Mostly it is," I begin, but he's no longer listening. Instead, he watches James, who approaches us, staggering.

"You were wise, tall man," he says to Wolfe, his speech slurred. "Best not to postpone the wedding to mourn dearest daddy."

Wolfe's eyes descend into icy slits. "What do you mean by that?"

"If something were to happen to you *after* the marriage, I'd have to wait for the official mourning year to be over before I could wed her myself."

I stare at him, flummoxed, not by his apparent interest in making me his bride, but his reference to something happening to Wolfe.

Wolfe, on the other hand, seems only interested in the former. "You're married, you fool," he seethes. "And this isn't a nation that allows you to choose."

"Papa said I could."

Wolfe draws himself to his full height, gazing daggers at his cousin. A minute later, though, and with obvious effort, he turns away, ushering me toward our usual table.

"Why would he—" I begin, only to have Wolfe wave aside my words with a snort of derision.

"He's drunk. Don't pay him any mind." Good advice, I

think to myself, but then Wolfe adds, "Why is it he's so smitten with you, anyhow?"

"I don't have any idea."

"I thought at first he was just trying to rile me, but now—"

"Wolfe," I interrupt, catching him by the arm before he deposits me into my seat. "I don't care about any of that. Why did he allude to you *dying*?"

"The drink," he replies, completely nonplussed. He sits himself opposite me and briskly picks up his newspaper, burying his nose between the pages and blocking me from view.

I sigh. That supposedly innocuous exchange with James leaves me far more unsettled than it leaves my fiancé.

Tonight, Evie dines with her mother. James, whose head now rests on the table as he snores, and King sit across from them. The Queen sits with Aubrey and Morocco looking as tranquil as ever. Aubrey grumbles loudly about her pregnancy while Morocco shouts to a servant about a triple-tiered cake—I can hear both of them over the doleful sonata played by the strings.

With little else to do and without making it obvious, I watch King closely out of the corner of my eye. His fingertips press together in front of his face. He is completely motionless, and yet his eyes are set on the viscount, the one I share both a table and a future with.

twenty

. . .

AS SOON AS the main course is finished with, the royals clear out of the dining hall with the guests at their heels. Only Wolfe and I remain.

He smooths out the paper and fixes me with his gaze. "You're attending the funeral, yes?"

It's the second time he's asked, I note, and quickly I assure him.

"Do you need to ready yourself?"

I glance down at my mismatched outfit. Frankly, I'm not sure I could fashion anything more appropriate, even if I were to try. "No," I say, watching him closely to gauge his reaction.

He stands abruptly. "A walk, then," and he motions to the door.

Silently I follow him toward the back of the palace. It's uncharacteristic, this, but it's a distraction from the evening ahead, and I think it must be for Wolfe, too.

As we step outside, sans cloaks, I smile. A warm front pushes against my cheeks. It greens the grass, and calls out the songbirds. The birch trees that hollered all winter long wave easily in the breeze, their long branches covered not with snow but buds. It makes me feel calmer, and I can tell by the way Wolfe's posture changes that it does for him, too.

"Were you able to track down your friend?" he asks as we head toward the newly constructed chicken coop.

I nod. "She's safe, at least."

"At least?"

"Safe, but scared. Paranoid, even. It makes me wonder how many others feel the same way following the broadcast."

"Fear can be a great motivator."

"It can also be a great tool to wield control."

He concedes this as we step inside the chicken run. "My uncle is rather paranoid right now himself."

"I've noticed. It's hard not to take some satisfaction in that," I add under my breath.

Half his mouth carves into a rare smile. "I know what you mean."

"Have you been using this opportunity to win back his trust?" I pry.

"Both stoking his fear and offering comfort," he confirms. "Plus a myriad of half-baked solutions. At the very least, more than James can offer, consumed with his love life as he is."

"You best make sure I'm never wed to that man."

He lifts his head and considers me. "I'd sooner die than see that happen."

Part of me is touched by this, and relieved, too. But part of me recoils at the mention of death—there's too much talk of such things in the air. It makes me feel a sense of foreboding, and I think of the way King was staring at Wolfe in the dining hall just now. I shake my head and say, "You're not allowed to die."

Another half-smile, but this time he masks it by turning toward the feed bin in the corner. "They look hungry, yes?"

I watch the chickens pecking at the ground and agree.

Together we scatter feed, then check the nesting spot for eggs. At first, it feels comfortable, even familiar, but I think of the kiss I placed on him, I think of our wedding just around the corner, and the purple wig I'm expected to wear, and my face burns.

He sighs deeply. "I suppose it's time," he says in a heavy voice, and I remember what he speaks of, I remember that this isn't about me, or a kiss, or anything except for his grief.

I rest my hand for a moment on his arm, and then we walk back to the palace, side by side.

———

AN ORGAN HAS BEEN BROUGHT in for the occasion, and its somber music echoes through the corridors of Strath Glen. In the ballroom, it's almost deafening.

Right now, Wolfe pulls me through a crowd of mourners waiting to be seated, and I see for the first time how elaborate funeral wear can be in these circles. Black, as I suspected, is exclusively in vogue, making my brown cardigan feel frumpy. The fascinators worn by the women are towering arcs of black plumes, with delicate netting covering their eyes. The men wear tuxedos with silk bowties and handkerchiefs peeking out of their pockets. It's only Wolfe who wears his usual ensemble—a navy suit, freshly pressed, with a crisp white dress shirt underneath.

As I'm pulled deeper into the ballroom, one draped with black satin and bursting with white roses, I realize the rather uncomfortable seating predicament ahead of me. Surely Wolfe doesn't want—

"We're up there," he says, pointing to the front of the room where the other royals have gathered.

It isn't my first choice to sit with the immediate family, and I'm sure most of them don't care for it either, but part of me is touched, and for the first time since learning I'd been betrothed to the Viscount of Airo-Aurora, I feel, just a smidge, like I belong.

"What a hideous ensemble," Morocco seethes, and I'm brought back to reality.

"Someone open a window," gasps the duchess as she fans herself, and I realize how overpowering the scent of the roses are up here at the front. Several servants are tasked with throwing open the windows, which causes the black satin draped along the perimeter of the room to billow ominously. And then, a man with the look of a priest takes the stage, tapping the microphone and causing the smattering of chatter to quiet. Seats fill as small talk is abandoned. Wolfe grabs my arm and seats me next to him.

I sit at the end of the front row, and on Wolfe's other side is Evie and the duchess, then the Queen and King. The other royals sit in the row behind us, and I realize this is why Morocco tuts her tongue with such fervor.

"She thinks she's awfully special, sitting up there," she hisses to Aubrey.

"Ladies and gentlemen," begins the priest, and off he goes, reciting the same words offered up thousands of times prior. A life well lived. A holiest of unions now underway in the afterlife. The eternal light leading the way forward.

I don't bother listening—not when I've heard it all before, and at the worst of times. Instead, I observe Wolfe discreetly: the bend of his neck as he stares at the floor, the mouth pressed into an even and unbending line, the slow and focused blinks as he maintains his composure. Evie, next to him, weeps quietly as the duchess pats her hand.

I am steady, for Wolfe's sake, even as I itch to go. To remove myself from sadness, pain, and memories.

It isn't until an hour later, after many speeches have been delivered by various members of the aristocracy's social circle, that I hear it.

The others do, too.

It's the sound of honking horns, and I vaguely wonder if there's a traffic jam down below—perhaps even an accident. But the honking is continuous, and then there comes another noise, too.

One I've heard before, and my spine straightens.

I glance at Wolfe, but he's as stony-faced as ever, impossible to read. Next, I look at King. He hears it, wafting through the open windows.

Protests. Outcry. Unrest.

Every cell in my body expands with hope. My pulse surges, so much adrenalin courses through my veins it's difficult to sit still.

But I do, of course I do, keenly aware of the need to not draw attention to myself with King so close. *King.* I watch the way his eye begins to twitch. I watch him turn pink, then the shade of a beet. Next, with a sound somewhere between a shout and a shriek, he's on his feet, moving as fast as his feet will allow toward the door. The priest pauses in his endless sermon, the royal family exchange terse, worried glances, and then they, too, are on their feet. I join the fray.

But my excitement ebbs as soon as I catch the look on Evie's face. Really, I realize, the timing couldn't be worse. This evening, after all, was supposed to be about saying goodbye to the duke—Evie's father, and Wolfe's. Nothing else.

My heart aches for them as we hurry after King, who predictably makes his way to the front doors, and I feel guilty, too.

And then King wrenches open the towering doors to the palace, my thoughts are silenced, and all of us pour onto a balcony bathed in the warm light of dusk. With a sharp inhale, I see that beneath the pink-tinged sky, the city of Airo-Aurora's streets are full of thousands of shouting people, their din amplified by the continued honking of hundreds of cars and buses.

Elation, and a great torrent of satisfaction—that's what I register. Because it worked—our plan worked, and now, surely, King will see that he must capitulate. He must step down from his position, he must abandon the program that brought about this unchartered level of unrest.

But as I watch him out of the corner of my eye, I notice something. His jaw is set, his eyes are slits of steel—he doesn't look like a man defeated. He looks like a man made angry, very angry, and I hope my reading is wrong. I hope the senior aristocrats can talk some sense into him.

As for the others—the members of the family unfamiliar with King's dark secrets—they look floored and confused. Once again, I'm met with a wave of guilt. Funny—never did I think I'd experience such a jumble of emotions. Never did I realize that doing the right thing would be so hard. And never did I dare to think that my heart may somehow be attached to this strange family known as the Rocksavage clan.

Just as I'm ruminating on how this moment could feel so bittersweet, the people down below catch sight of the fully-occupied balcony, they spot the sparkle of King's ruby crown, and a roar erupts like a freight train, the protestors surge forward, a broken levy spilling onto palace grounds.

The fear is immediate, and it's visceral. It radiates across the balcony, then the greencoats are shouting, and we're being shoved inside, the towering front doors are locked, they're barricaded, and despite the shouting of some green-coat or another, King dashes into Devonshire with the rest of us on his heels, he beelines to the front windows as the parrot screams, and all of us jostle for position so we can see what's happening below.

Citizens flood the property, they surround the base of the stairs, where they're met by a brigade of greencoats with weapons drawn, and I remember that, technically speaking, I'm a member of the Rocksavage clan, the aristocracy, so I, too, am the enemy. Yes, my life's in danger just as much as the rest of the residents, and I feel a push-pull sensation in the pit of my stomach.

I stand with the people down below, and against them. I wish for them to breach the barrier, to storm the castle, to seize the country's ruler. But there's genuine fear there, too. There's a kernel of foreboding.

Devonshire Commons is sealed closed as a debate takes place between several greencoats about whether the underground parking garage is the safest spot for us. Evacuation routes are also discussed, but ultimately dismissed.

"The army," King calls over the mayhem. "When are they scheduled to arrive?" and my ears bend to hear the response.

"Only the bluecoats are briefed on that, sir," replies a greencoat with red hair. "I could place a phone—"

"Do it, do it," King seethes, knocking Aubrey out of the way as he returns to the window. His knuckles blanch white as he grips the windowsill.

"Papa," says James. "They're calling for your resignation. Step down, and I shall take the throne."

I remember Wolfe's contention that James is easy to manipulate, and once again, I find myself filled with hopefulness.

But King's reaction is swift. He grabs James by the collar of his shirt. "Say it again, and I'll see to it that the throne goes to Aubrey," he hisses, making his position perfectly clear.

"Papa!" exclaims Aubrey. "First a party planner, and next the chief of a dynasty—count me lucky!"

"Shut up," King hurls at her as he stares through the window.

"Your cigars," comes Gerard's voice.

"Not now," King snaps at his most faithful servant. "Where the hell are the blackcoats?"

"Approaching from the west," replies Wolfe in an even tone. I press my nose to the window beneath his arm and see that he's right. A brigade of blackcoats on horses storm the streets, attempting to drive protestors away from the palace.

"Issue orders to have the blackcoats arrest them all," King says.

"But Papa," counters James, in a show of boldness, or stupidity, "there are far too many of them to be rounded up by a few fellows in black. Or blue, for that matter. Why, the entire city's turned out for your head."

King steps back from the window, breathing hard. He grabs the statue of a bust positioned in the corner and hurls it across the room. It shatters into a thousand pieces.

"Oh dear," the duchess mutters as the Queen waves blithely out the window.

"Brother, what's going to happen?" Evie demands, pulling on Wolfe's sleeve. Panic lights her eyes.

"We're going to go to our quarters and go to sleep, much like any other night," he replies in a calm voice. "The authorities are perfectly competent and well-prepared to keep Strath Glen secure." With that, he walks across the room and swings open Devonshire's door.

Immediately there comes a new swell of noise, and Wolfe snaps the door shut. He turns to our group, and all of us, even King, are now silent. He clasps his hands behind his back, looking as stately as ever. "It would seem, given the circumstances, that all the guests present for my father's funeral are now trapped within the palace."

"Blasted high hell," says James.

"How are we supposed to get said beauty rest now, cousin, hmm?" Aubrey shouts.

"Is there enough food supply to feed everyone if the protest lasts for days?" I ask.

"We can eat those damn chickens," counters Morocco with derision.

"Their continued egg production is far more valuable," Evie points out.

"The army should arrive before we are out of food," Wolfe assures us. "In the meantime, all guests should be escorted back to the ballroom—"

"No," says King suddenly. "Scatter them across the first floor. Tell them to make themselves at home, anywhere."

Aubrey gasps. "Not here in Devonshire!"

"Not the study!" says James.

I almost echo them with a cry about the library but catch myself just in time.

"Uncle," says Wolfe. "Why do you propose such a thing?"

"If the palace is breached, those lunatics will get their hands on the guests first, don't you see? It buys us time."

"Surely," says the duchess in a tone reminiscent of her son, "you aren't suggesting we offer up the people who came tonight to honor my late husband as edible scapegoats—"

"Not at all," replies King, sounding more jovial than before. "It's simply a matter of happenstance. After all, what else to do with them?" With that, he snaps his fingers at Gerard and heads toward the door. "Escort me to my chambers," he grumbles to the greencoats.

There's a loud bang, then shrieking from down below, and the rest of us rush to the window, King's departure already forgotten about. A car is overturned—the source of the bang—and is currently burning.

"What madness," says Morocco in a scolding tone. "Whatever could they have their knickers in a knot over?"

Evie and I exchange a glance, and I remember that even though she knows nothing of the override chip program, she was sympathetic to the White Ribbon Movement, she endeared herself to the idea of a free Airo-Aurora. I have a feeling if her life circumstances were vastly different, she, too, would be marching down below.

"Wherever is your husband?" Morocco suddenly demands of Aubrey.

She twirls around and gasps. "And he was holding my bag!"

"We really ought to placate the guests," the duchess says, checking her watch.

"We need more greencoats on the scene," comments James, staring at the action down below. "Why, that fellow made it all the way to the palace walls before he was shoved down again. I've always said to Papa we should install a moat," he laments, "and it looks as though I was on the nose."

"I'll make the request," says Wolfe. "I'll also communicate to the authorities that they aren't to fire—"

"Enough with that hippie nonsense," Aubrey shouts. "Do you not see the hoodlums out there? If any time is a time for bullets...now is that time!"

"It will just rile people up even more," replies Wolfe in an even tone. With that, he vanishes out the door, into the hall and what sounds like mayhem in its own right.

"And I'll tend to the guests," says the duchess. A second later, she, too, disappears.

Evie and I look at each other. The Queen is busy watering plants, James is shouting, "Shoot him," through the windowpane, and Aubrey and Morocco are comparing manicures. We are, as far as I can ascertain, the last level heads remaining.

"I suppose your mother will be back shortly with some of the guests," I say to Evie, trying to offer her some semblance of comfort.

She nods.

"I'm sorry the funeral was interrupted. It really was a lovely ceremony."

"Oh, sister!" she lays her head on my shoulder and weeps. "It's too much—all of it!"

As the initial adrenalin I experienced begins to fade and weariness sets in, I have to agree. I pat her on the back, wondering to myself if Agnes has joined the throng outside, or if she still hides behind the curtains. I wonder, too, where Aunt Jo is—if she's safe. I wonder how much longer it will take for the army to arrive, and what will happen when all those citizens are met with soulless machines—armed ones.

The ironic part is that their guns might not work at all, but the people of Airo-Aurora don't know that and, frankly, neither do I.

And then the doors are thrown open, and the duchess sweeps inside with the guests, black boas and fascinators dominating Devonshire as mourning returns. Evie is ushered into the group where condolences are frequent, and Aubrey quickly joins the fray in a show of tears. Morocco and James call for aperitifs.

I go back to the window, but dusk is drawing to a close, and it's difficult to see what's happening down below. And then there's an ear-splitting sound—a crash, and suddenly it's raining glass—and something smashes into the lamp next to the sofa. A rock, thrown through the window, and everyone is screaming and pushing in unison out Devonshire's door, retreating toward the back of the palace.

"They have the place circled!" someone shouts, and suddenly the wave I'm caught in grinds to a halt, stationed around the majestic imperial staircase in the middle of the palace.

"What about the rest of the guests?" Evie shouts.

"Alex," calls the duchess, "round up whoever you can from the library. I'll warn those still in the ballroom."

I nod, running toward my favorite room in Strath Glen, feeling far more vulnerable than before, and exposed. But wasn't I the one who incited this violence? I *wanted* this to happen.

Just as I throw open the library door, another rock sails through a window, showering my beloved books with shards of glass. "Everyone out," I shout, before the occupants of the room can register a reaction, before they can even ascertain what just happened, but it doesn't take them long, and I'm almost trampled as they spill into the corridor.

With the others from the ballroom now ushered into the main corridor, space amongst the Ming vases becomes limited.

And then my shoulder is seized, I see that it's Wolfe, and he says curtly in my ear, "The army isn't due to arrive for another day, however, my uncle has authorized the use of force to dispel the protestors, and the blackcoats are now equipping themselves with water cannons, tear gas, and rubber bullets. If they fail to dispel the crowd with all that, real ammunition is sure to be used. Can you think of any avenue to convince the protestors to go home?"

"Meet their demands," I say swiftly. "Convince your uncle to step down, or at least to abandon the override chip program that—"

"My uncle is a stubborn man, one determined to hold onto power until it is quite literally wrenched from his hand."

At that moment, screams lift from the streets below, a torrent of them, and Wolfe and I exchange an uneasy glance. I turn for Devonshire, determined to see what's happening, but Wolfe grabs my hand. "We'll have a better vantage point from upstairs," he reminds me. "It will be safer, too."

I hesitate, then, like well-oiled machinery, we're navigating through the crowd, Wolfe using his considerable height to cut a slither of space through the chaos. Up the stairs we go, through a world of black and white, until we reach the row of windows—the same ones Monsieur uses when I and the other servants slip outside for an evening away from the palace.

Wolfe's right. The vantage point is better, and from here, I can see that many streets are clogged with people, not just the one directly in front of the palace. Fires burn, peppered throughout the city, but that isn't what captures my attention. No, it's the cube truck down below spraying water at the protestors. It's the teargas being fired by the blackcoats. The popping sound of rubber bullets.

"Aces, isn't it?" calls a jovial voice, and I look over my shoulder to see King striding our way, his crown askew, his walking stick missing, but with that Cheshire grin returned to his face. "Do you see my brave men and women out there, doing god's work? Do you see those hoodlums scattering?" He lets out a cackle of laughter. "Me? My heart's a flutter!"

"Yes," I agree, as he stands next to me and stares down at the city. "A great relief," I add, mostly for effect.

"I do hope I'm sending a stern enough message," King says over my head, addressing his nephew.

Wolfe is silent for a minute, his eyes dissecting the scene down below. Finally, he turns to his uncle. "Only time will tell. For now, spilling their blood would incite even more violence, even more desperation. I think you've played your hand nicely, indeed."

It's the first time I've heard Wolfe be less than earnest, less than honest. Right now, his words are theater.

King, meanwhile, claps his hands together. "Well said, my boy," he gushes. He turns on his heel and adds over his shoulder, "Time to tell my guests that their King has the situation under control."

Once he vanishes downstairs and a smattering of applause lifts from the first floor, I murmur, "Is it a good thing the protest is ending, or a bad thing?"

He looks at me from the corner of his eye. "I'd think the answer would be easy for you."

"Yes, well…"

"Yes, well, what? Perhaps you now realize the danger the palace's occupants face should the entire citizenry rise up?"

"The rest of us wouldn't be in such a precarious position if your uncle would do the right thing." I stare out the window and sigh. "How will change come to Airo-Aurora?" I mutter, more to myself than to Wolfe. I watch the tear gas and the water cannons clear the streets until I lean back on my heels, feeling deflated.

Defeated, too, because right now, change feels more unlikely than ever.

twenty-one

. . .

THE NEXT MORNING, I press my nose into the windowpane and survey the streets below. Signs of civil disobedience are aplenty—scorched cars, refuse scattered here and there, abandoned signage. But nowhere are the people.

I can't help but wonder, was that it? Was that the grand fallout from the national address? And now, nothing?

I suppose so. The ingenious plan crafted with Neo and the others has failed, and quite miserably. The only thing it accomplished, I suppose, is to ruin King's day. But that's not enough, it's not even close to enough, and, besides, now he knows he can squash any protest. He knows that he'll have the added security of his army soon, too.

Despite falling woefully behind lately in my cataloging work, I know today will be another write-off, and I resolve to stay here, tucked inside my quarters, where I can nurse my wounds. Regroup. Perhaps catch up on some sleep, too.

But by midday, my nose is once again pressed to the window, and this time the streets hold more than last night's refuse. It's an unending stream of people, all of them disheveled, filthy, and walking in eerie unison, just like I witnessed at Ashville Range.

I didn't think it was possible to feel worse, but as my stomach nosedives, I realize how wrong I was. The army has arrived—mindless machines brandishing guns—a terrifying thought. But more than that even, is the fact that beneath the computer chips controlling their every move, they are human. Humans with consciences, and beliefs, and feelings. Humans who deserve respect—and the filthy, emaciated soldiers down below are clearly being deprived of that.

Right now, they stand in rows in front of the palace, their hands clasped behind their backs, their chins lifted. Hundreds of them, with more and more still pouring in. And it strikes me, suddenly, that these people have nowhere to go. Nowhere to sleep. Mavericks before King got his claws into them, I suppose they're used to it, but still, it doesn't sit well with me, and surely it won't with the rest of the population, either.

———

AS SOON AS I enter the dining hall that evening, I roll my eyes. Tonight's theme is clearly the theme of war, and something more distasteful I can't imagine. An army green parachute hangs from the ceiling, and what looks like a fully operational helicopter sits in the corner. The chairs are fitted with khaki canvas, while the centerpieces are large ammunition replicas.

"Oh, sister," cries Evie, yawning as she clenches her fingers around my arm. "What peculiar times, can you believe it? Have you seen today's new addition? They're standing guard in front of the palace this very minute—have you noticed?"

I nod.

"What a relief to think of the added security they bring.

Why, some of last night's protestors came a little too close to Strath Glen for comfort, didn't you find? The servants have been frantically sweeping up glass and repairing the windows all day long—my!"

"Evie, before we talk about all that—how are you?"

"Oh—that? I—I'm fine, so long as I keep my brain occupied with other things. Such as the new addition of the soldiers, for instance."

"Yes, that," I say, taking her lead. "Where are they supposed to sleep?"

She cocks her head. "What an astute question, sister! The thought never crossed my mind, not in the slightest."

"What didn't cross that pea-brain of yours?" James demands, pulling up alongside us and elbowing Evie playfully.

She flicks him across the forehead. "Don't you call me pea-brain," she declares. "Why, we were simply wondering where all those soldiers are to sleep. Surely we must find a way to house them!"

"Papa said they're most comfortable sleeping outdoors," counters James. "Pleasant time of the year, anyhow, compared to the last couple months."

"But what about showering and all that?" cries Evie.

James shrugs. "They don't look too bothered by matters of hygiene, cousin. And the kitchen will see to it they're fed."

"Alex," Wolfe says, joining our group. "A word?"

I agree and follow him to the helicopter. And it's there that I notice King standing in the corner with a goblet of wine in his hand. He speaks to a bald fellow I've seen here time and again, but once again, his gaze follows none other than Wolfe.

"Why is it that King is always watching you lately?" I ask at once. "Have you done something to ruin his trust in you? Besides the weapons fiasco, I mean."

"Nothing," he replies, sounding unconcerned. "I take it you've noticed the addition—"

"Are you absolutely sure? Because lately, I've noticed him staring at you—"

"It's in your head. Things are perfectly civil between the two of us, I can promise you. Now, to business. Harbor's Minister of International Affairs would like to meet to discuss a potential trade agreement tomorrow, mid-morning. Are you available to charter me?"

For a moment, I'm distracted from my worries concerning King and the soldiers, and I simply stare at him. "You...want me...to act as your pilot? After—"

"Your skills were every bit as proficient as I expected. Your insubordination too," he adds with a frown. "Anyhow, it's no matter to find someone at the Sky Center if you're not interested. What say you?"

What say me. I itch to say yes. The opportunity to fly a helicopter again is more appealing than anything else I could conjure up in my imagination. A chance to get out of the palace, too. But I think about King's unusual interest in Wolfe, and I find myself shaking my head. "Tomorrow morning, I plan to speak to the Queen," I lie, "in an attempt to persuade her to give schoolchildren access to the library once a month. After all, she did allow the National Gallery to borrow those works of art."

"How could I forget that," he says dryly, and I know he's referencing Patrick. "All right, I'll call the Sky Center now and have them ready a pilot." He makes to leave with his normal brusque fashion, but he hesitates a moment. He bends toward me, pushes my hair back, and says quietly in my ear, "My uncle has scheduled another broadcast for Sunday evening. He and James have been somewhat cagey with the details, but I believe he will publicly hold Neo responsible for the override chip program. It is my hope that following this, he will dismantle the program. In the meantime, I haven't heard or seen anything that would lead me to believe that my uncle is inordinately suspicious of you. In fact, you have done well to keep a low profile lately. I should have tasked you with overhauling the library months ago."

I catch him by the arm. "No. That can't be right. He promised the citizens a most public execution, remember?"

"Young love," sighs a familiar voice. King places his arms around both of us. "Whisper whisper, kiss kiss. The good old days—I remember them well! Only my most brilliant Mainframe would think to put the two of you together, hmm? Go on, continue your secrets while I watch."

I stare at him, my eyes wide. This man. This malicious man is going to kill my friend Neo in front of the entire citizenry?

King's false grin vanishes as he sees my expression. "Whatever's on your mind, little bird?"

"She was in the middle of informing me about a laudable idea to open Strath Glen's library to the nation's schoolchildren," Wolfe says quickly. "It really would cast you in a more favorable light, Uncle."

"You don't say," exclaims King. "Is this true, doe-eyed cotton-tail?"

For the time being, I swallow my hatred and my anger. I force my face to soften. "It is, King," I say with a small curtsy. "I've been working on organizing the library for weeks now, although I must admit it's not quite ready—"

"And you think it kosher to have schoolchildren traipsing around the place at all hours of the day?" He blinks theatrically.

"Not at all," I assure him. "I was thinking that the library may be open to them only once or twice per month."

"Daisies! I don't mind the idea at all—what an asset you are! No wonder James' head is spinning!" He taps me on the shoulder, then carries on through the crowd.

Immediately I lean toward Wolfe, my features hardening

over with concern. "Neo may have an override chip implanted in his brain, but he still breathes."

"I don't wish to see him executed either," Wolfe assures me. "But I don't see what can be done about it. My uncle has promised the public the wrongdoer, and Neo is the only guilty party they've found. Thankfully," he adds pointedly.

I shake my head. "This won't do. I can't let it happen, I just can't."

"If you meddle, you know what will happen."

Wolfe's right. It's dangerous to meddle. So dangerous, it's downright stupid. But I can't sit idly by and let someone be killed, so I guess I now have two reasons not to charter Wolfe to Harbor in the morning.

As if he can read my mind, he says, "Do I have your word that you won't meddle when I'm away?"

"I think sticking around here to babysit me is untenable for both of us."

He sighs. "If it helps, I believe if it were easily ascertainable who Neo's accomplices were, they would have been brought to justice by now. That being said, continue to be vigilant, Alex."

"And you, safe travels in the morning."

He lifts his hand as though he's going to stroke my hair, then tilts it at the last second so that it lands on my shoulder. "You're sure you don't wish to come with me?"

I nod, but inside I'm suddenly unsure. It isn't that I'm particularly fearful of King right now, and it's not that I'm any less determined to investigate King's suspicious glances Wolfe's way, or to find a way to stop Neo's execution. It's simply that I don't want him to go.

The ridiculousness of that thought is enough for me to turn away.

———

THE NEXT MORNING, with Wolfe gone, I steel myself to finding answers and resolutions. Then I head for Bishop's Aisle. I don't have a plan, not really. Eavesdropping had been on my agenda, and still is, but that's only so I can ascertain King's true feelings toward Wolfe. Because although Wolfe may think that their squabble about the weapons is water under the bridge, I've been subjected to enough of King's side-eye glances to know that all isn't well. The more pressing question, of course, is how I'm to stop Neo's execution. Warning Neo is pointless, given the override chip in his brain that precludes him from disobeying or, frankly, from being remotely difficult. Yes, the chip in his head will dictate that he meets his fate without a fuss. So how, then, am I to intervene?

Perhaps the best option is also the simplest. Talk to King. Convince him that executing Neo won't win him support from an irate public. In fact, it may even stir up more unrest. Neo is, after all, a member of the citizenry. And what if people don't believe King's contention that he was behind the override chip program? He clearly wouldn't have the connections and the resources to make such a vast program come to life. Yes, King may be wise indeed to spare Neo's life...

How to broach the subject is another matter. Especially considering the personal risk. At no point can I make King suspicious that I have ulterior motives. That perhaps Neo and I are partners in crime, and my palms turn tacky at the thought.

The answer hits me: Wolfe. The warning should come from Wolfe. Not only does King trust him far more than he does me, but this is the type of advice King's right-hand-man would typically make. Then again, James has usurped that roll, hasn't he? And that brings me back around to the problem of King's cold gaze following Wolfe around the room.

I lick my teeth as I stare at King's office door, one currently sealed shut. And then, as if by magic, it swings open, and I hear James' voice grow louder.

"I'll be back in an hour," he calls as I dart out of sight, down the servants' stairs.

"We need to discuss Sunday night, you jackass!" shouts King.

"I need to take care of a personal matter first," James replies. Then he grumbles to himself, "You insipid old fool."

I return to Bishop's Aisle only when I'm sure James is inside his office. His door is open, I note, and so is King's. I could come back in an hour and hope to find a way to listen in on their conversation, but I don't want to waste an opportunity, either. What personal matter must James take care of?

With sudden jangling coming from his office and the sound of footsteps, I retreat into the shadows and watch as he sets off for the staircase. I look back at King's office, then follow after him.

I expect James to disembark at the second floor, where his quarters are located, but instead, he continues down to the main floor. He turns the corner, walking briskly, then makes another turn, this time toward the back door of the palace.

Now intrigued, I pick up my pace, noting as I approach the door that he's left it propped open with the brick. Cautiously I peer through the opening, noticing for the first time the tents littering the backyard. Makeshift barracks, I suppose, for the Maverick army.

Funny—I've been so focused on what's happening down in Airo-Aurora's streets, I've missed all this.

Not spotting James, I push the door open wider and slip outside. For a minute, I'm overwhelmed by the sight—hundreds of tents, and plenty of soldiers, too. I suppose they must work in shifts at the front of the palace while the others rest. Far more disturbing than that, though, is how quiet it is. Despite the sea of people waking up or traipsing in and out of the woods, none of them speak. None of them register any sign of life at all—no smiles, no eye contact, nothing but the simple execution of basic functions.

It's easy to spot James through the crowd. Not only is he the only one not wearing army green, but he babbles incessantly to a young woman while everyone else is quiet. It's clear that he beckons to her, and eventually, she stands, following slowly after him, her gaze down.

My own narrows. Then I'm striding toward them, zigzagging between tents, stepping across pots, pans, and scattered canteens. Twice I almost step on an actual person. My progress is slow, and by the time I'm halfway through the crowd, James and the Maverick he escorts have reached the guesthouse.

He unlocks the door, and they vanish inside. Perhaps the Mavericks have been using the guesthouse to take their meals. To use the facilities. Perhaps there's nothing untoward happening in the slightest. But I do know James, I know he can't be trusted, and I push even faster.

I've never been to the guesthouse before. I've never even been close, given that it's on the opposite end of the grounds as the stables. Glancing up at it as I climb the front steps, I see that it's a stately place with painted wood siding, a large veranda, and blinds that match the national flag. Typically it's filled with the guests of the aristocracy, but not today.

I twist the door handle—locked. I knock, I knock incessantly, until my knuckles ache, and there comes the sound of footsteps from deep inside the house. The door creaks open, and James' eye presses into the opening. When he sees it's me, he pulls it all the way open with a wide grin. "Whatever are the odds!"

I step inside without waiting for an invitation. "Are the M—" I catch myself, but was it in time? James must know that the soldiers are Mavericks by now, given his and King's sudden closeness, but I'm certainly not supposed to be privy to such information. I cough into my fist and begin again. "Are the men and women of the army staying here?"

"What—here? God, no," he says swiftly, as though it's a preposterous idea.

The sound of running water switches on upstairs, and both of us look toward it. "Who's that?"

"Oh, that?" He blinks for a moment. "One of the soldiers. Generous boy that I am, I thought I'd let her take a shower."

"That is generous," I agree. "I'll go round up others in need of a shower and we can form a line."

The surprise cuts clean across his face, but I'm out the door before he can counter the suggestion. Already I'm yelling instructions to the troops, but it doesn't take long to realize that none of them even lift their head. They must take orders only from certain people, or through pre-programmed decisions in their override chips. So, how did James convince the young woman to go inside and bathe?

I approach the nearest soldier, a middle-aged man currently rubbing wax into his boots.

"Your turn to shower is next," I say calmly. I gesture to the house and motion for him to follow me. "Come on, your turn."

It takes several more minutes of cajoling him, but finally, he makes it to the guesthouse. The young woman has finished and, I'm relieved to see, now fully clothed. Attractive, too, and I frown at James as she walks mindlessly out the door.

"What?" he queries, his eyes widening in a show of innocence.

I say nothing. Accusing him of having dubious intentions is pointless; he'll simply deny it. But how much longer until that woman—a girl, practically—is victimized? What kind of monster is James? And what kind of hellscape have I stumbled into?

I head back to the palace, unable to stomach being in his presence any longer. I go wait in the servants' stairs, just off Bishop's Aisle, instead. Soon James will return, and he and King will discuss the next broadcast. The broadcast where Neo is going to be killed.

Yes, I need to hear every second of that conversation. It will give me something to work with—some angle to use to convince King to take a different course of action, beyond what I've already crafted. James walks by just then, his hands in his pockets, whistling casually. A rush of nerves hit me, that and foreboding, and I watch from the shadows as he strides into King's office, kicking the door closed behind him with his foot.

I groan.

How am I supposed to hear anything with the heavy door sealed shut?

"What are you doin' here, aye, miss?"

I whirl around to see Rebecca standing there, holding a tray of biscuits. "Are you taking those to King?" I ask at once.

She nods.

"You're in and out a lot, are you?"

"Aye, of course, miss."

"What have they been discussing lately, if you don't mind me asking?"

"I can't be gossipin' 'bout the family," she cries. "Though the King himself has been on and off them phones all morning."

"Speaking with?

"Someone at the Mainframe sounds like. Tryin' to get a better read on what happened at the broadcast is my thinkin'."

My heart races. "Any luck?"

"He's been in a right foul mood, so I'd say not. Bet these cookies will cheer him up some. Go on, you've got me gossipin'!"

"Please, Rebecca," and I block her path. "I desperately need to get inside that room."

"Aye, well I don't think it's gonna happen, miss. Move now—I gotta give the King his biscuits."

It's risky and wild, far too dangerous. And yet...it's my only hope of finding out what King's up to. And the niggling feeling in my stomach tells me there is nothing more important than that. I grab hold of Rebecca's arm.

"Miss?"

"I need to swap outfits with you."

She stares at me as if I've gone mad. "Swap outfits. What are you talkin' 'bout?"

"Please, Rebecca. Put on my dress, then go straight to my quarters. Hide there until I join you. If I'm caught, I'll say I pulled the outfit from the laundry."

The girl looks less than certain.

"Please, Rebecca—you won't regret it."

"Is anyone comin'? Won't look so good if I'm caught in my skivvies!"

Peering around the corner, I shake my head. Quickly we strip down and trade clothes. I coil my long hair into a tight bun, then take the platter of biscuits in one hand, smooth my starchy apron with the other, and walk quickly to King's office as Rebecca disappears down the stairs.

I take a breath. And then another. Relax, I remind myself. The last time I wore the outfit of a maid, it rendered me completely invisible. Today will be no different.

Still, it's impossible to stop the tremor in my hand, or the band of sweat forming around my hairline.

With one last deep breath, I push open the office door and slip inside with the tray held out in front of me. Emulating the way I've seen other servants carry such trays,

I use both hands, carrying the tray out in front of me, my back perfectly erect and my chin held high. In my peripheral vision, I see that King and James sit around one of the countless coffee tables spread across the room, taking their tea. I angle around the furniture so that I draw up behind them, noting as I do, that James flips through an X-rated magazine full of nudes while King contemplates a series of thick files spread out on the table in front of him. Carefully I hold the tray under his nose.

"Splendid!" he shouts, scooping up a handful of biscuits. When I shift the tray to James, he takes one without removing his gaze from a particularly busty redhead. I step back while they munch happily, watching, waiting.

"You've only a few days to decide, Papa," James says between bites. "Make a decision already so you can program the army to assassinate the correct person. Certainly, you know my two cents on who the lucky fellow should be."

"Your two cents are based on your own little whims, not what's best for the palace," he snaps, his delight to receive sugary treats waning almost immediately.

"It's the best solution, Papa, and you know it. We need someone high-rank to appease the people, and besides, Matthew needs something to do now that he's not doing any more runners."

"Matthew's useless," King says from the corner of his mouth, "as you well know, aside from acting as my daughter's bag boy. Gerard, my cigars!" he barks over his shoulder.

Amazed, I scan all corners of the room for the lurking, solitary figure, assuming I'd missed him. But no, he's nowhere to be seen, so I walk to King's towering desk, pick up a familiar-looking box, and present it to King whilst remaining deliberately out of sight.

There comes the sound of a sparking match, and a long coil of smoke snakes its way to the ceiling. The box is handed without regard around the back of the chair, and carefully I return it to the desk. Next, I remove a duster from the waistband of Rebecca's uniform and begin dusting the desk, making sure to stay out of their eyeline.

"He has allies, strong ones. His death will raise questions," King murmurs.

"What kind of questions, Papa?"

"Questions of legitimacy, you fool. The international community frowns over willy-nilly executions, don't you know?"

"Willy-nilly? Why, it's for implanting chips illegally in people's heads, of course!" he cries happily. "We're nothing short of the heroes who caught him, wink, wink. I'm so pleased you decided to confide in me, Papa."

"You shall inherit the throne, my boy. Best you have an idea what's going on. Soon we'll get those chips in your head out of commission so we don't have to worry about another traitor the likes of that boy *Neo*. Now, where did that servant put those biscuits?"

I lay down the duster, pick up the platter, and hold it once again under King's nose, moving quickly so he doesn't cast his gaze in my direction. It's amazing, frankly, how arrogant these two men are. To think so little of the servants that they don't bother to lay eyes on them. To think the servants are so subhuman that they don't need to mask their conversations around them, or hide their X-rated magazines.

"It's a shame to have such disloyalty, I agree," continues James. "But really, the threat from that boy has already been neutralized. And to execute him won't be enough to calm the people, you see that, surely? A lowly technician, slaving away at the Mainframe, phhsh. But a high-ranking official of the Rocksavage clan? It's beautiful!"

That's when I finally read between the lines and clue into what they speak of. Who they speak about. So dumbstruck am I that my entire body begins to tremor and shake.

My tendons, ligaments, and muscles go numb. The cookie tray smashes to the ground and showers King in biscuits.

Feeling as though I'm moving in slow-motion, I do the first thing that comes to mind.

I cover my face with my hands to shield my identity, then sprint toward the exit.

With my back to them, I throw open the door and take off at full speed.

I race down the servants' stairs two at a time, I run through the House of Mirrors so fast that my face flashing in and out of reflection becomes dizzying.

I streak past Rebecca, who warms herself in front of the fireplace, still wearing my cardigan and gown, through the closets, and into the washroom. I place my hands alongside the sink and will the room to stop spinning. I breathe, in and out. Only when I'm certain I'm not going to be sick do I lift my gaze and stare at myself straight in the eye.

That niggling crumb of uncertainty—well, I have my answer now. In three days, my fiancé is to be executed.

twenty-two

. . .

THE REST of the day is spent alone in my quarters. I sit at the window, waiting for Wolfe's return. As I ruminate, I consider the problem from all angles. It's the army that will execute Wolfe, James had said so himself. The army controlled by the override chips, so perhaps—perhaps it's the override chips that must be destroyed. The Mavericks acting in their own accord wouldn't murder someone simply because Airo-Aurora's King tells them to. Besides, Wolfe has friends among the Mavericks.

And yet, hadn't Timothee said that introducing a virus to destroy the override chips is too risky? That it may even make the situation worse? It would destroy the link between the chip and the Mainframe—that's what he had said, but it wouldn't necessarily destroy the override chip itself. No, instead, an empty chip would be left running, creating a mindless machine operating without human intelligence or artificial intelligence. But...what if instead of targeting just the override chips, the entire system is targeted? What if the entire system is destroyed?

It would mean the end of the Selection. It would mean that people may choose for themselves who they marry and what they do with their lives—and don't I want that? Certainly, in my early days here at Strath Glen, I did. I suppose lately, as my placement here at the palace has grown more bearable, my attention has been diverted to the override chips alone. But if I'm being true to myself, don't I believe in the right to choose?

Yes, I do believe in that. The right to choose one's own destiny. One's own path. I run my tongue behind my teeth as I consider what else it would mean. The avoidance of the wedding in a few weeks to Wolfe, for one.

But that's not all, I realize. It would mean that all those memories stored at the Mainframe would be gone. Wiped clean. It would mean that I'd no longer have the ability to visit my parents' memories, and I can't have that. No, there must be a way to attack the chips while leaving the memory bank intact.

And then there's the *how* of the whole thing. Because introducing a virus won't be easy without Neo's help. Timothee had said himself that the Mainframe has more firewalls and other measures to stop a security breach than any other entity. So, if this has any chance of working, we'll have to find a way inside the Mainframe first. Risky, yes, but not impossible with the help of Jill...

Is the idea even feasible? Is it possible to ready something with so little time? I'll have to track down Timothee as soon as possible to ask him, but right now, I wait for Wolfe.

Finally, as the afternoon draws to a close, the long nose of the behemoth arcs its way onto the grounds, and my heart beats uncomfortably in my chest. Wolfe has returned. Wolfe, who has a giant bullseye on his back, and once again, I feel like I'm going to be sick.

I smooth my gown and breathe in and out in an effort to calm myself. Cooler heads prevail. Now is not the time for theatrics. Besides, the last thing Wolfe needs to do right now is worry himself over me. Already he has done far too much of that, busying himself watching over me when really, it's him that's in danger.

I swallow, and I wait, and I wait, and it feels like an eternity. Finally, I hear the door from the corridor swing open, and a second later, he strides inside our shared quarters. He pauses upon seeing me. "I thought you'd be in Carnegie," he says as he sets down his bag.

"I'm not remotely hungry."

He nods slowly. "Is everything alright?"

"No. No, it isn't."

He frowns. "Need I be worried?"

"Definitely."

"He knows of your—"

"Not me," I interrupt. "You don't need to worry over me." I put on some music and motion him toward the couch.

He takes a seat next to me, looking pensive. "You look rather unwell," he comments, studying my face. "As if you've seen a ghost."

"I wish that was the problem. You should know that I took the opportunity today to play the spy inside King's office. You're wrong that Neo is to be executed Sunday night. He's far too low in seniority to pacify a rowdy public. He and James have discussed it and have decided that a senior ranking official's head must roll." I bite down on my lip at these words to stop the tears that suddenly prickle behind my eyes. I draw myself straighter and say, in as level a voice as I can manage, "It's you."

Wolfe doesn't display any reaction whatsoever. His body is completely immobile, his features are unchanged, even his eyes remain the same. Meanwhile, I feel like the entire contents of my stomach could empty themselves onto my lap.

Finally, he sighs in a shallow, slightly perturbed way. "I see." He stands abruptly and smooths his jacket, then disappears into the closets.

I stare after him with my mouth hanging open. That's it? That's the only response he can muster to the news that he's to be executed in three days? Does he really expect to head to dinner instead of brainstorming ways to keep himself safe?

But when he emerges again, I see that attending dinner isn't on his agenda at all. He wears the same outfit as the one he dons during his morning hunt. A quiver is slung around his back, and he carries a bow.

"What are you doing?" I ask, even though it's plainly obvious.

"Dusk is as good a time as any for a hunt," he replies calmly, as though I hadn't just delivered to him the news that he has seventy-two hours of life left. That his own family is going to sacrifice him in front of all the nation. The thought isn't just chilling, it's sickening.

I stand and stare at him, exasperated by his nonchalant attitude. I start to protest but think better of it. "I'm coming," I say instead.

"You can't ride a horse."

"I'll share yours."

"I need room."

"I'll sit behind you."

His mouth tightens, but after considering it for a minute, he nods his head. I grab my cloak, and we head silently for the door.

————

OUTSIDE, the wind has swept up, but it's mild and smells ever-so-slightly sweet. We walk carefully around the barracks, and I think of telling Wolfe what happened earlier with James. Now isn't the time, though. We need to focus on one thing right now, and that's saving his life.

I stand off to the side of the stables while Wolfe readies

the horse. I lift my gaze over the city of tents and consider the back of Strath Glen. Somewhere along the way, I had fallen in love with the old building—its beauty, its unusual way of coming alive. Right now, though, it looks like it did when I just arrived. Cold and uninviting. The most heinous plot underway colors it black.

"I draw with my right arm," Wolfe says coolly as he returns with a large and impressive mare. "Lean to the left while I shoot, and don't make a sound."

Without waiting for agreement, he picks me up and places me over the saddle. He swings himself on in front of me, and I wrap my hands around the quiver.

"Hold me, Alexandra," he instructs curtly. "Both arms, with all your strength."

I reach around him and hold on tight, a good thing as the horse bursts into a gallop away from the barracks, veering toward the woods. Once tucked deep inside, I find it's a different world than before. No more snow—just a bare forest floor not yet covered with summer's growth. The crisscrossing branches overhead are weighed down not with ice, but with burgeoning buds, the squirrels chasing each other up and down the trunks. And against all odds, I feel something resembling peace in here. Peace, and the hope that everything will be okay.

Eventually, Wolfe pulls at the reigns, slowing us to a walk. As a fox darts between trees, he removes an arrow from the quiver, nocks it, loosing the arrow deliberately into the tree.

Next, he dismounts the horse in one motion and wrenches the arrow free. His face is cool and disinterested— I get the sense he's many miles away. A heartbeat later and the bow is drawn toward the ever-darkening sky. Once again, he pauses, firing not at the passing bird, but at a tree.

"Can we talk about it?" I finally query.

"No."

I drop to the ground, and when he returns to the horse, I block his way. Despite the aggressive way he stares at me, I don't move an inch. "Go back to Harbor," I whisper, realizing it's the only foolproof way to keep him from being publicly executed Sunday evening. "Go now—pretend to be busy with a work mission."

"And leave you in the wolf's lair?" he growls.

"I'll be fine—"

"You don't know that."

I shake my head. "I'm just a girl from Quire. They aren't going to gain a thing by executing the likes of me."

"You don't know that," he reiterates. "Come with me."

My eyes widen at the proposition. Not one I expected either, and one that holds appeal. Finally, though, I shake my head. "I need to do something here. Something that will ensure the army won't murder you the second you return. Something that will mean you'll never have to return—not if it's not safe."

"What are you talking about?"

"I'm talking about introducing a virus into the Mainframe. A virus that would destroy the entire system."

He pulls away with a half-laugh. "I doubt very much that's even possible. Besides, it would destroy the foundation that our society is based on—"

"I know exactly what it means. Free choice—something we should've had all along."

"And you expect me to go hide in another nation, take refuge there, while you undertake such a dangerous mission? Do you not know me at all?"

"Wolfe—"

"If you're caught interfering with the Mainframe, which you undoubtedly will be, you'll suffer the same fate as your friend Neo, and there's nothing I can do to stop that if I'm hiding like an impotent child in another country."

"Be that as it may," I say, standing taller, "I would still feel much better with you far removed from danger."

He raises an eyebrow as he considers me. I think he may even agree. Then he says in a brisk tone, "It is out of the question. Do not mention it again."

"Then you will die!"

"Perhaps your plan to dismantle the system will be effective and the army won't respond to the Mainframe's direction. In that case, I'd readily accept a dual with my uncle or cousin."

"But, as you said, it's unlikely that the plan will be a success—"

"There's the ammunition you switched out," he reminds me. "It's feasible that an assassination attempt will fail—"

"And what if it doesn't?"

"Then you will be without a troublesome and unwanted fiancé," he snaps. "Just as you've been working toward all this time. Consider it my wedding gift to you."

I stare at him, my mouth open, dazed. "My *wedding gift*? Is that some sort of sick joke? Because I don't find it at all funny," I shout. "Oh, and I'll be sure to remember it when I'm forced to wed *James* instead." I turn for the horse, but he grabs me by the arm.

"What's that supposed to mean?"

"That's his intention," I retort. "Surely you can see that. Do you really think he can't get permission from his father?"

His face sours, then he laughs darkly. He says nothing, but he throws down his bow and quiver and sits on the forest floor, looking suddenly defeated.

"Wolfe?" I ask, and I'm unable to mask the alarm in my voice.

"Yes?"

"Are you okay?"

"I've been better." He sighs. "When you were playing the spy in my uncle's office, as you put it, were you outed?"

"I don't think so."

"Good. Neither King nor James can suspect that we know of what they intend to do, or I'll be locked in the dungeons until the address."

I kneel beside him. "We'll figure out a way to stop this from happening." My voice sounds certain, even though I know it's an uphill battle, a daunting one with shockingly little chance of success.

He studies me. "You're doing okay with all this?"

"No," I admit. "I just can't believe they would betray you like this. They're *family*."

"Their loyalty or betrayal alike doesn't mean a damn thing to me," he seethes. "Your allegiance, on the other hand..."

We glance at one another in a brief, explosive way.

"We should head back before the sun disappears on us entirely," I whisper.

He simply nods.

twenty-three

. . .

THE NEXT MORNING, I wake early. Friday. I need to go to Hallah. I need to go there the second it opens to speak to Timothee. Once I've done that, I'll try once again to convince Wolfe to hide in another nation. And if that doesn't work, I'll attempt to convince King and James that a public execution—any execution, frankly—is ill-advised. That it would spark more outrage amongst the citizens.

Tracking down Monsieur is task number one, since leaving by foot against King's orders, and while the palace is surrounded by soldiers, sounds less than ideal. Less than intelligent, too. I go first to the basement, where the servants reside.

"What made miss so upset, like?" comes Rebecca's voice, and it takes a moment to realize she speaks of yesterday, after I overheard that seismic conversation in King's office.

"Oh, I was just feeling scared and overwhelmed, that's all. The protests aren't something I had to deal with in Quire."

"Not something we've had to deal with here, either," replies a passing servant—one of the cooks.

"Aye, it's a strange time at the palace, ain't it?"

I must agree. "I'm looking for Monsieur Sawyer. Have you seen him?"

"Go on, you're always after him. Probably sneakin' a roll in the kitchen, like."

I thank her, then speed around the corner, careening into the kitchen and nearly knocking over a dozen trays full of biscuits cooling.

"Ah—Miss Alex. Making a fine entrance as always, I see," says Monsieur.

I grab the biscuit from his hand and wrap my arm around his. "You must take me to Hallah at once," I whisper tersely.

"Right now?"

I check my watch and nod. "We can't afford to waste even a single minute."

"Whyever not?"

I'm at a sudden loss for words. Monsieur Sawyer has become a friend over the months, there's no doubting that. And he thinks highly of the viscount, I know that to be true. But revealing to him the truth could put him in danger's way, and besides, how much help could he offer even if he was so inclined? "I can't say," I tell him. "But please, I'm begging you to take me right now. And I ask that you be discrete as possible, too."

He angles toward me, better to look me in the eye and gauge my earnestness. Finally, he nods. "Alright, then. Will you at least give me my breakfast back?"

I hand the biscuit over, then we're both moving briskly through the underground hallways, and finally out into the garage. We board the behemoth silently, and then we're off, my stomach not simply full of butterflies, but twisting into knots too. My hands shake so badly that I have to sit on them. Because although I've woken with clarity as to what I have to do, I've also gained more clarity on the direness of the situation, too.

Once we arrive, I run inside the building without bothering to avert my eyes or take precautions. There isn't time, and inside, I stride right over to Timothee, who's just beginning to open up files on his computer. His coffee sits untouched next to him.

"I need to speak to you," I say under my breath. "Quickly."

His eyes round in surprise, and the quip forming on his tongue dissolves when he spots the look on my face. Immediately he stands, and I lead him into the stairwell.

"What's wrong?"

"King plans to hold my fiancé responsible for what happened during the national address. He intends to execute him Sunday evening, during another broadcast."

"Shit."

I nod.

"What can we do about it?"

"Destroy the entire system. If targeting the override chips is too risky, let's destroy it all."

"Whoa, you're serious?"

"Very."

"To destroy all of it, though…It would mean that everything changes. Everything."

"It would mean free choice. And without all of Airo-Aurora's dissenters turned into mindless zombies. Without the army, too."

"What about all those memories? People don't want their family members to vanish, and there's no way to preserve those memories if everything else is destroyed."

I hesitate. I was hoping that wouldn't be the case. I think of my mom and my dad. I think of visiting those times when we surrounded the dinner table, laughing. I cherish those moments above all else, where it actually feels like we're together again. But. But…they aren't real, that's the crux of it.

Wolfe is.

And, maybe it has made healing and moving on that much more difficult. Maybe the people of Airo-Aurora would be better off without the memory bank. Besides, those memories of us surrounding the dinner table—they'll live on inside of me.

I turn to Timothee. "If that's the cost of freedom, and saving lives, so be it."

"But how will it help your fiancé? I mean, the King may still want to hold him responsible, right?"

"So long as we can do this before Sunday night, King won't go forward with the broadcast, I'm sure of it. He'll be too distracted with his beloved Mainframe gone. Besides, there will be so much pressure for him to step down, he won't have the opportunity to pin anything on Wolfe. And, don't forget the army is the one set to do the executing. Once those override chips stop working, the Mavericks will be gone."

He swipes at his lip, one now touched with sweat. "If it's sequenced right, there are fewer risks than if we just targeted the override chips. But the personal risk is huge. Don't forget what happened to Neo," he reminds me.

"I know. But if it works..."

He rubs his temple. "I didn't sign up to be a revolutionary, Alex. And time is going to be an issue," he adds, checking his watch.

"Can you skip work today? There's so much that rides on this. Not only would it save Wolfe from being killed, it would mean Neo would be back to normal, too. And..."

"And?"

"And you know your brother didn't kill himself. He died because of the system. He was unhappy because of the system. Destroying it is what he would've wanted."

The silence seems to stretch forever. But finally, he nods.

"So, I design a virus potent enough to bring down a massive system, then what?"

"Come straight to the palace and ask for me. I'll get in touch with Jill, and the three of us will go straight to the Mainframe to install it. Good?"

Slowly he nods. He's risking his life for this project, and I think he knows it. But I refuse to back down. I refuse to accept the possibility that this will not work. This is for Wolfe—it must work.

We part ways a few minutes later, me retreating to the behemoth, Timothee going to collect his belongings and skip work for the rest of the day.

"Satisfied, Miss Alex?" Monsieur asks once I fasten my seatbelt.

"As satisfied as I can be, given the situation," I reply.

"And which situation is that, precisely?"

"A private situation, Monsieur," and I shoot him a look. "Although, once it's safe to do so, I'm happy to divulge."

"Count me excited, Miss Alex. How is your aunt doing?"

"Fine, so far as I know. Why do you ask?"

"Just wondering how she weathered the recent protests."

I'm silent. With a rush of guilt, I realize I've barely considered it.

"Miss Alex?"

"Yes, I wonder that myself."

"A detour?"

I swallow. I don't have time to be sidetracked, and Wolfe doesn't, either. But already Monsieur turns the behemoth up Central Boulevard, making the decision for me.

I opt to say nothing, considering how much gratitude I already owed to the chauffeur for taking me to Hallah. Besides, I reason—I can speak with Jill later, and I use the ride through the city to visually scour each street, each business, each home—searching for signs of unrest, dissidence, a fresh wave of protests—but there's nothing but passing cars, a few shoppers. Even Agnes' posters are frayed, some of them covered up by other news and advertisements for yard sales.

I frown. The momentum that began after the national address has stalled, that much is clear, and even though I'm disappointed, I'm not surprised. Not with the military might currently surrounding the palace, and I can't help but feel that the planned assassination of Wolfe is completely unnecessary.

King really must have lost all trust in Wolfe when he ordered the weapons with the slowest delivery time, and wasn't that partly my fault? Or is it James whispering in his father's ear, intent on making me his bride?

Suddenly Monsieur jams on the brakes, and I smash my nose against the seat in front of me. "Speak of the devil!" he shouts merrily, swinging open the door before I can even see straight.

I'm ushered onto the sidewalk, and my aunt wraps me in a hug. "What a treat!" she shouts, ruffling my hair. "You've a keen eye, Monsieur Sawyer," she adds as she lets the heavy mailbag rest on the ground.

The chauffeur blushes, then dives into a deep bow. "Did Quire see any of the protests that clogged the streets around the palace?" he asks.

She shakes her head. "Everyone I know who took to the street headed downtown, so far as I know," she replies, and I breathe a sigh of relief. It would seem my aunt is safe, tucked into this quaint little suburb. "I read in the paper that the palace grounds were breached. Is that true?"

I wave my hand. "Nothing to worry over, Aunt. The authorities cleared away the protestors with ease."

"And now I hear the King has fortified the place with an army of sorts?"

"Of sorts, yes," I agree.

"The whole thing is keeping me up at night," she says, fanning herself. "Monsieur, will you look out for my Alex?"

"It would be my pleasure," he agrees, saluting her.

I stare at him for a moment, then refocus on my aunt. "Did you see the national address? The one from which all this upset stems?"

"Of course I did. What a bizarre thing. And the Queen wasn't the only one, from what I heard."

"Far from it," I agree.

"They're saying some of the chips are malfunctioning. Hope mine don't act up," she adds, patting her head.

My brow lifts. "Oh, is that what they're saying?" My brain twists around this bit of news. Malfunctioning chips, a far more palliative explanation than the truth. And yet—if that's the official story—why hold Wolfe publicly responsible? Because either King or James want him dead, that's why.

Another thought occurs to me. Here I've been trying to hide the fact I know what King and James are scheming. But perhaps that's the wrong tactic. Perhaps I should be warning all of Wolfe's allies...

"Anyone home in there?" Aunt Jo calls, waving her hand in front of my face.

"Sorry," I say. "Just...thinking of something."

"Clearly. And how's that charming fiancé of yours, anyways?"

Normally I'd zero in on the term 'charming'—an odd choice, certainly. But right now, with the weight of the world seemingly on my shoulders—it's all I can do not to lose my composure. "We should be going," I say hurriedly, pulling Aunt Jo close to my chest and using the opportunity to wipe away a tear—one I think Monsieur notices.

She kisses my cheek, then turns for Monsieur and shakes his hand, thanking him once again for the impromptu visit.

Blushing for a second time, he swings open the door and ushers me inside.

"Are you quite alright?" he asks, studying me in the rearview mirror as we pull away from the curb and head downtown.

I realize how deeply I long to tell him everything. He will share my feelings, my indignance, my horror—I know he will. He'll believe me, too.

"Miss Alex?"

"Everything is fine, sir," I respond in the clearest and most level voice I can manage. I close my eyes for the rest of the ride.

———

AFTER THANKING Monsieur for his generosity, I head straight for the towering front doors. I need to speak with Jill, desperately, and not simply because I need to tell her the plan, or what's at stake. No, I need someone I can talk to. Talk, and share, and sob. Burdening Wolfe with my feelings is vastly unfair, considering how impossible it must be for him to contend with it himself, and nobody besides Jill and Wolfe know the truth here at Strath Glen.

"That was some protest, eh?" she asks as soon as I step outside. "Not bad, considering how unpracticed Airo-Aurora folks are."

"It seems to be all over with now."

She shrugs. "They change things," she says, nodding down at the soldiers standing shoulder to shoulder in front of the palace.

I shiver at the sight. At the thought of the order they'll receive, to assassinate Wolfe. "I need to tell you something," I say quietly, and I can tell I have her full attention. I proceed to explain the public assassination of my fiancé slotted for Sunday evening.

"You're kidding. He's probably the most respected person in there," she adds, gesturing to the palace. "What kind of messed-up family is this?"

"I spoke with Timothee this morning," I continue, "and he's now working on a new computer program. A bug, actually, that will destroy the entire system."

"Everything?"

"Everything," I agree. "Once it's ready, we'll need your help breaking into the Mainframe to execute it. That means I need a way to reach you this weekend."

She gives me details on her weekend plans and how best to reach her. "We'll have to be extra careful this time, considering what happened to Neo. Although," she adds, pausing to spit over the banister, "I guess if the virus works, we won't have to worry about that at all."

"Things will definitely change around here," I agree.

"It'd be nice to see this army clear out. Are they the ones who are supposed to kill your viscount?"

I nod.

"And the protests will be able to continue, too, with the army gone," she points out. "But what if they still want your fiancé's head to roll, even if the virus destroys everything?"

"I'm counting on King having other priorities—the Mainframe's like his child. But if I'm wrong, well, without the chips recording everything we say and do, he could at least go into hiding. He could start fresh, somewhere else."

"Without you."

I nod and try to ignore the push-pull sensation in my stomach.

"When do you think Timothee will be ready?"

"He's taking the day off work so he can tackle it," I explain. "So, hopefully, by tomorrow."

"I'll be glued to the telephone," she promises, and then I wave goodbye, heading back into the palace feeling more discombobulated than before.

Because now there's nothing to do but wait. I must sit here, on pins and needles, with my fiancé's fate hanging in the balance.

Agnes, I realize, with a lurch. I'll need to speak with Agnes at some point. Because her underground network is the perfect tool to spread word quickly that King is behind the override chip program, that he's planning on executing a scapegoat, that protests demanding his expulsion from the throne should continue in full force.

But I can't ask for more protests with the army still here, and besides, Monsieur has already been accommodating enough. I should check in on Wolfe, that's what I will do. I head to the kitchens first to make a pot of tea, and that's when I notice the rest of the palace.

Everyone, seemingly, is caught up in wedding preparations, and the reality of the situation makes my stomach sink. After all, it's a wedding unlikely to come to fruition, either because the Mainframe has been destroyed or, far, far worse—because the groom is dead.

Multitudes of décor is currently being delivered to the palace, garlands are being strung along the corridors, and life-sized fairies now hang from the ceiling in the ballroom where the reception is to take place. The ceremony itself, seemingly, will take place at the top of the imperial staircase, under the rotunda—an admittedly majestic setting for such a moment, with my veil apparently set to cascade down all twenty-seven steps. Tailors once again descend on the palace, though this time it's for the benefit of the royal family, a group constantly determined to upstage one another in how splendid they appear.

I suppose it's a blessing, as I seem to be the very last person on everyone's mind. I traipse up the stairs behind manicurists who are apparently late for an appointment with Aubrey, then carry on to Bishop's Aisle. I grab the tea tray from the dumbwaiter, observe that King's office door is sealed shut, and knock on Wolfe's door.

"No Claudia?" I ask when he finally swings it open, an attempt at a joke. One glance at his face, however, tells me he isn't in the mood. To call his expression stormy would be an understatement, not that I can exactly blame him. "I brought tea," I add, pouring him a cup and placing it next to the towering stack of paperwork positioned in front of his chair.

He takes a seat, but still, he says nothing.

"Have you reconsidered my original proposition?" I ask tactfully. "The one with the international angle?" I add.

"I believe that matter has been settled."

I had been expecting this and decide not to push it—at least not yet. "Are you really tending to your day-to-day work responsibilities right now?" I ask, eyeing the stack of paperwork next to him.

"Not quite. In fact, I was planning on sending for Monsieur Sawyer—I'd like a word. Would you happen to know where he is?"

"Not at the moment, but I wouldn't mind a lift to see Agnes—perhaps if you do track him down, you could mention it?"

He nods in a distracted way, not like himself at all.

"How are you, er, doing?" I ask after another minute of silence stretches between us.

He grimaces—perhaps an attempt at a smile. "Fine, Alexandra. And yourself?"

"Fine," I assure him, though my stomach aches with the unknown, my pulse is quick with fear. I am far from fine, and I know Wolfe is, too. We drink our tea in silence.

Finally, once our cups are drained, Wolfe stirs. "Can your meeting with Agnes wait until the morning?"

My brow lifts with surprise. What, precisely, does Wolfe want with Monsieur that will take all afternoon? I know better than to ask, just as he knows better than to ask why I want to see my friend in the first place. I bow my head. "It can wait until the morning, yes." We stare at each other for a moment, and then I'm gone, taking the servants' stairs to the second floor, disappearing into my quarters, where I collapse on the bed. It had been good to see Wolfe, but it had made me nauseous, too, thinking of Sunday evening. So nauseous that right now, I wait for the room to stop spinning.

He isn't working on his usual duties—hadn't he said that? And the unusually long meeting with Monsieur? Might he be up to something? Something to fix the problem of his scheduled assassination?

I can only hope.

twenty-four

. . .

THE NEXT MORNING brings with it storm clouds and broody echoes of faraway thunder. Despite it being Saturday and, from what I can surmise, quite early, Wolfe's side of the bed is already empty. I stare at the rumpled covers and sigh. And, as the heavy, sobering snippets of reality hit me, so too do the questions.

Will the virus that Timothee is crafting be ready today? Will we soon be sneaking into the Mainframe to change Airo-Aurora in the most drastic, most just way possible? Will the end of the Mainframe spell the end of King's reign?

In order to tip the odds in my favor—that the people of Airo-Aurora will see King as the villain he is and demand his ouster—I need to speak with Agnes. With that in mind, I draw myself up and stumble toward the closet as thunder rumbles closer. Maybe, if I'm really lucky, Monsieur will tell me what his lengthy meeting with Wolfe entailed yesterday afternoon.

"Sister!" Evie shouts the moment I step into the House of Mirrors. "I feel like I haven't seen you in absolute ages," she gushes, sounding more like herself than in recent days. I suppose that the healing process has begun, I realize, with a rush of relief. And then it hits me. If King is successful in executing Wolfe tomorrow evening, she'll be without her brother, too. The thought makes me ache all over. "Sister?" she echoes, her delicate brow scrunching with concern.

I decide then and there not to burden Evie or her mother with King's evil plan, not when they're already grieving. No, Wolfe and I will find a way out of it, it's that simple, and I force myself to smile. "You have far too much pep in your step considering this weather."

"April showers," she remarks breezily. "And guess what I just realized? Not only do I have your wedding to look forward to, but your birthday, too!"

In all the mayhem of the last few weeks, the thought that my birthday is just around the corner—on the same day as the wedding, in fact—had completely slipped my mind. I will be turning eighteen, too—not an insignificant milestone. And, if Timothee, Jill, and I are successful, that additional surveillance that kicks in when a citizen turns eighteen will never come to fruition. "I suppose we'll have to celebrate doubly hard," I say, patting her arm.

"Oh, no, sister. We must do something special—something exquisite. But my, what a dilemma trying to think of something when it will take place in the shadow of your special day. Already your nails will be done, and your hair, and so on, and etcetera! And I know Aubrey's taste is far different than your own, but really, your wedding is shaping up to be an exquisite affair. She really is pulling out all the stops. Come—let us explore the ballroom." She grabs my hand before I can decline the offer, and we're off, spinning through the House of Mirrors, tripping down the grand staircase, and, finally, into the recently transformed ballroom.

The black netting and gauze that had cloaked the room during the funeral have vanished, along with the white roses. I peer at Evie out of the corner of my eye, but her delight seems genuine—I don't think she associates the room with her father's death in the slightest. Such relief hits me with this small observation that I barely notice the array of bubblegum pink décor that now dominates the space, and yet, there it is.

Satin ribbons a meter wide twist around the windows, and the ceiling now features several dozen hanging bird-cages, all of them painted a bright pink.

"They'll be full of pink parakeets on your big day—isn't that tremendous?"

My eyes widen at this revelation, but I'm determined not to worry Evie in the slightest. "It shall be quite a spectacle," I gush obligingly. And really, why should I care? There's virtually no chance the wedding will even happen.

"Have you and Aubrey discussed the main course?"

I shake my head. "We haven't discussed anything," I admit.

"Oh, sister—and it's all my fault!"

"No, no," I immediately assure her. "It's not your fault in the slightest. I'd prefer someone else to make the decisions, anyhow, and besides, planning a wedding is the last—"

"Oysters!" shouts a voice from the hall, and as we turn in unison, Aubrey steps into the ballroom and tosses a ball of confetti into the air. "Oysters on ice! Oysters bathed in hot sauce! Oysters swimming in lemon juice!" She spreads her arms wide. "Isn't an oyster bar at the wedding ta-da?"

"I didn't think pregnant women were allowed raw seafood," Evie says under her breath.

I have to hide my smile. It wasn't so long ago that she idolized every move Aubrey made.

"Evie, darling, I absolutely want your input on center-pieces," Aubrey continues, sweeping past me and enveloping Evie in her silk shawl. I wave goodbye and head downstairs to the servants' quarters, once again intent on finding Monsieur. When he's nowhere to be found, I head to the underground garage, where I immediately spot him polishing the rims of the behemoth.

"What can I do you for, Miss Alex?" he asks without taking his attention off his work.

"I was hoping for a lift to my friend's house in Quire," I explain. "Perhaps Wolfe mentioned it?"

Monsieur says nothing, instead attacking a smudge with particular rigor. Finally, he stands. "You're ready now, I take it?"

I bow my head, and a minute later, we slip outside and into the elements. Rain batters the limousine, and flashes of lightning fill the west sky. "Are you quite alright?" I ask, after giving him Agnes' address.

"I've been better," he says levelly, then stares at me for a second too long in the rearview mirror.

"Care to elaborate, Monsieur?"

"Not at the moment, Miss Alex."

"Does it have something to do with yesterday's abnormally long meeting with Wolfe?"

Another weighted glance through the rearview mirror, then he returns his attention to the traffic, ignoring me completely.

I frown. I've never known Monsieur to be so lackluster, so withdrawn. Whatever Wolfe told him has had a profound effect.

Thunder rumbles closer as we draw up in front of Agnes' house. "I won't be long," I assure him, but as I step along the walkway toward the front door, I hesitate. It's fear that does it. A crippling wave of anxiety. Because what if Agnes is no longer Agnes? What if her role in the White Ribbon Campaign was outed? What if the bluecoats got to her?

But this is what King wants. Fear, leading to inaction. So, with that firmly in mind, I continue up the path and ring the doorbell.

Silence and stillness, then the slightest shifting of

curtains, and I almost yell out with relief. It's Agnes. Real, still-paranoid Agnes, and when she inches open the door, I push inside and embrace her in a hug.

"What's that for?" she asks once I release her.

"Just relieved you're safe."

"Oh, I'm taking precautions—don't you worry about me."

"Are you back to work?"

She shakes her head, then, seeing the look on my face, smacks me across the arm. "I don't want to end up like Neo!"

"Speaking of that, I need to talk to you about something," and I drag her to the loveseat. "Timothee's working on a virus to destroy the entire system," I whisper.

"All of it?"

"All of it."

"So...no more Selection?"

"Even the memory bank will be wiped out."

She stands. Then sits again. "You're serious, Alex?"

I nod, watching her carefully.

"This is...That is..."

"Is this happy Agnes? Or upset—"

"Happy," she assures me, grabbing my hand. "That would mean I don't have to work at the nursery anymore! It would mean I could divorce Miller!"

I'm not completely surprised, but my eyes still widen. "Are those things you want to do?"

She gives me a look. "Do you think I started the White Ribbon Campaign because I was bored?"

"Good point."

"What can I do to help?"

"Well, if everything goes according to plan, Timothee will finish creating this virus today, or maybe even tomorrow. We'll install it right away at the Mainframe with Jill's help. Not only would it get rid of the army, but it should distract King from his current plan, which is to hold a national address tomorrow evening and, uh, execute Wolfe."

For a minute, she's motionless. Then her face contorts. "What?"

"I know. He's going to blame what happened to the Queen on Wolfe, then have the army kill him."

"But you don't want that to happen—"

"Of course I don't want that to happen!"

"Shhh," she reminds me. "Okay. Okay, so what can I do?" she asks.

"I need you to spread word that King's behind the override chip program and that he's trying to pin it on his nephew. I also want people to know that even if we manage to destroy the Mainframe and Selection system, we won't have true freedom, or permanent freedom, until King is ousted."

"And you're sure the army will be gone? Because I'm not sending my supporters to be massacred."

"If Timothee's virus works? Positive."

"Okay," she agrees, smoothing her jeans. "Wild that it wasn't that long ago we were getting ready for our Selections, right?"

"True."

"Shit's really hit the fan."

"That's one way of putting it."

"How come you aren't scared?"

"I am," I tell her. "I'm very scared."

"Yeah? Well, no one would ever know it. You're braver than I am, Alex."

Despite the direness of the circumstances, a smile flits across my face. Something approaching contentedness fills my chest, and for a moment, I feel safe, calm, and confident that everything will work out. Then there comes incessant and impatient-sounding knocking from the front doors, and the moment is lost. "Monsieur Sawyer," I assure Agnes.

"Promise me you won't get caught at the Mainframe and end up like Neo?"

"Promise," I say, hiding the way I shiver. Monsieur taps his watch once I swing open the door, then retreats to the behemoth. "Good luck," I whisper.

"You, too." She squeezes my shoulder, then I head to the limousine with the sound of locking mechanisms echoing from behind me.

twenty-five

. . .

BY LATE AFTERNOON and with no word from Timothee, I grow uneasy. To make matters worse, tensions in the palace become more unbearable by the second. Wolfe strides from room to room in a mood matching the storm clouds overhead. Monsieur has yet to regain his sunny disposition, and King can be heard from all corners of the palace yelling at various servants rather than his typical singing of arias. Even James seems preoccupied when I spot him in the hall, nodding curtly at me instead of his usual cocktail of juvenile behavior and unwanted advances.

By the time all of us gather for dinner, the storm outside has stalled directly above Strath Glen, and I can barely contain the feeling of pins and needles inside my stomach. Why isn't Timothee finished with the virus yet? Will he finish before the address? What if he doesn't?

I stare at Wolfe through the warm glow cast by a dozen chandeliers. He registers no fear, no outward change in his demeanor, but I spot his tells: the tightness in his jaw, the levelness of his brow, the darkness of his eyes. Even his posture looks more unnatural than usual, determinedly erect—brittle, even.

Yes, it's a question I have no choice but to consider. If the virus isn't ready in time, what do I do? Begging Wolfe to flee the country won't work—he's made that perfectly clear. Perhaps I should set my sights on *him*—and I turn so I face none other than King.

Right now, he schmoozes with a couple I've seen here plenty of times before, wearing a smarmy expression. But when he turns away, his features harden, and I see the stress written clearly upon them. Perhaps he has something resembling a conscience. Some sliver of emotion that dreads the slaughtering of his nephew. The son of his recently deceased brother.

It's foolish to jump to such conclusions, I know that. This, after all, is a heartless man, an evil one. But, if I'm right, if some part of him is questioning the execution, perhaps I can tap into it. Perhaps I can convince King to abandon the plan...

I loop my fingers together and sigh. The virus will be ready in the morning, that's what I tell myself, and all the rest is needless worrying.

"I take it you saw your friend Agnes today?" queries a voice from way up high.

I turn to Wolfe and nod. "Monsieur took me."

"And did you manage to pry any information from him?"

"I can assure you," I say with a hint of a smile, "he showed total discretion."

"Good."

"I noticed he was more serious than usual. More somber, even. Would it be a leap to assume it has something to do with your lengthy meeting with him yesterday?"

"Dinner is being served," he replies levelly, his steely eyes not wavering in the slightest.

I make a point of looping my arm through his as we walk to our usual seats. "We're on the same team," I remind him in an undertone.

"Indeed. And yet our tactics couldn't be more mismatched."

I withdraw my arm and cross it over my chest, fixing him with a look. "You're really not going to tell me?"

Once again, he looks deflated. "I'm afraid, at this point, there's little to tell."

"Sister! I just had the most touching, most splendid idea concerning your fast-approaching wedding! Are you dying with excitement?"

At that moment, there's a flash of lightning, bright enough to lift easily over the countless chandeliers, followed by an ear-splitting crack of thunder that rattles the silverware. A heartbeat later, the power is cut, and we're thrown into velvety darkness. Evie gasps, others shriek, but all that's barely audible over the stentorian rain. I don't scare easy—Agnes is right; I am brave. But with a murder plot in the air, with my fiancé's time left on earth down to its final twenty-four hours, a bolt of fear ramrods down my spine.

"Wolfe?" I call.

"Sister?" echoes Evie.

And then there's a scream, a blood-curdling one from the other side of the room, and chairs are scraping, and a hand wraps itself around my arm, dragging me toward the door in one swift motion.

Once I'm shoved through the threshold, I realize the dark is even less penetrable in the corridor. A hand still grips my arm, a hand I assume belongs to Wolfe, and when I hear Evie whimper next to me, I realize he must be pulling her along, too.

"Wait," I say, resisting the unrelenting march forward. "Do you really think there's anything to fear? Or is everyone simply panicking because of the dark?"

"Sister, you're truly not scared?"

"Either option is a possibility," comes Wolfe's morose

voice. "I don't believe waiting around to see which is true holds much merit."

And then the lights switch on, and our small group and all the rest take a visual hold of our surroundings. Nothing seems to be amiss, nothing askew, except another scream echoes from the dining hall, this one just as blood-curdling as the last.

Wolfe, Evie, and I glance at each other. Wordlessly making the decision in unison, we turn and head back into Carnegie.

It's the last scene I'd ever expect to meet my eyes. One that makes my stomach solidify into a rock that pulsates uncomfortably.

Bent forward on the table and surrounded by a pool of blood is Butch, killed with a penknife in his back.

Aubrey shrieks hysterically as King watches on, his expression even-keeled and detached. Evie buries her head in Wolfe's shoulder, the Duchess bustling toward her at once. James and Morocco stand off to the side, looking tense and, for once, speechless. Dear Matthew holds the paper in front of him, not seeming to notice the horror in the slightest, and the Queen rearranges a flower bouquet.

"How will we find the murderer?" the duchess demands as she transfers Evie into her own arms.

"It's impossible," King says swiftly. "A room full of people and killed under the cover of darkness." He pats Aubrey on the head. "Gerard, have the blackcoats attend immediately to clean up this mess," and ever so slightly, his lip curls at the grisly sight in front of him.

I wonder if it's as obvious to everyone as it is to me that King is the culprit.

Feeling nauseated, I shuffle backward toward the door. The whole thing is too much. Too awful in its own right, but made all the worse by the planned execution hovering in the wings. And if King can kill this easily, with such an absence of remorse, Wolfe doesn't stand a chance.

King will not take pity, he will not be swayed by a girl from Quire. And with still no sign of Timothee, failure and the specter of death loom large, casting shuddering shadows along the old walls.

I seal myself in the closet to gather my breath. To slow my racing heart.

A sharp rapping comes at the door.

"I'll be right out," I call.

Wolfe clears his throat when I finally swing open the door. "You're upset," he remarks.

I roll my eyes. "Of course I'm upset. Aren't you?"

"It's gruesome—"

"What about tomorrow night?" I continue. "You see how heartless he is, don't you?"

"Indeed."

"Well? Don't you realize what's at stake? Don't you have any desire to save yourself?"

"I do—"

"Then why aren't you doing something? Why are you still here? Pretend you have an international mission, and go! Just—just go!"

"To have the national address postponed to another date? How long do you think I can keep the ruse up?"

"Go and don't come back until things have changed," I plead with him. "Until the Mainframe is destroyed, or King has stepped down. Stay away until it's safe to return!"

"And what if that day never comes? I'm to live in hiding for the rest of my life? What difference does it make to you, whether I'm living abroad or dead? In both cases, you will, seemingly, be forced to wed my cousin."

I stare at him. "There's a difference, Wolfe."

The hardness in his stance deflates, and we stare at each

other, more exposed than before. "How is your plan to destroy the Mainframe coming along?" he asks quietly.

"The virus isn't ready yet. I don't know when it will be ready, and I don't know if it will even work. But if you go...if you pretend you have a work meeting and force the broadcast to be delayed, it will buy us the time we need."

"Perhaps. It would also appear to be a strange coincidence to my uncle. So strange that he may take the time to review my feed. And yours."

"Wolfe—"

"I will sooner die than be thrown to the prisons, have an override chip implanted in my brain, or, far worse, witness any of those things befall you. Now, best to get some sleep and hope for a miracle in the morning."

twenty-six

. . .

THE NEXT MORNING, after a few feeble scraps of something resembling sleep, there comes no miracle. No change in circumstance whatsoever, aside from the ticking clock, marching ever forward, closer and closer to this evening.

I stare down at the streets below, observing with despair how ordinary it all looks. How life continues on, no matter my personal anguish, or Wolfe's. I look, too, for signs of Timothee, but of course, there comes none. And I don't have his personal address, I can't even check in on him to see how he's making out. To see whether there is any chance of our plan working, or whether I need to craft something different.

With Wolfe already gone, I flop down on the bed and consider the problem from all angles for the thousandth time. The duchess. The only remaining senior aristocrat with any sway. And I have witnessed her placate King before. I have seen the closeness the two of them share.

Of course, going to his mother won't please Wolfe. And, to be fair, if it held any chance of success, surely he'd already have done so. And then there's the fact that she just lost her husband...

But I can't sit here and twiddle my thumbs, and besides, I'm running out of options. I rush to the closet, get dressed, then step into the House of Mirrors. With an unpleasant thumping in my chest, I turn for the duchess' private quarters, the ones she shared with the duke, until recently.

My knocks go unanswered. Another dead end.

"Whatever are you doing, child?" echoes a voice. I turn and see Wolfe's mother walking toward me, her red dress drifting behind her and alighting the black and white checkerboard hall with color.

I hesitate, paralyzed by self-doubt. Is confiding in this woman the right thing to do? The answer isn't clear-cut, but, as Wolfe's mother, I decide she has the right to know. "Searching for you," I explain, "as I'd like a word."

"You have my ear," she says, stopping in front of me, her gaze scrutinizing.

"Somewhere private, madam."

Her brow creases, but she motions me forward into a small entrance hall similar to Wolfe's, then into a living room dotted with antiques. "Tea awaits," she says, and I glance around, looking for the tea service. "For me, child," and she looks at her watch pointedly.

"I—I'll be quick," I say, clearing my throat. "I believe something dire will happen this evening, without your intervention."

A knock sounds at the door just then, incessant and thunderous.

"Excuse me," she says, drawing open the door to none other than Wolfe.

We stare at one another, and I see that he isn't surprised to find me here. And, if that's the truth, he's come on purpose.

"I need a word," he says curtly, motioning to me.

"Your fiancée was just about to tell me about something most dire—"

"My fiancée is confused," he says swiftly, ushering me from the room.

Out in the hall, Wolfe says nothing. Instead, he marches to our own quarters, and only once we're tucked inside does he round on me. "I warned you, did I not, that exposing our position could result in me being locked away until the broadcast—"

"It's your *mother*—"

"My mother who is still grieving the loss of her husband."

"She'll soon be grieving the loss of her son, too," I counter, my voice every bit as sharp as his. "What else am I to do when you refuse to do the sensible thing and flee?"

"There's no need to worry my mother, after all she's been through."

"She may be able to talk some sense into your uncle!"

"Nobody can talk sense into him, don't you see that?"

"It's worth a try," I hiss. "Anything is, at this point."

"You overheard chatter, yes, I don't deny that. But much can change hour by hour, let alone day by day."

"You're saying you may not be in danger?" My voice is incredulous. But part of me is hopeful, too.

He lifts his hand. "I am in the dark, just as you are. But it *is* feasible that plans have changed."

I'm forced to agree.

"For the time being, please do not disturb my mother on this matter, or anyone else."

Reluctantly, I promise. "How did you know I was there?" I call before he can reach the door.

"I've friends around here, just as you do." Then he's gone, and I'm left wondering what to do now.

A moment later, I'm out the door myself, this time headed for the front doors. I'm not familiar with either guard on duty, but I approach them nonetheless. "Has anyone come calling for me? A boy around my age?"

Both of them shake their heads.

"Do you think they would allow him to approach the front doors?" I ask, nodding down at the row of Mavericks standing shoulder-to-shoulder at the bottom of the stairs.

"Don't know, right?"

Of course he doesn't know, and I kick myself for just realizing it now. It's possible, perhaps even likely, that Timothee has already finished the virus—that he's already tried to reach me but wasn't allowed to approach the palace because of the army encircling it.

I sit down on the front step and resolve not to move a muscle for the rest of the day. Because if my theory is correct, surely he'll try again. I scan the property, back and forth, but nowhere lurks a solitary figure trying to get the attention of someone inside the palace.

I keep waiting. Caterers come and go, and stylists. The Mavericks check their credentials, then let them pass by. Timothee, though, wouldn't have any credentials or any reason to access the palace whatsoever. So, I stay vigilant, willing Timothee to appear through the apple grove. An hour slips by, and another. I yawn, my stomach growls, the surge of adrenalin from earlier is long gone, but still, I wait.

Eventually, though, the sun slips lower in the sky. Almost dinner, and still no Timothee. The realization makes me sick to my stomach, and I shudder and shake at what lies ahead. Dinner and a show. Sustenance and an execution.

I instruct the guards on duty to come find me if they see a dark-haired young man attempting to approach the palace, then step inside.

Right now, it feels as though I'm viewing it for the first time. The decorative columns, the glittering floor, the towering Ming vases. The parrot shrieks, "Always a killer!"

from Devonshire, and I think of King—always a killer, indeed.

The palace bustles with its usual rhythm, one I now know well. Milliners storm past with hat boxes. Dear Matthew and Morocco do shots with guests inside Devonshire. James climbs the imperial stairs, followed by acrobats, and the Queen mindlessly glides from room to room carrying an armful of flowers. Aubrey is the only anomaly, donned in black, a handkerchief clutched in her hand and used liberally. Her anguish is as real as her love for Butch, but it doesn't faze the rest of Strath Glen's occupants. And, seeing as how Butch was never part of the royal family, there's no service, no reference to him whatsoever.

I step along the hallway, feeling nothing but revulsion for this place. How I long to buckle myself into a helicopter right now, the sparkling green beast at the Sky Center, and whisk Wolfe to safety. Maybe I'd stay with him, too. But it wouldn't take long for the Mainframe to determine our location, and how much longer after that until we're deported back to this hellscape? I sigh as I drag myself along the House of Mirrors.

A minute after I enter the quarters shared with Wolfe, the door swings open. Wolfe stands there, wearing his usual navy suit and pressed white button-up. He's paler than usual, and he looks ragged, deflated, and defeated. But his back remains rigidly upright, and he nods curtly at me. "Ready for dinner?"

My eyes narrow. "You're actually going?"

"I have no known reason not to attend," he says in a pointed tone.

Tears prickle behind my eyes, and I feel a sudden rush of anger. All I do, though, is turn to the window.

"Will you," he pauses to clear his throat, "be attending?"

"I won't," I say, and there's a hardness to my voice. "I'm

done keeping up appearances. I'm done playing games."
Suddenly I wish I'd stopped ages ago.

"Is there anything I can say to persuade you otherwise?"

I glance at him over my shoulder. "No."

"Are you angry with me?"

I survey the grounds before I respond, still hoping fruit-lessly to spot Timothee.

"This isn't my fault," he continues. He clears his throat a second time.

"The fact that your uncle decided to pin the blame on you? No. No, that isn't your fault." I round on him. "But it is your fault you're here instead of hiding safely in another country as I asked. As I pleaded!"

"I've explained myself—"

"It's not good enough!" I shout.

He stares at me for several seconds, then scowls. "If the roles were reversed, do you know what you would accuse me of?"

"What?"

"Caring not about you—the real you—but rather my own position within the palace. Rest assured, I wish to see you wed James as little as you, but I'm afraid my hands are rather tied." With that, he turns on his heel, slamming the door hard enough to rattle the moldings.

Inwardly I reel. Is he right? Is my concern and anger borne out of selfishness?

Before I can unpackage the question, or even attempt to, I see a flash of movement down below, from where I've been keeping a vigilant eye. Dark hair, and I gasp.

Timothee.

That's Timothee rushing toward the palace steps. That's Timothee being swallowed up by the army—and immedi-ately I pivot, I dash to the door, shooting through the House of Mirrors faster than I've ever moved, down the imperial steps three at a time, and, finally, bursting through the towering front doors. Every cell in my body swells with anticipation. I feel like I'm floating, both dead and alive. I spot Timothee through the throngs of army-green-clad arms, and I move nimbly down the stone staircase as I shout his name.

He stops struggling against the Mavericks once he spots me. And when I'm close enough, I see that his eyes shine with brightness, they shine with excitement.

My stomach inflates like a balloon, filled with joy, and it expands to my chest, even to my head. I feel like I'm floating. I'm so delirious, so full of excitement, and relief, relief, relief.

"You finished?" I shout as I elbow my way toward him through the army.

"Only just now," he hollers back. "And that's with no sleep, either!" He yawns, then gestures toward the Mainframe. "We need Jill, don't we?"

"There's a telephone booth that way," I say, pointing to the east. But the back of my cardigan is grabbed before I can take a single step.

The Maverick holding me has empty eyes, but his grip is unrelenting. "You stay," he says in a voice devoid of inflection.

"What? But why?"

He doesn't reply, instead dragging me back, closer to the palace. I shoot a nervous look at Timothee. "We can get Monsieur Sawyer to give us a lift off the grounds," I suddenly shout the idea, bringing with it a flood of relief.

But when Timothee makes to follow me up the steps, the army once again intervenes.

So, Timothee isn't allowed in, and, as per King's orders, I suppose, I'm not allowed out. And right now, time is of the essence, making it all the more infuriating.

"You go to the telephone booth," I instruct. "Call Jill and have her meet you at the Mainframe. I'll meet up with you guys there as soon as I can," and then I'm dashing up the steps and through the now-empty corridors of the palace, everyone having already congregated in Carnegie. I go straight downstairs, and once I'm surrounded by stone walls and flickering torches, I call for my friend. I shout his name over and over again so that when he finally rounds the corner, his brow is drawn with concern.

"What in good god are you going on about?" he demands.

"I was looking for you."

"I rather deduced that."

"I need a favor. Right away."

He rolls his eyes. "I suppose I could've deduced that, as well."

"It won't take long. I simply need a way to get off palace grounds straight away. The Mavericks won't let me."

"Who won't let you?"

"The uh—the army."

"Oh, yes—the army," he echoes, and his gaze is scrutinizing.

"How much has Wolfe told you?" I suddenly ask.

"I was rather wondering the same thing."

"I'm quite capable of fact-finding on my own accord," I say as I motion toward the garage.

Still, he doesn't move.

"Please, Monsieur. It's a matter of life or death."

Now his gaze narrows even further. Then, without another word, he marches toward the garage at a brisk pace, leaving me to once again ponder how much my friend knows. After all, if anything would warrant a question, it's my most recent declaration.

Two minutes later, we roar into the elements.

"Slow down, Monsieur," I call to him. "You'll attract attention—"

He lays on the breaks and grumbles. "Do this, Monsieur.

Do that, Monsieur. Jump here, Monsieur. Jump higher, Monsieur."

"Nonsense," I say as we pass the front of the palace and the row of Mavericks who stare at the behemoth. My stomach cinches as I wonder how advanced the Artificial Intelligence is that powers them. Will they deduce that it's me back here? Will they stop the limousine?

"I'm authorized to come and go, Miss Alex, so do relax," Monsieur says as if he can read my mind.

Still, I angle away from the window in case one of them glimpses me through the tinted glass. It's eerie—*they* are eerie, and it's no wonder there have been no more protests since they arrived. Human in all the obvious ways, and yet there's something distinctly inhuman about them, too, and even though I know the reason for that, it doesn't make it any easier to swallow.

"Where am I dropping you, Miss Alex?" Monsieur asks once we make it to city streets.

"Here will do," I say, staring up and down the street, trying without luck to locate Timothee.

"Let's take you around the corner to be safe, hmm?"

I return my attention to Monsieur. Then I nod. "Thank you."

He pulls the gigantic machine around the block, letting me out only once the palace is blocked from view. "Until next time," he says, tipping his hat.

I wave goodbye, then take off along the sidewalk, moving as quickly as the spring shopping crowd will allow. There. There's Timothee, standing on the corner, his head swiveling as he looks for me.

"About time!" he shouts once he spots me. "Now, all we need is for Jill to hurry up."

"Did you speak to her?"

"She's on her way to the Mainframe right now," he confirms.

I exhale with relief.

"Keep your eyes peeled for the bus," he adds.

"The bus?"

"She doesn't have a car. Do you?"

"I have Monsieur," and I scan the streets for the behemoth.

"It's too late," Timothee continues. "She already left. All we can do now is wait."

He's right. Besides, the chauffeur and his limousine are nowhere to be found. We walk toward the Mainframe, our pace leisurely even though our reality is anything but. "How long will it take to unleash the virus?"

"Not long. But breaking into a computer might take hours."

"What?" I say, coming to an abrupt stop. "Did you say *hours*?"

He nods. "I had Neo with me last time, don't forget. All he had to do was log in. Without him, I have to guess at the password."

"Guess," I echo, feeling suddenly faint.

"I have a program that tries about a thousand passwords a minute. It might take no time at all," he points out.

"Or we might never crack it."

"We can install the program on multiple computers. Somebody will have an easy passcode to crack."

"It's half past six already."

"What time is the broadcast?"

"Eight o'clock."

His jaw clenches. An hour and a half. It's not much time. It's not much time at all, and the balloon of hope in my stomach deflates, the empty space it leaves behind filling immediately with dread. "The Mainframe's closed," he says, staring around the empty parking lot. "Think we'll attract attention loitering here?"

I shrug. I don't care, not at this point. Instead, I stare at my watch and at the streets, willing the bus carrying Jill to appear.

Time passes, and the worrying grows worse. Finally, twenty minutes later, she gets off a city bus advertising a daycare service. "Damn traffic," she mutters once she's within earshot.

"We need to be quick," I say. "Just a little over an hour until the broadcast begins."

She pulls out a ring of keys from her pocket. "Anybody watching?" she asks as she leads us to the front door.

"Other than the Mainframe? Not that I can tell," replies Timothee.

"And that will be deleted soon enough," I add, sounding both hopeful and desperate at the same time.

"What's the plan if there's a greencoat inside?" asks Timothee.

Jill shrugs. "Cross the bridge when we come to it."

Once we're inside, butterflies fill my stomach and give me the boost of adrenalin I need. Now is not the time for fear or worry. It's the time for action. Once we scan the hallways for signs of movement, Timothee and Jill begin forward, and I'm reminded they've done this before. I follow after them, our footsteps silent across the polished floors.

Suddenly, like a clap of lightning, a thought strikes—an idea, an important one, and I grab Timothee's sleeve. "Do you have an extra memory stick?" I whisper.

He pulls three from his pocket. "This one has the passcode breaker on it," he says, holding up a blue one. "This one has the virus," he adds, pointing to a red one. "And this one is extra, but that doesn't mean I want it lost."

"I'll guard it with my life," I promise as I pocket it. "I'll meet up with you in a few minutes," I add as I edge toward the Visitation Room.

"I'll keep the door open for you," grunts Jill as she enters the passcode needed to gain entry to the rest of the building.

I nod, but already she's gone, and I feel a surge of appreciation for my friends. There isn't as much on the line for them as for me, but that doesn't mean they're taking this mission any less seriously.

Next, I think about my parents—how can I not? So many hours logged away in here, watching them through tears. But time goes on, and life does, too. Besides, their memories are imprinted on my brain, and nobody can take that away from me.

It isn't their feed that I pull up.

I work quickly, knowing precisely the date and time I'm after, transferring the snippet of video onto the memory stick, then securing it in my pocket. I say a silent goodbye to my parents, try to ignore the heaviness in my chest, and walk out the door, headfirst into a large brick of a person.

"Busted," Sedaris says slyly. "I knew there was something fishy about you. Knew it as soon as I saw you trying to break in last time."

"I was simply looking for a technician to speak with," I explain.

"And this time?" He makes a show of checking his watch. "After hours and officially closed. That counts as breaking and entering, right there."

"It's not for selfish purposes, I can assure you. If you'd just agree to look the other way this one time—"

"And lose my job in the process—"

"You never saw me. We were never here—"

"*We*?" he echoes, spinning on the spot. His gaze darts back and forth along the hallway.

"Me...and Wolfe," I blurt out. "And I can assure you, you're far more likely to lose your job by intervening in the viscount's affairs."

"Why would the viscount be snooping around this boring old joint?"

"He, uh, wants to visit a memory, that's all. But a man of

his stature, attending during opening hours...You can see why that wouldn't appeal."

Sedaris pokes his nose into the Visitation Room and scans it more closely than before. "So where is he?"

"Oh, he'll be here any minute." I take a seat inside the room, an effort to keep Sedaris away from the important work Timothee is currently doing. Sedaris pulls up a chair, too, crossing his arms and fixing me with his gaze.

Unfazed, I check my watch. Now less than an hour until the broadcast begins. How are Timothee and Jill making out? Have they been able to access someone's computer yet? Or is the passcode breaker still running, fruitlessly scouring thousands of letter combinations with no end in sight?

It pains me to not know what's going on, but what to do about Sedaris? There has to be a way to lose him—and I'll need to soon. Because if Timothee can't install the virus in time, I'll need to stop the execution another way.

The minutes don't just tick by, they vanish. Forty-five to go. Forty. When there's only thirty minutes left until the national address, I pick up the sound of footsteps. Sedaris sits straighter. Jill rounds the corner just then and stops short.

"What are you doing here?" he shouts, lurching forward in his seat.

She places one hand on Sedaris' chest and forces him to remain seated. "I was wondering what the hold-up was."

"Any progress?" My voice is desperate.

"Not yet," she says, and I'm filled with a sinking feeling that burns, and aches, and throbs. When I finally blink back the tears, I notice that Sedaris is handcuffed to the chair.

"Come on," she says to me as she pushes him out the door, rolling him toward the back of the building.

"What the hell's going on? Who's that?" Sedaris yells as we wheel into the room where Timothee sits hunched over a computer.

"Any luck?"

"Not yet. These things can take a while. Lot of possibilities for passwords, right?"

"Do you have the program running on every computer?"

He nods. "All are up and running. It's a waiting game now."

"I know what her password is," Sedaris says from the chair he's fastened to. He nods toward a corner computer, closest to the window that looks upon the vast computer collection.

Immediately I round on him. "Who? How?"

"The girl that sits right there. She's cute," he says, shrugging. "I've watched her enough times to know what's up."

"So, what is it?" Jill demands. "What's the password?"

"Let me go first."

"He's full of shit," she says, waving his words aside.

I lift my palm to quiet them both. "You're married," I say to Sedaris.

"No shit, Sherlock. I hear your wedding's not so far away, either."

"But you have feelings for another woman. You must if you watch her that intently."

Now he's silent, simply staring at me, frowning.

"If you give us the password, if it works, do you know what will happen?"

He shakes his head.

"The entire Selection system—the entire Mainframe—will be done. Gone. It'll be a new Airo-Aurora. A free one, where we can marry—and divorce—whoever we like. We can choose our own career too."

"That's what all this is about?"

I nod.

"So all that about the viscount visiting—"

"I made it up. Please, Sedaris. If we don't get that password now, we won't have another opportunity to create real change."

"I don't want to get in shit for this. Destroying the Mainframe? It'll be the biggest crime to hit Airo-Aurora since its inception!"

"It will eliminate the army, meaning people can protest —they can demand lasting freedom. And besides, there will be no evidence you helped once the memory bank is wiped clean."

"Yeah," adds Jill. "And if you don't cooperate, all three of us will put all the blame on you." She spits on the floor and crosses her arms.

He rolls his eyes. "Sundayfunday," he finally mutters.

"Pardon?"

"That's her password. All one word. Can you unlock me now?"

Timothee leaps toward the corner computer, knocking down several desk chairs along the way. He strikes several keys to stop the passcode program from running, then enters the information from Sedaris.

None of us breathe. Not a single sound. No movement. Then the screen changes and Timothee lets out a loud cheer. "In," he says triumphantly. Jill starts toward Sedaris to remove the cuffs.

I pull up a chair next to Timothee and watch the screen. I watch the clock, too. Just fifteen minutes now. "What's next?" I ask.

"Basically, the virus inserts itself into another application's code so when that application runs, it executes the virus' code and spreads it to other programs. Once it spreads, it executes the payload—the part you care about."

"But—that sounds like it'll take ages."

"Shouldn't take more than a few minutes. There are only two programs running, functionally speaking. The one that runs the wireless collection of data from all us Airo-Aurora underlings and the override chip program that essentially works in the opposite direction, feeding data to the chips."

"And the payload?"

"That's when the virus unleashes itself. It's three-pronged, remember?"

I shake my head.

"First, it'll encrypt all the data currently stored here, then delete it, basically turning all the people with override chips into complete robots—much like our interesting friends, the Mavericks. During the second prong, the virus will scramble the data-collecting program, meaning these little micro-recording chips in our brain have nowhere to send the data to. Finally, for the third prong, the virus will disable and delete the override chip program."

"How long will all that take?"

"I really don't know. It's my first large-scale virus."

I nod, thinking. The virus will impact people like the Queen first. And if King notices, he'll know another breach is happening. And that might spare Wolfe, but what about Timothee?

"Now that the virus is installed, can we leave?" I suggest tactfully.

He shrugs. "I'd rather monitor things."

"But if King notices his wife acting differently, he'll realize what's happening. And don't forget he has the army at his disposal."

"The army can't get inside here," Sedaris says.

"How do you know?" Jill replies with a snort of derision.

"There's a back door," Sedaris counters. "Even if I'm wrong and they storm the front of the building, we go out the back. No big deal."

I glance at Jill, and she nods.

"You two stay here," I say, pointing to Timothee and Sedaris as I stand. "Jill and I will go to the front steps. If

King gives the order, Jill will sprint back to warn you. Good?"

"Good," Timothee agrees, not taking his eyes from the computer. Sedaris looks less than sure, but he doesn't make to leave, either.

"Get that payload working as fast as possible!" Jill shouts as we round the corner and head for the front doors.

We lock them behind us, then poke our way through the spruce trees and the apple grove. Once we reach the road allowance, and I consider the scene at the top of the stairs, I feel more faint than ever. It's the camera crew setting up equipment, the front door swung open wide, the trickle of royals slowly gathering. It's the Mavericks, too, three-deep, standing in front of the palace steps, the very steps we need to climb if the virus doesn't work, and I need to take a last-ditch shot at saving my fiancé.

And I realize in that moment that I'm not so intent on saving his life for selfish reasons, no. I care for him in some capacity—of course I do.

"How are we going to get past the army?" I ask.

"Two feet and a heartbeat."

"But the—"

"They see me all the time when I report for work. It's never an issue. Either they know my face, or they're programmed to defer to the greencoats. Watch," she adds over her shoulder as she strides toward them.

I scramble to keep up, and, just as she said, they part ways to make space for her. They don't impede my progress, either—more facial recognition, evidently. And then we're jogging up the steps, and when I reach the top, none other than King stands there, considering me with eyes that glint darkly. "Wherever were you, little cottontail?" he asks innocently.

Can he really be so heartless? So heartless that he's

completely indifferent to the upcoming execution? Or is it possible I'm worrying for nothing?

"Well, my dear?"

"Strolling the grounds," I say promptly. I gaze across the balcony. Nowhere do I spot Wolfe.

"Ah, the grounds, the grounds," he echoes. "Given your love for the grounds, perhaps you should sleep there with the army, hmm?"

I stare right at King. I stare, and I see something menacing flickering behind his eyes. As if it's a threat he currently casts my way. As if that will be my future once Wolfe is out of the way.

"Keep your eye on the Queen," I whisper to Jill. "If she starts to behave out of the ordinary, get her inside and away from the others before they can see. King can't be suspicious."

She nods. "What are you going to do?"

"Look for Wolfe." Look for Wolfe so I can make one last plea for him to vanish. And then, at that very moment, he appears on the balcony, marched through the front doors by two thick-bodied Mavericks.

"Brother, whatever is going on?" cries Evie.

"Places, everyone!" shouts the cameraman.

"No more chitchat," snaps King as he smooths his robes and positions himself in front of the towering front doors, practicing his smile. The other members of the royal family stand off to the side, including the Queen. Wolfe and the Mavericks stand off to the side, too, and despite trying to capture his attention, Wolfe refuses to acknowledge me with his gaze.

Finally, I turn to Dear Matthew and the Queen, desperate to see any change, no matter how slight—an indication that the virus is unleashing its payload, that the army will abandon their post at any minute. Nothing. My entire body thrums with nerves, it shakes with fear, and dread, dread, dread.

The men working the camera count down with their fingers, then yell, "Action!"

"Good evening," King says in a simpering voice. "My fellow citizens of Airo-Aurora, during my last address, I was alerted just as you were to a most egregious breach to our system of governance. Alarmed and outraged, I took it upon myself to find the source of the problem—and I'm thrilled to announce to you tonight that I've succeeded in my mission. That's right, I've discovered that it's an override chip implanted in the brains of some of our citizens, with the capacity to control their behavior. That, gentlewomen and gentlemen, is what you witnessed last week. Was it me who ordered the introduction of these override chips? Is it me who developed something so ghastly? Why, of course not, and I pledged immediately to find the twisted person responsible for such a reprehensible program. Tonight, I'm pleased to announce that, indeed, I've discovered the culprit. A high-ranking official, just as you'd expect, and a member of the family, too." He holds up his hand theatrically and gestures toward Wolfe. The cameraman maneuvers the camera sideways until they have a clear shot of him standing wedged between the Mavericks.

Wolfe doesn't seem to notice. Instead, he stares down at the street below, seemingly lost in thought. He doesn't struggle against the men who grip him, he doesn't register any reaction whatsoever.

Evie and her mother, however, do, and their panicked shrieking cuts like a knife. They proclaim his innocence with fervor, realizing just as the rest of the nation does that King intends to have him executed on-air, as was promised.

"Silence," King mouths at them, directing his walking stick at their heads—a warning shot. Then he gestures to the cameraman, and the camera swings back to him; he assumes his regal posture at once. "I can assure each and every one of you that, from this day forward, there will never again be such an egregious breach of trust or privacy. But first, gentlewomen and gentlemen, we must eliminate the disease that first infected us. I present to you, the execution of the viscount!"

The duchess screams. Evie sobs. Even Aubrey and Morocco look horrified. I cover my mouth as my legs turn to jelly. My plan has failed.

I look desperately at Jill, my friend, my rock. But she isn't paying attention. In fact, she's staring at something over my shoulder, and when I turn, I see it's the Queen. She doesn't watch the drama unfurling in front of her, but she doesn't smile as she normally does, either. The first phase of the virus must be complete—a small triumph, but it's not enough—it's not nearly enough.

And then Wolfe clears his throat, the camera moves to him, and all superfluous noise disappears like it's been sucked into a vacuum. "While I deny any and all responsibility associated with the override chip program, I accept my sentence."

"Yes," says King, sounding unsure, "well, you have no choice in the matt—"

"However, I make a simple request, one granted to even the lowest of prisoners, and that's to say my last words."

With the camera on him and the sound of Evie and the duchess sobbing in the background, along with my own labored breathing, King, through a clenched-tooth smile, nods.

Wolfe holds up his hands for silence. He clears his throat. Then he launches into a recitation of what sounds like an international treaty on national defense. I peer at him, wondering what relevance these words have, and then it hits me. Time. He's buying time, and I can't ever remember feeling so hopeful.

For the next few minutes, I watch both the Queen and Mavericks standing on either side of Wolfe. I will the virus to be quicker about its work. I imagine the army awakening. I imagine the tide turning and washing King out to sea where he belongs.

But as the sun inches lower along the horizon, as shadows lengthen and Wolfe drones on, King steps forward.

Before I can intervene, Wolfe once again holds up his hand. "I'm not finished," he says simply before delving back into his admittedly dry speech.

I try to use the additionally bought time wisely, knowing it will soon come to an end. I wrack my brain for a solution, one more immediate than the slow-moving virus, but nothing comes to mind. I turn to Evie and the duchess, but they've been corralled into the corner with a greencoat standing in front of them. I try to catch Wolfe's eye, thinking perhaps something will reveal itself there, but he stares straight ahead, still droning on about duties, taxes, and tariffs.

"Let's get on with it," James calls from the wings. He yawns widely.

King, buoyed by this, steps forward. He shoves his walking stick into Wolfe's chest—a hard strike. Wolfe grimaces, then, in a rare show of anger, wrenches the stick from his uncle's hands and hurls it over the banister.

Immediately the Maverick next to him draws his gun and pushes it against Wolfe's head.

twenty-seven

. . .

STARS CLOUD MY VISION. I feel faint, and all noise and light filter unevenly through my brain as I slump against Jill. It won't work. Nothing will save Wolfe. My plan failed—it failed *him*. Someone who doesn't deserve to die, not in the slightest.

Wolfe doesn't move, but I can see his chest rising and falling. I can feel his fear, and it makes everything inside me whither. And then, just as I find my feet, just as my brain switches gears and begins searching for a last-ditch solution, one that doesn't involve waiting for the virus or hoping the ammo jams the gun, just as I'm about to burst forward—I hear Jill grunt in my ear—"Look."

I don't see anything out of ordinary—not at first, but then Jill points at the Mavericks that line the steps staring down at the city. They lift their feet curiously, they turn their heads. I stand straighter. I forget to breathe. And then I see that the man holding the gun to my fiancé's head...he, too, is looking around, considering the weapon with skeptical curiosity.

Every cell in my body expands with a renewed sense of hope, one that's so powerful it feels like it's radiating light, and everything around me comes into intense focus, crystal clear, shining and pulsating with energy.

At that moment, there's a commotion down below—the behemoth coming screeching around the corner, racing up the drive toward the front steps. Monsieur jumps from his seat and throws open the doors, ushering out at least a dozen men and women, some smartly dressed, some in uniforms of their own, and all of them completely unfamiliar.

The Mavericks don't bother asking for credentials, and as these strangers march up the steps, the cameramen twist the equipment around to capture them.

"What's this?" shouts King from the top step.

"You are hereby under arrest," says the most important-looking of the lot. "For breaching articles 6 through 8 of the International Treaty of National Defense, articles 19 through 23 of the Treaty Governing Artificial Intelligence, and for plotting the murder of Wolfe Rocksavage, the Viscount of Airo-Aurora."

"Ready your weapons!" King screams at the Mavericks, and I'm not sure whether he means to levy the weapons against Wolfe or the intruders. Regardless, his order fails miserably. Not a single Maverick reacts, and I realize that the virus' payload has been unleashed, and no matter what happens on these steps right now, life in Airo-Aurora has been fundamentally changed. No more record of all we say and hear. No more memories stored in perpetuum on machine. No more military, no more rebels turned into mindless machines.

"Lock him up!" screams a voice from the balcony, and I'm floored to see that it's the Queen pointing the finger at her husband. A lively one indeed.

And then the uniforms brought in by Monsieur step forward at this, and I can almost hear Airo-Aurora inhaling in unison as King is placed in handcuffs.

The Queen, the duchess, and Evie cheer, and the rest of the dignitaries shake hands with the viscount. Eventually, he motions them inside and away from the cameras. James follows after them, looking so confused, so dazed, I almost feel badly for him.

Evie darts between her mother and the greencoat, racing across the balcony toward me. "Whatever just happened, sister? I know you hold all the answers—tell me everything."

"It's a long story," I warn her.

"I'm all ears."

"Your uncle," I begin, as the camera crew pack up their things and the Mavericks scatter, "has been using the override chips to subdue a discontented population. He also used them to turn the Mavericks into his own personal army. He and James placed the blame on your brother, as you saw this evening."

"Tell her the good part," says Jill, elbowing me.

"My friends and I dismantled the chip program just now and, along with it, the entire Mainframe. And the foreign dignitaries," I add to a flabbergasted Evie, along with the rest of the royal family that listens to my every word, "must have been Wolfe's doing." I smile broadly. "He really is grossly astute. And, of course, we can't forget Monsieur Sawyer—whisking them here in the nick of time."

For a while, the others are too shocked to say anything, and I don't really blame them. I barely understand what just transpired myself, despite having a large hand in all of it. But one thing is clear...Wolfe is safe. He's *safe*. He will not be executed. I will not be forced to wed James, sleep outside, or face Evie after losing both her father and her brother.

Success has never tasted sweeter. My relief has never been so profound. And even though I can't visit my parents' memories any longer, I feel them with me here, now, atop this balcony. I feel their pride mixing with my own, and as dusk settles around us, so does a new dawn.

Finally, the royals sputter to life, and I'm reminded that even though so much has changed, much stays the same.

"My James had nothing to do with it!" hollers an indignant Morocco.

"I'll have my husband's head," the Queen shouts as she turns on her heel.

"Not if I get him first," calls the duchess as she rushes after her.

"It's as if my family doesn't love me in the slightest!" Aubrey cries. "First my uncle, then my Butch, now this? Doesn't anyone care that I'm with child? Stress isn't good for the baby!"

"What happened to Butch?" Dear Matthew asks, looking as if he's just woken from a long sleep.

Jill pulls on my arm, and without another thought, I follow her down the steps as the remaining Mavericks begin to head toward the tree line.

"The tents King had you sleeping in are around back," I tell them. "You may as well keep them—they're full of supplies. And, oh," I add before they can go, "if those guns don't work properly, it's because the ammo's the wrong size. If you can trade for the right gauge, though, you'll find hunting much easier."

I spot Timothee poking between the apple trees, and I forget about the Mavericks and the weapons. I run full-speed toward him. "It worked—you did it!"

"And by the skin of your teeth, too," adds Jill, grinning.

"*We* did it, more like," says Timothee, ruffling my hair. "Outliers to the rescue."

"We did it," I agree. "And others, too," I add, thinking of Wolfe and Monsieur, Agnes—even Sedaris. "And all the brave protestors, too."

"Neo should be back to normal," says Jill. "We have a lot to fill him in on."

"Yeah," says Timothee, "I guess he's really the master-mind behind all of this."

I grin. "Who would've thought. A girl from Quire, betrothed to a viscount in order to tear it all apart with her friends."

All of us grin, silently digesting it.

"So, no more Mainframe," says Jill eventually. "What does that mean for our current jobs and mates?"

"I guess it depends on who takes the throne," says Timothee, staring up at Strath Glen. "And how much unrest all of this causes."

"I have to go," I blurt out, suddenly remembering something. "But, uh—thank you, both of you, for everything. You risked your lives—"

"Hey," says Jill, kicking my boot. "Don't get all sappy on me or I'll have to punch you."

"You really care for him, don't you?" adds Timothee before I can go.

"Wolfe?"

He nods.

"I suppose over the past few months, he's become as much a friend as the two of you have," I admit. "Considering what we've been through, Wolfe—and the two of you—will always have a special place in my heart."

With that, I turn for the palace, rushing up the front steps and through the towering doors. Quickly I climb the imperial staircase, passing over the spot where me and Wolfe are supposed to wed—*were* supposed to wed, I remind myself, and I slow for a moment to gaze up at the rotunda, its windows now velvety black with darkness. The end of a chapter.

With a deep breath, I carry on to Bishop's Aisle. When I walk into King's office, I see this is where everyone has congregated, as I expected.

"Oh, good," remarks Wolfe in his typical detached way of

speaking. "I was going to have someone fetch you."

I lift an eyebrow.

"My colleagues here from the neighboring countries of Myopia, Harbor, and the United States are keen to know what has become of our system of governance and what our governance will look like going forward. As I am not privy to what happened at the Mainframe with your friends, perhaps you could fill everyone in."

"A virus has destroyed all the data stored there—data collected over the past fifty years from all of Airo-Aurora's citizens," I explain. "The programs allowing for wireless transmission of information both from and to the Mainframe have also been destroyed, meaning that data collection in Airo-Aurora is over, along with the ability to control a person using artificial intelligence."

"How will spouses and jobs be selected, hmm?" queries James from behind King's desk. He has taken up the throne without a second thought for what will become of his father, and it is in that moment that I see him for the man that he is: not inherently cruel or sinister, just recklessly indifferent to the feelings of others—a sociopath.

King, meanwhile, stands in the corner in handcuffs, looking distinctly put out.

"How will spouses and jobs be selected?" I echo. "Through free choice."

"Nonsense," replies James. "I plan to re-establish the chip program, even if it must be built from the ground up. Free choice leads to mayhem, any fool knows that. Don't worry, don't worry," he adds to the foreign dignitaries, "I have no plans to do as Papa did and breach your articles of international who-dinky and whatever-you-call-it. But, all engagements and careers chosen at the previous Selections stand. Except for yours, girl from Quire. You'll marry who I say you will, and it just may be a King!"

Wolfe stands from his chair at this, but I step forward

and open my mouth before he can. "That isn't for you to decide."

"What does that mean?"

"It means you are not the true ruler of Airo-Aurora."

"But of course I am! With Papa being carted off to jail, he surrenders the crown to the next in line!" He picks up the crown and studies it, kissing each ruby in turn, finally placing it on his head.

"You colluded with King to place the blame on the viscount and have him executed, all so the illegal override chip program could continue. I overheard the conversation myself when I was dressed as a servant, serving you biscuits. And this," I reach into my cardigan pocket and pull out the memory stick, borrowed from Timothee, "This contains the recording of that conversation lifted from the Visitation Room before the data was deleted. A recording that will ensure you spend the rest of your days behind bars. It follows, then, that you shall abdicate the throne at once."

The silence in the room is thunderous. James turns a violent shade of red, while King grinds his teeth. Wolfe simply stares at me before clearing his throat, having recovered from the shock before the rest. "I believe the articles surrounding throne entitlement were amended several years back when the Queen started 'getting too big for her britches', to quote my uncle."

"Too big for her britches?" echoes one of the foreign diplomats. "How so?"

"Demanding more of a role in governance, I believe. It's probably what kick-started the override chip program in the first place, isn't that right, uncle?"

King stares at the floor with his lips puckered.

"You'll find the proper papers in the desk," Wolfe continues.

Several dignitaries surround James, placing him in handcuffs and pocketing the memory stick that has proof of his and King's wrongdoing. I make a mental note to buy Timothee a new one, then watch as the desk's drawers are emptied, and the office fills with loose-leaf and the sound of many voices reading out clauses, trying to sort out who the throne now belongs to.

In the midst of it, Wolfe edges closer to me. "Are you alright," he asks in his normal, brisk fashion.

I nod. "I am now. And yourself?"

Just then, one of the dignitaries lifts a stack of papers into the air. "According to Clause 8, the throne should pass to his daughter Aubrey. However, given Amendment 13—C.4, which precludes a woman from taking the throne, transference proceeds to the King's living brother."

"The King's brother," explains Wolfe, in a somber voice, "passed away recently."

"Then to his son," the man finishes.

I turn to Wolfe, my jaw slack.

Wolfe merely bows his head at the news. "That would be me."

"Surely there's a mistake," cries James, sounding furious.

"No mistake," the man says as he continues to leaf through the papers.

"I'll contest it. I'll fight such a ridiculous result for the rest of my—"

"You'll be behind bars, I'm afraid," the man says curtly.

"There should also be an investigation launched into his sexual abuse of certain members of the Maverick army," I add, motioning to James. "And King should be investigated for the murder of a young man who goes by the name Butch."

"Those accusations will never hold water," James replies lazily, waving his hand. "As the true King, let my first order of business—"

"You are not the true King," says Wolfe swiftly. "And I'll

see to it that both you and your father are imprisoned until the day you die."

"And you, dear King," says one of the dignitaries to Wolfe, "do you intend to carry on with this chip program?"

Wolfe turns and stares at me. Finally, he shakes his head. "Free choice," he concludes, "shall from this point forward be a cornerstone of our governance."

And just like that, I feel the shackles of an unwanted future fall to the floor. Just as I wanted from the very beginning, I can wed who I want. I can choose a career that is most fitting.

All of my sparkling Airo-Aurora can.

———

I GO DIRECTLY from King's office to my quarters. For a while, I just stand there, studying the sumptuous and vast space, ignoring the way I yawn. Really, I should spend some time relishing my success. I should enjoy the luxuries that the palace offers, ones that in the morning I will be deprived of, now that I'm no longer betrothed to a viscount, or destined to serve as his handmaid. I finger the gowns in the closet and turn it over in my mind. Tomorrow. Tomorrow, I will return to my aunt's house in Quire, I will pull on the menswear that had been my hallmark look before all this madness began. And in the future, I will be whoever I want to be.

I collapse into bed, the pull of sleep too much to resist, and fall fast asleep.

twenty-eight

. . .

HE SLIPS his hand through mine as we twist between the carnival crowd. A summer breeze pushes my hair from my face, and off in the distance, the sun begins its hazy descent to the horizon. The sky burns orange overhead, and this is what I focus on as Patrick squeezes my hand tight. I glance at him over my shoulder, and he takes the opportunity to kiss me. I kiss him, too, then return my attention to the sky.

But from the other end of the carnival, there comes a fuss, and my interest is piqued. I drag Patrick past the carousel, and the Ferris wheel, around the ring toss game, and past the candy floss vendor, until, through the crowd, I spot Jill dressed in her olive-green uniform. I edge closer so I can wave at her, and that's when I notice the sparkling limousine. And from that limousine emerges a shadowy and grim figure that reaches to the sky.

My stomach twists into a thousand painful knots as I lay eyes on him. He looks regal as ever, even more so, brought with the passage of time. Then he reaches his hand behind him, I spot a gloved hand rest delicately in his. Claudia emerges from the limousine wearing a bubble-gum-pink taffeta dress, her stomach rounded with the late stages of pregnancy.

I stare at them, rooted to the spot, even as Patrick—the boy all of Quire thought to be my perfect match—pulls at my arm. On and on he tugs, but I can't move, not even an inch—

I wake to find my face and hair wet with tears. I push my heavy hair from my eyes and stare around the room. It had been a *dream*—just a dream.

Outside, the sun shines proudly, and inside, the other half of the bed is cleanly made. If Wolfe came to bed last night, he has already started his day.

I waste no time.

Still wearing the clothes I wore yesterday, and with my hair a mess, I push out into the House of Mirrors without a backward glance. I take the servants' stairs up to Bishop's Aisle, then run all the way along the corridor to Wolfe's office. Voices murmur from inside, but I knock sharply nonetheless.

A second later, the door pulls open. Surprise registers across Wolfe's face at seeing me. Inside, the woman occupying the seat across from his turns, and, just like in my dream, I see that it's Claudia.

twenty-nine

. . .

I HAVE to bite my lip to stop the tears.

I take a step back, and another. Then I turn, I retrace my steps as quickly as my legs will allow. Wolfe calls my name, but I don't slow down, not even as I hear his footsteps echoing after me. What an idiot I am, to be swayed by a *dream*.

He catches up to me inside the walnut-lined entrance hall that leads to our quarters, stopping me from moving any farther by reaching his long arm past me and shuttering the door. "Alex," he says again, gentler this time.

I study my fingernails. "Yes?"

"Tell me why you came to my office just now."

I let out a small laugh, feeling so foolish I could cry. Somehow, though, I lift my gaze to his. "It was nothing of importance," I assure him.

"I don't know what it is you're thinking," he beings. "I never really do." He swipes his mouth. "But before I get too far, I believe that gratitude is in order."

"Gratitude?"

"Yes, Alexandra. Gratitude. For saving my life. For saving the nation from James, too."

I wave my hand to brush his gratitude aside.

"Apologies, then. For not having a full and frank conversation with you last night. You were sound asleep when finally my uncle and cousin had been removed from the palace and Doctor Lebwitski had been rounded up. I didn't wish to wake you."

"I'm not interested in your apologies, either."

"Right. Well, then." He coughs into his hand. "You should know, perhaps...I mean, in the interest of transparency, I summoned Claudia to my office first thing this morning to make something clear."

"I'm sure she was delighted to learn that not only is the Selection system and all its rules gone, but that you're now King, too."

"That isn't why I summoned her."

"Oh?"

"I wished to inform her that just because she was no longer obligated to marry her fiancé, I remain, ah-hem, engaged."

"You remain engaged, you say?" I echo. "But you don't have to be—"

"I know I don't have to be," he barks, pulling from his pocket a handful of change that he begins to methodically sort and count.

"Wolfe," I sigh, and I vow to be direct. "What exactly are you saying?"

"You're ascribing in me courage I do not possess," he mutters, still not looking at me.

I frown. "On the contrary, you have stared death in the face, you have acted as a double agent, you have taken it upon yourself to protect me since day one when you had more reason than anything to hate me, and you have persevered through a personal tragedy that would shatter all others. You are the most courageous man I know."

He goes stalk-still. "You're going to make me spell it out? So be it. Who is at the epicenter of all that, hmm? I had no other option but to calmly face death with you watching in the wings. Only with your aid did I take down my uncle. Knowing you inspired in me the need to keep you safe. I have only moved past tragedy with your steadiness next to me. I am nothing without you."

"Perhaps," I whisper, over my thumping heart, "we can be courageous together."

He deposits the change back inside his pocket and nods —just once, and curt as ever. And then we gaze at each other, this time more freely than before. More freely than ever before.

Slowly, as if giving me every opportunity to object, Wolfe's hands wrap around the back of my head, he tilts his large face down to mine. He kisses me softly, then releases me as though he's fearful of my reaction.

I don't hesitate in my response. I draw him to me so that we hold each other tightly, so tightly no air can separate us. He lifts me off the ground, I kiss him with abandon, my insides exploding with sheer joy as that stern and sullen mouth parts to make room for mine. When he sets me down again, I notice that his face has filled with color and he breathes deeply.

"Wolfe?"

His eyes dart to mine, and he kisses me again—once, twice, three times. "I would die to keep you safe. I will do anything to make you happy. Do you see that now? Do you understand how much I love you?"

I stare up at him, aghast. Yet slowly and sternly, I nod. And me. What are my feelings? Is there any remote possibility that I love him?

Of course, there is. In fact, I've had feelings for him for far longer than I cared to admit. That's why I had gone straight to him this morning after my dream, in order to rectify what would have been a devastating mistake...

"Marry me, Alexandra. Please. Marry me."

epilogue

. . .

I SHAKE hands with the kindergarten teacher, then wave to the children as they file out of Counterdown Abbey, books clutched in their tiny hands. Me and Rebecca exchange an exhausted smile. At the far table, the duchess and Marylin, previously known as the Queen, review a series of documents over tea, thoroughly relishing their portfolio in international relations, the same one the duchess watched her husband perform for decades. In the year since King's departure, Wolfe had hired not only women in the palace to perform critical functions for the nation of Airo-Aurora, but also help from outside palace walls, a small step in the march toward democracy that he has committed to.

I check my watch. He should be back any minute from his trip to Harbor, a free trade deal now well in the works, a trip I'd typically pilot him on myself if my services weren't needed in the library.

Indeed, over the past ten months, I'd opened it to the public, just as I'd hoped. And there have been other changes, too—dinners in Carnegie Reserve are no longer the overrun, gaudy displays of wealth for the nation's most well-heeled.

Instead, they are an opportunity for the royal family to welcome volunteers into the palace to thank them for their service. They're also a time for intimate family dinners, often enjoyed with close friends. Aunt Jo and Agnes now spend a great deal of time at Strath Glen, my aunt still delivering post by her own choosing, and Agnes now living solo with a new job at the city paper. Even the Rocksavages themselves have undergone a transformation.

The absence of King and James is the most obvious— both of them awaiting trial on a great many international war charges, in addition to many crimes committed against national law, along with Doctor Lebwitski. If they ever see the light of day again, there is no longer a place for them at Strath Glen, or even in Airo-Aurora. Dear Matthew moved out, leaving Aubrey to raise her young son George alone, while still grieving the senseless loss of Butch. Morocco continues to reside here, critical of the changes Wolfe and I impose on the palace, but grateful for our decision to allow her to stay. The former Queen has proven herself to be a tremendous asset in all things related to governance, and she's quick to keep the ladies of the palace in line when it comes to "dicking about."

It's been a good influence for Evie, now more committed to her studies than before, though still very much enjoying her games of seduction with neighboring boys. With the weight of an impending Selection gone, so too are her bouts of anxiousness.

As for the wedding, it had been postponed, given the unusual circumstances, and is now set to unfold in only a week's time, planned with precision from front to back by Evie, helped along with my far more enthusiastic input.

Half of the servants chose to leave their employment at Strath Glen, and after considerable discussions with Wolfe, we decided to raise the wages of the servants who remained and now allow them to live off-site if they so choose. With fewer servants tending to their whims, the Rocksavage clan has begrudgingly grown accustomed to doing more household chores themselves.

"Miss Alex!" shouts Monsieur Sawyer as he holds open the library doors for Aubrey and George. "You wished to speak to me, I believe?"

"Indeed. I heard through the grapevine you've asked my aunt to accompany you to next week's wedding."

"Oh, and Miss Alex doesn't like the idea?" He stares at me, mockingly aghast.

I indulge him with a small smile. "Your choice, Monsieur," I admit. "Though I warn you that if you cross her, she'll tear you to shreds."

He stares at the ceiling as though he finds the idea particularly enticing.

"You dog!" and I swat him. "Don't you think it'll make things uncomfortable when you're both walking me down the aisle?"

"Oh, me, me, me. What a princess you've become."

"Darling, do recommend another picture book for my little Georgie-Pordgie," Aubrey calls as Marylin bounces George on her knee. "He absolutely adored the one with the elephants!"

I oblige, and a few minutes later, Rebecca bustles in carrying a bouquet. "Aye, your viscount—oh, sorry, miss—your king, like. He's returned. In your quarters now, miss, just so you know. And he brought you these!" She holds out the bouquet, which I lift from her hands.

I stare down at a simple bouquet of small white flowers—baby's breath.

"Those aren't for the wedding, are they?" Evie cries as she walks through the door. "They'll never last, sister—my!"

I shake my head, and a minute later, I'm running up the imperial staircase. Sometimes it's hard to believe that the towering figure I spotted on my first morning at Strath Glen

—the one with the shoes that clicked like money and the scowl contorting his dark eyes—that soon we will be husband and wife, and this time not because of computer chips or Mainframes, or revolutionaries like Neo who orchestrated the whole thing in the first place.

No, we shall be husband and wife because we *choose* to be, and my pulse races at the thought.

I push inside our shared quarters and find him fixing a drink, sporting a navy suit and looking as regal as ever. "After all this time, you remembered," I breathe, lifting the bouquet between us.

"That they're your favorite?" he asks, considering both me and the flowers.

I nod. "My mother used to plant extra all across the city so she could bring them home by the bunches."

Half his mouth pulls back with the hint of a smile. "Why, of course I remembered. It's hard not to pay attention to a young woman once she announces her proficiency at playing piano, commandeering a helicopter, and...what was your third pursuit again?"

"Very funny."

"Something to do with books, if memory serves me?"

"Something like that," I say, grabbing him by the lapels and tugging him close. "I missed you."

His brow arches. "Alas, a problem with an easy answer— a rarity for us," and he sets down his drink, picks me up, and kicks the door shut, sealing us blissfully in a world of our making.

a look at: wise wolf books young adult starter library

Strap in and enjoy a rollicking ride through fairytale worlds, criminal empires, and more with eight sizzling series starters from some of Wise Wolf Book's newest young adult storytellers.

From authors Sorboni Banerjee and Dominique Richardson–*Red As Blood*:

When Penny Zale mysteriously disappears from a psychiatric hospital, leaving behind only clues in the form of letters and her severed braid, her friends Raven, Aarya, Dawn, and Elle must navigate a treacherous world of wealth and deception to find her.

From Nova McBee–*Calculated*:

In a world where numbers hold great power, seventeen-year-old math prodigy Jo River is betrayed, kidnapped, and forced to use her talents for a criminal empire.

From Lee Matthew Goldberg–*Runaway Train*:

After the devastating loss of her sister, a 16-year-old girl decides to escape her neglectful parents and embark on a 90's adventure, fueled by music and a desire to avoid her sister's fate.

From Jerri Chisholm–*The Sordid Selection*:

The realization that one's ideal career and partner are not what they seem throws Alex Egelton into a tumultuous world of palace intrigue, deceit, and mystery, as she unravels cryptic clues that hold profound consequences.

From L.J. Martin–*Two Thousand Grueling Miles*:

In a quest to survive and protect his family while moving west, young and determined Jake Zane faces the grueling challenge of a 2,000-mile journey on the Oregon Trail, accompanied by a mute escaped slave and hundreds of others. Along the treacherous trail, they must conquer the wilderness, face wild animals, harsh weather, and hostile encounters, while disease and accidents pose a threat to their journey and dreams of a better life in the west.

From Chelsea Bobulski–*All I Want For Christmas is the Girl Next Door*:

In this heartwarming YA holiday romance novel, Graham Wallace finds himself caught between a decade-long love for the girl next door, Sarah Clarke, and the realization that some wishes are better left unfulfilled.

From Tamara Girardi–*Gridiron Girl*:

Julia Medina, determined to become the starting quarterback for Iron Valley High School's football team, faces challenges and controversy as she defies expectations and confronts gender biases.

From western author Chris Mullen–*Rowdy: Wild and Mean, Sharp and Keen*:

After a devastating tragedy leaves him alone and adrift, thirteen-year-old Rowdy embarks on a perilous journey of survival along the Mississippi River, where he discovers his inner strength and determination as he fights for justice.

These page-turning stories await, so dive in and let your imagination soar!

AVAILABLE NOW

about the author

Jerri Chisholm is a YA author, a distance runner, and a chocolate addict. Her childhood was spent largely in solitude with only her imagination and a pet parrot for company. Following that she completed a master's degree in public policy and then became a lawyer, but ultimately decided to leave the profession to focus exclusively on the more imaginative and avian-friendly pursuit of writing. She lives with her husband and three children, but, alas, no parrot.